"I FOUND THE GLORY . . .

. . . didn't I?" he wheezed, and with a strangling cough he began his final struggle. Gideon's eyes burned with tears as he held Quincy tight—held him until he felt his friend give up the fight and go limp in his arms.

The sound of gun thunder intruded on Gideon's grief, and he remembered then where he was and what was happening. He glanced at the melee of riders silhouetted against the bloodred sun, but that scene did not hold his attention for long. The enemy was all around him. His only ally now was the darkness.

"Goodbye, Quincy," he said, choking on emotion as he let go of his friend and in a crouching run made for a thicket of catclaw a few yards away.

His plan was to wait, four hours if need be, until he was certain that the Mexicans were long gone. Then he would locate the North Star in the night sky and head for home.

Not that he expected to make it. But a person had to try.

THE MARAUDERS

Jason Manning

SIGNET
Published by the Penguin Group
Penguin Putnam Inc., 375 Hudson Street,
New York, New York 10014, U.S.A.
Penguin Books Ltd, 27 Wrights Lane,
London W8 5TZ, England
Penguin Books Australia Ltd, Ringwood,
Victoria, Australia
Penguin Books Canada Ltd, 10 Alcorn Avenue,
Toronto, Ontario, Canada M4V 3B2
Penguin Books (N.Z.) Ltd, 182–190 Wairau Road,
Auckland 10, New Zealand

Penguin Books Ltd, Registered Offices:
Harmondsworth, Middlesex, England

First published by Signet, an imprint of Dutton NAL,
a member of Penguin Putnam Inc.

First Printing, June, 1998
10 9 8 7 6 5 4 3 2 1

Printed in the United States of America

To

MAMAW

The Grandest Lady

Chapter 1

On the day he died, Bob Carnacky woke up in a foul mood.

For one thing, he had a pounding headache that threatened to split his skull wide open. For another, his mouth tasted like the inside of an old shoe. His stomach felt bloated and queasy, seeming to perform slow rolls. And it took him a little while to determine whether the room really *was* tilting back and forth like a ship tossed by heavy seas.

His condition, however, didn't alarm him. He knew why he felt like this. Quite often he woke with a hangover. Getting drunk was an old habit. And he knew how to solve his problem. A little "hair of the dog" would cure what ailed him.

But when he groped blearily for the bottle of tequila on the table beside the bed he misjudged and struck it with a hairy forearm, knocking it from its perch. The bottle shattered when it hit the floor. Carnacky muttered a vile curse. Then he cursed again when he realized the bottle had been empty. Not even the worm was left.

The bottle shattering and his gruff profanity awoke the Mexican girl who lay in the bed beside him, and she sat up with a start. Carnacky glowered at her and tried in vain to remember just who the hell she was. She was young, with small breasts which she hastened to cover with the soiled sheet. But Carnacky wasn't interested in her breasts anymore. Just mildly disappointed that he couldn't recall any of last night's frolic, which he must have enjoyed.

"What's your name again?" His voice was half-wheeze, half-croak.

She told him, and then he remembered some of it—at least the part about how she had come to share his blanket. Had to do with her brother, whatever *his* name was. One of the greasers Carnacky had locked up in the Brownsville jail. Drunk and disorderly—yes, that had been the charge, and the Mex hadn't had the money to pay a fine, so Carnacky, as he was wont to do whenever the opportunity presented itself and he was in the mood, had made an arrangement with the greaser's sister.

It was a crying shame, Carnacky mused, that he couldn't recollect having his pleasure with this young spitfire, but he waxed philosophical, secure in the knowledge that there would be another time. He could arrange to have her brother arrested again, for something or other. Besides, greasers were too damned ignorant to learn their lessons. Jesus or Paco or whatever the hell his name was would screw up again, that was guaranteed.

She started to ask him, then, about her brother, and he curtly told her to shut up. Carnacky liked to think of himself as a man of his word. He'd made a bargain and he would keep his end of it. Paco or Jose or whatever his name was would walk out of jail a free man today and the unpaid fine would be forgotten. So there was nothing to be gained by further discussion of the matter. Just shut the hell up.

Now that the room had ceased to roll and heave, Carnacky swung his horse-bowed legs out of bed and tested his ability to stand. He was a brawny man, with a great deal of hair on his back and chest and legs and face. Numerous scars bore vivid testimony to his proclivity for violence. In his forty years he had been a soldier, a slave trader, a placer miner, a scout, and a scalphunter. He'd fought in the Mexican War, and he'd fought the Comanches, too, and he had even clashed with tribesmen on the Ivory Coast of Africa. He boasted that he wasn't afraid of any living thing and so far he hadn't given any evidence to the contrary.

Which was why they had made him sheriff of Brownsville, one of the most violent places in the world. Take a border town in 1859 with Mexicans and Texans rubbing elbows, and you had a recipe tailor-made for bloodshed. It hadn't been all that long ago that Texas had fought for and won her independence, and only a dozen years back there had been that little fracas called the Mexican War, during which Carnacky had accompanied Winfield Scott and the United States Army to Mexico City and given the greasers a good whuppin'. Fond memories for Bob Carnacky, since as an irregular scout he'd had ample opportunity for raping and looting, General Scott's standing orders notwithstanding. What Ol' Fuss and Feathers didn't know wouldn't hurt him. That had been Carnacky's motto.

When General Zachary Taylor brought his army down to the Texas border at the outbreak of the war, he had established Fort Brown on the Rio Grande directly across from the Mexican town of Matamoros, and Brownsville had grown up in short order around the fort. Located near where the Rio Grande emptied into the Gulf of Mexico, the town had quickly become a thriving port. The population these days hovered somewhere in the vicinity of two thousand souls, most of them of Mexican extraction. But that was okay by Carnacky, who had nothing but contempt for greasers, and was firm in his conviction that they were a subhuman species. In spite of being the minority, Americans dominated the commerce and politics of Brownsville, and that was as it should be, were you to ask Bob Carnacky's opinion.

This being July, it was hellish hot even in the morning, so Carnacky had the window open, and now, standing by the bed naked as the day he was born—and a lot uglier—Carnacky wiped at the perspiration on his hirsute belly and felt a sudden, undeniable urge. He went to the window and pulled back the ragged, dusty curtains and cursed again as the sunlight seared through his tender skull, but he stood his ground and relieved himself out the window. When he was finished he looked at the girl, who still sat on the bed with the blanket pulled up to cover her breasts, and he leered at her.

"You stickin' around for seconds? Get dressed and get out of here, then. I'm a busy man. Got things to do. So get thee to a nunnery."

She dressed swiftly and was gone before Carnacky had finished pulling on his soiled and faded underriggings, and as she fled from the sheriff's house, two men walking down the street witnessed her fast exit.

"I see Bob's been at it again," remarked Charles Stoneman, his tone of voice registering mild amusement.

Samuel Burkin shook his head. Being one of Brownsville's most talented lawyers, he often found himself associated with the sheriff, and no one's opinion of Bob Carnacky's value to humanity was lower than his.

"That man is disgusting," he replied.

Stoneman smiled. "When Brownsville becomes a civilized place to live, we'll hire a civilized peace officer."

"Carnacky is the type of man who can single-handedly put back the process of civilization at least a hundred years."

In the weeks to come Sam Burkin would remember those words and marvel at how accidentally prophetic he had been.

Bob Carnacky was on his way out when his visitors arrived. Thumbing a forgotten suspender onto his shoulder, the Brownsville sheriff looked Burkin and Stoneman up and down with a half-cocked smile. Burkin knew exactly what the lawman was thinking. He was thinking that here were two self-important fools who felt compelled to wear their black broadcloth suits and waistcoats and cravats in all this heat and dust because they *thought* they were big fish in this little backwater pond. And Burkin was dismayed to find that Carnacky's expression *did* make him feel foolish. That was one reason he didn't like Carnacky. The sheriff made him feel like something less than a real man.

"You gentlemen come to see *me*?" asked Carnacky, feigning humility and astonishment. "To what do I owe this honor?"

Stoneman cast a glance along the street. "Mind if we talk inside, Bob?" he asked, smooth as silk.

Carnacky's beady, sun-faded eyes squinched up suspiciously, but his shrug was one of manifest indifference, and he turned back through the door with the two men in black frock coats on his heels.

Burkin had never been inside Carnacky's house before, but the condition of the two-room clapboard shanty that Brownsville had provided for its peace officer was every bit as horrible as Burkin had imagined it would be. Carnacky lived like a pig. There was clutter everywhere, and not a single stick of furniture undeserving of a bonfire. The place had a rancid smell to it, a smell of cheap whiskey and unwashed flesh that nearly overwhelmed the young lawyer, who was by nature a fastidious man.

"You carryin' that whiskey flask on you, Charles?" Carnacky asked Stoneman with a sly, sidelong glance.

"Brandy, old fellow."

Carnacky held out a beefy hand. "Beggars caint be choosers. Give it here."

Stoneman lifted an eyebrow, but he produced the silver-scrolled flask and Carnacky drank half of its contents like water. When he was done he belched and gasped and, looking with considerably more equanimity upon life in general, surrendered the flask to its owner.

"Breakfast," he said, much amused with the look of astonishment on Burkin's face.

"Bob, you know the elections are coming on," said Stoneman. "That's why we wanted to have this little talk."

"We? You mean you and my old buddy Sam here?"

"I mean the Reds in general. We've discussed matters and decided you might want to think about being a little more—shall we say, circumspect?—with the Mexican population of Brownsville."

"Hmm. Circumspect. Ain't that a rich word?"

Burkin was becoming annoyed. Carnacky did that to him. The man had a wondrous knack for getting under his skin. Clearly the sheriff was mocking them. Stoneman surely knew this. Charles was an extremely perceptive man. He had acquired that talent from his father, one of New York's most prominent bankers. And he had demonstrated it time and time again while becoming, in the span of a few short years, one of the leading property owners and entrepreneurs in Brownsville.

But Stoneman's skin was thick, and he didn't wear his feelings on his sleeve. He was too sly for that. So he ignored Carnacky's impertinence and nodded earnestly.

"Yet you know what I mean," he told the sheriff. "You tend to play a bit rough at times with the Mexicans."

"If they don't cotton to it they ought to get across the river where they belong."

Burkin wanted to remind Carnacky that the Mexicans had been here long before the first Americans had moved in, but Charles didn't give him an opening.

"That's entirely beside the point, Bob," said Stoneman reasonably. "The Mexicans are here. They are citizens. And that means they have the right to vote."

The light of understanding dawned in Carnacky's faded eyes. "So that's what all this hemming and hawing is about."

Wearing a tolerant smile, Stoneman nodded.

Brownsville had two political factions, the Blues and

the Reds, and the leaders on both sides were Americans of wealth and influence. Stoneman was joined by men like Richard King and Mifflin Kennedy, both of whom were trying to establish ranching empires in the vicinity, as the guiding lights of the Reds. The Blues followed the lead of men like Stephen Powers, who had been a confidant of President Martin Van Buren and who had served his country ably as a minister to Switzerland. The members of these factions wore red and blue ribbons when election time rolled around; today, both Stoneman and Burkin had red ribbons pinned to the lapels of their frock coats.

Carnacky was not politically inclined. He considered all politicians to be crooks and frauds who tried to mask their lust for power behind high-sounding declarations of concern for the welfare of the common folk. The Blues and the Reds were all Democrats—there wasn't another national party in Texas, as few people in this part of the country would dare admit to an affinity for the new Republican Party, with its abolitionist and free-soil slant. If there was an issue that distinguished the Blues from the Reds it was southern rights and secession; New Yorker Stoneman and his colleagues were proponents of states' rights and strict construction and generally in favor of the expansion of slavery, while the Blues were stout Unionists who claimed that the South's best interests could only be served by turning a deaf ear to the secessionists and states' righters and remaining in the Union.

As for Carnacky, he didn't lose any sleep over the fate of the Union in these troubled times. So long as he got his wages and plenty of liquor and an occasional woman, he was perfectly content to let the world around him go to hell in a handbasket.

But he was wise enough to know that a man who held a position of official responsibility, as he did, could not entirely divorce himself from the politics of the day. The unvarnished truth remained that he owed his present situation to the auspices of Charles Stoneman and other Reds. At the moment, they were Brownsville's dominant faction. If he wanted to keep his job he would have to play along with their little games. Stoneman didn't need to remind him that were it not for his good offices, one Bob Carnacky would be just another wharf rat or mercenary for hire. As sheriff, Carnacky had never been burdened by the idea that he had a duty to the citizens to maintain law and order. But he was well aware that he *did* have a duty to his benefactors—one of whom stood before him in the person of Charles Stoneman.

"So what is it you want me to do, exactly?" asked Carnacky.

He couldn't avoid sounding a little sarcastic. He resented Stoneman's wealth and power. The man was a pompous stuffed shirt, arrogant and vain. But that didn't mean Carnacky underestimated him. Stoneman was also a hard-as-nails cutthroat beneath that urbane and polished exterior. He would destroy anyone who crossed him. Only he didn't need a gun or a knife to get the job done. So Carnacky had to swallow his pride and act subservient.

"We just think it would serve everyone best if you showed our Mexican neighbors some leniency," replied Stoneman. "For the time being."

"You mean until the election is over."

Stoneman shrugged, as though that went without saying.

"What about them that break the law? You know

there are a lot of those pepper-eaters that do. You want I should cat-foot around them, too?"

"Of course not. You must do your job. That is what you're getting paid for."

"What we're wanting you to do," said Burkin, dryly, no longer able to hold his tongue, "is not to take such obvious relish in beating some poor Mexican half to death when you arrest him for relieving himself in the street."

Remembering that he had just urinated out the window, Carnacky smirked.

"Well, I can do that," he said. "But it stinks like last week's garbage. The greasers ought not to be allowed to vote in the first place, if you ask me. And it's a sad day indeed when white men have to butter up a bunch of damned Mexicans just so they'll make their mark on the right ballot. I won't ask you what kind of promises you plan to make to them so they'll vote for the Red ticket, because I know good and well you have no intention of keeping those promises. Don't get me wrong, though. I ain't criticizing. A greaser don't know what it means to keep your word, anyway."

Burkin was fuming. Carnacky might as well have come right out and called them lying scoundrels. But before he could issue a barbed retort, Stoneman turned to him and gestured at the door.

"We'll be going now," he said. "Don't want to keep you from your rounds, Sheriff. You see, Sam? I told you Bob was a reasonable man."

As they headed back up the dusty street toward the better part of town, a scowling Sam Burkin shook his head.

"We ought to get rid of that man, Charles," he said. "He is wicked and brutal and one day he will do something incredibly stupid and cause us no end of trouble."

"When that happens we *will* get rid of him. And when we do, it will demonstrate to the people that we put the good of the community before loyalty to one of our own."

Burkin envied Stoneman's ability to turn every eventuality to his advantage. "Carnacky is not one of us," he said.

"For the time being, though, he suits our needs. Most Americans here don't think any better of the Mexicans than he does. And they're worried, too, because the Mexicans outnumber them three to one. They like having a man of Carnacky's temperament around. They see him as a fellow who is tough enough to keep the Mexicans in their place. They wouldn't want a peace officer who caters to the Mexicans all the time. Who concerned himself overmuch with Mexican rights."

"Carnacky would die before he conceded that a Mexican *had* any rights."

"As far as I'm concerned, they don't."

"You're in the wrong there, Charles. They *do* have rights, and if Carnacky keeps trampling on those rights they will rise up one day and demand justice."

Stoneman chuckled. "You're an alarmist, my friend. Actually, I do concede that they have one right—the right to vote for Red candidates come Election Day."

"I'm curious to know what you plan to promise them this time."

"Oh, I don't have any idea, frankly." Stoneman made a ne'er-do-well gesture. "Does it really matter?"

* * *

The long draft from Stoneman's brandy flask had helped cure Carnacky's hangover, but it had also put him in the mood for another good stiff drink, or two, so he resolved to visit his favorite watering hole on the way to the office. It was a detour he was accustomed to making.

Clad in a red muslin shirt and suspender pants with the legs stuffed into mule-ear boots, Carnacky left his house. He wore the red shirt, he joked, so that the greasers, who as everyone knew were pitifully poor shots, would have something to draw a bead on. He carried his customary array of weapons: a staghorn-handled Arkansas Toothpick, a Winchester Volcanic Repeating Pistol, .38 caliber, and a Sharps 1852 Slanting Breech carbine. The latter he carried in the crook of his right arm, while the other two rode under his belt. A man who made enemies with such aplomb as Bob Carnacky was a fool to leave home without plenty of firepower.

Heading for Grindle's saloon, Carnacky mulled over the visit by Stoneman and Burkin. The fact that for all intents and purposes Charles Stoneman owned him rankled the sheriff, and made his foul mood even worse. It didn't matter that Stoneman and the others who ran this town gave him a pretty free hand except when the local elections rolled around. That Stoneman felt he could come into his own home and tell him how to do his job cut Carnacky's pride to the quick.

It was nearly noon, and there were wagons and riders and pedestrians on the street, and all of them gave the scowling Brownsville sheriff a wide berth. In this section of town most of the inhabitants were Mexican. Carnacky didn't mind that he lived here any more than a fox would mind setting up shop in a chicken coop. Better here, where he got the respect he deserved, than on the other side of town where Stoneman and his kind lived, and where Carnacky knew he would be treated no better than dirt.

Grindle's was on the edge of the business district, several blocks from Carnacky's house, so by the time he arrived at his destination the salutary effects of Stoneman's brandy had worn off and the sheriff's head was pounding again. He figured hell had to be cooler than Brownsville, Texas, on a July day. The sun was driving red-hot spikes through his brain.

Cutting through an alley strewn with trash, Carnacky turned the corner to the front of Grindle's, and as he did so he collided with an old Mexican, who crumpled like a rag doll at the sheriff's feet. Carnacky stumbled over the body and dropped the Sharps carbine and slammed a shoulder into the wall of the saloon before regaining his balance. With a vivid curse he retrieved the Sharps and whirled and cocked one leg back with the notion of driving the toe of his boot as hard as he could into the fallen man's spine. In that instant he recognized the Mexican. His name was Lopez, and he was a harmless old drunkard who Carnacky had never bothered with before. Reason being that Lopez had no money and no comely daughter or wife and Carnacky wasn't about to let him stink up the jail and get his meals on the county dole without there being any hope of profit in it for the jailkeeper.

But that wasn't why Carnacky refrained from breaking a few of the old man's brittle ribs. No, he was recalling what Stoneman had said to him—and he looked around to see whether he was being watched. Of course, he was. There were a few people along the street, and they were all spectators. Teeth clenched in a snarl of impotent rage, Carnacky muttered another curse, then turned abruptly on his heel to enter Grindle's establishment, leaving the half-conscious Lopez twitching and grunting incoherently in the dust.

Josiah Grindle was behind the counter, as usual, dusting shotglasses which one of his daughters, both of whom served as barmaids, had just washed in a water barrel out back. Most of the time Grindle didn't pay Carnacky much mind, but today he watched the sheriff closely, and the expression on Carnacky's face brought a surreptitious smile to the bartender's usually pinched and sour features.

"Morning, Bob," said Grindle pleasantly as he placed a glass and a bottle in front of Carnacky.

Carnacky laid his Sharps on the bar and mumbled a bad-humored something as he filled the glass from the bottle.

Looking quite pleased, Grindle leaned against the back bar. "May I assume from your demeanor that Charles Stoneman came to see you this morning?"

Carnacky remembered then that Grindle was one of the leaders of the Reds. He knocked the tequila back in one long gulp, hissed at the burn of the liquor going down, and slammed the empty glass on the bar. "Maybe I'll just take my business elsewhere," he said belligerently. "A man ought to be able to have a drink in peace, without others poking their snouts into his personal affairs."

"No need to get your hackles up, Bob," said Grindle, smooth as China silk. He stepped up and refilled Carnacky's glass, all the way to the brim. "Have another, on the house."

As Grindle well knew, this was one offer Bob Carnacky would never refuse.

"Don't take it personally," said Grindle, as Carnacky drank. "It's just politics. That's all it is."

"Maybe next time some drunk greaser is tearing up your place, or putting a pigsticker through your eyeball, Josiah, I'll handle it different. Just politely ask him to please be nice and cease and desist. And if he guts you like a fish, I'll respectfully request him to accompany me to the jailhouse. But I won't shoot his balls off, whatever he does, since I'd hate to deprive the Reds of another cross-mark vote."

"Now, now, Bob. That's uncalled for."

"You're laughing at me, Josiah, damn your hide. You think it's funny? You think Stoneman's pulled my claws? That he's the organ grinder and I'm the trained monkey? Is that what you think?"

Grindle was thinking that part about the monkey was very appropriate. But he could see that Carnacky's mood was getting uglier, so he reached for the bottle. Another shot of tequila was the last thing Carnacky needed. But Carnacky snatched the bottle away from him and poured himself another very tall shot.

"I'll pay for this one," snapped the sheriff. "Stoneman pays me for doing his tricks."

Grindle shot a quick look around the saloon. Two men sat at a table near the back, playing cards, one of them a professional gambler recently in from Galveston on the coastal steamer. Neither man was paying him or Carnacky any attention, perhaps intentionally. Grindle decided not to prod the sheriff further. He'd been of the opinion that Carnacky was roughing up the Mexicans a little too much in recent months, and as a businessman the saloon owner was concerned by rumors of growing discontent among the greasers. That Stoneman had put Carnacky on a short rein had pleased him immensely, but now he realized he'd been an idiot to gloat over it in the sheriff's presence. Carnacky was a hair-trigger pistol set to go off in his face.

"Sure, Bob," he said. "I just remembered I've got to tell my daughters to do something. Help yourself."

"You're too kind," drawled Carnacky contemptuously, and drank his third dose of nerve medicine as Grindle hastened to the end of the bar and out the back door, pausing to give the two card players a word of warning, glancing warily back at the sheriff as he did so. Carnacky hardly noticed as the two card players got up and slipped out the back way as quiet as church mice. He was thinking about Stoneman. Couldn't stop thinking about that supercilious bastard. The more he thought about Stoneman the more his blood boiled. By God, the people of Brownsville had hired him to do a job. Sure, maybe he never would have been elected without the help of Stoneman and the Reds party machine, but that was beside the point. He was Brownsville's peace officer and it was his duty to keep the streets safe.

He slammed the empty glass down again, grabbed his carbine, and went outside.

"I'll show him," he muttered. "Bob Carnacky don't kowtow to no man."

Lopez was just recovering from his previous confrontation with Carnacky when the Brownsville sheriff emerged from Grindle's saloon. The bewildered old Mexican had just enough time to focus on the dark scowl clouding Carnacky's coarse, bristled features.

But before he could lurch out of the way, Carnacky gave him a vicious shove, striking him in the shoulder. Lopez went spinning out into the street. Legs tangled, he fell on his back. Carnacky uttered an ugly laugh as Lopez wheezed desperately for air. The sheriff advanced on the old man. He wanted very much to kick something, and either a Mexican or a cur dog would do. Before he could strike Lopez, however, the old man rolled over on his side and suddenly puked all over Carnacky's mule-ear boots.

Something snapped inside Carnacky. Swearing loudly, he kicked Lopez in the stomach. Lopez tried to roll away, and Carnacky kicked him again in the spine. Then Carnacky lifted the old man up by the shirt collar and propelled him forward, just to watch him stumble and fall again. Carnacky rapped him on the head with the barrel of the Sharps carbine. "Get up," he growled. But Lopez couldn't get up. Infuriated, Carnacky hit him again, and the carbine's front sight opened a gash on the old man's cheek. "I said get up, you stinking greaser!"

The realization that someone or something was behind him—something big enough to throw its shadow over him—pierced Carnacky's blind rage, and he whirled to see a man on a white-maned bay horse.

"Pardon me," said the man, "but I must ask you to stop."

He was dressed like a *brasadero*, his legs shielded from the thorns of the brush country thickets by leather chaps, and wearing a short green jacket of brushed leather over a plain white muslin shirt. Big-roweled spurs were strapped to his boots, and a sombrero hung by its chinstrap down his back.

His hair was iron-gray and worn long to his shoulders, partially concealing an angular face with finely chiseled features and expressive hazel eyes flecked with gold. They were the eyes, thought Carnacky, of a mountain lion.

"I know you," said Carnacky, but he couldn't extract a name from his whiskey-befuddled brain to go with that face.

"Yes," said the man, his voice softly resonant, resignation dwelling in his expression. "And I know you. That is why I must ask you to stop beating this man before you kill him."

Carnacky laughed. "Well, how do you like that? A greaser telling me what to do. Now that's rich."

The horseman sighed and looked away for a moment. "This man, what has he done?"

"For one thing, he puked all over my boots. For another, he's stinking up the street. It's my job to keep the streets of this town clean." Carnacky caught himself. "Not that it's any of your business. I don't have to explain myself to you."

The horseman smiled faintly, still looking away, as though there was something down the street of far more interest to him than Carnacky and Lopez.

"Of course you don't," he said.

"So why don't you just ride on," said Carnacky.

Finally the horseman turned his attention back to Carnacky. His eyes had hardened.

"No, I don't think so. I think you are the one who should go away."

Carnacky blinked, questioning whether he could believe his ears. He wasn't accustomed to a Mexican speaking to him in that tone of voice. Though he racked his brain, the man's identity still eluded him.

"Just who in hell are you, anyway?"

"Caldero. Antonio Caldero."

"Oh yeah. That's right. You're the troublemaker. What are you doing in Brownsville? You're not welcome here."

"It was a mistake to come," acknowledged the horseman.

"You're damn right it was a mistake. We don't want your kind in this town. I think maybe I ought to arrest you."

Caldero nodded. "You could try."

That was enough to goad Carnacky into action. Bringing the Sharps carbine to bear, he advanced on Caldero.

"Get down off that horse and—"

The pistol appeared as if by magic in Caldero's hand. Carnacky had just enough time to identify it as a Colt Model 1847 Army Revolver. The .44 caliber six-shooter had been commissioned by Captain Samuel Walker for use by the United States government, and the weapon was more commonly known as a Walker Colt.

Then Carnacky was struck massively in the chest, and the next thing he knew he was lying on his back, staring wide-eyed into the sun. He felt no pain, just a quick-spreading numbness. It was as though he had been kicked by a mule. Only he couldn't catch his breath. The realization that he wasn't ever going to breathe again was followed by a blessedly brief explosion of panic—and then the brass-colored summer sky faded to black. Bob Carnacky was dead.

Antonio Caldero holstered the Walker Colt, dismounted, and went to the old Mexican who lay in the dust, curled in a fetal position. As he sat on his heels like an Indian beside Lopez, Caldero paid no attention to the body of the Brownsville sheriff which lay only an arm's length from him.

"Old man," said Caldero, in his native tongue, his tone one of gentle respect, "can you be moved?"

"Yes," whimpered Lopez.

Caldero took the frail, broken body in his arms, lifting Lopez as though the old man weighed no more than a feather, and draped him over the saddle of the bay, which stood as still as a statue, ground-hitched. Taking up the reins, Caldero heard a sound, a small sound that was loud in the dead silence of the street—it seemed as though Brownsville had caught its breath, frozen in time and place, the moment Caldero's pistol had spoken.

Turning, Caldero saw Josiah Grindle, framed in the doorway of his saloon. Grindle was looking at Carnacky's corpse, his lips pursed and his brows knit, as though he was pondering in terms of dollars and cents the ramifications of the shooting.

"Well," he said, when he realized Caldero was watching him with eyes veiled in impassivity. "Well, you've really opened up a can of worms."

Caldero just walked away, leading the horse. A hundred paces down the street he was approached by a middle-aged Mexican woman in a plain black dress, an *olla* of water, drawn from the nearby communal well, balanced on her shoulder. She was one of the dozen or so people who had witnessed the death of Bob Carnacky, all of them Mexicans. And all of them had vanished, but for her.

"Bless you, *Senor* Caldero," she said, her eyes moist with gratitude. "Bless you."

Caldero stopped in his tracks, and gave her a look filled with pity. He shook his head.

"I have not helped you. I have hurt you. More blood will be spilled now. Maybe it will be yours, or the blood of your loved ones. You will curse me one day. You will wish you had never heard the name Caldero."

"No, never," she replied, her eyes worshipping him. "You will protect us. This was destined to happen."

He walked on, consumed by the irony of it all—that the woman would bless someone like him, someone so cursed as he.

Not once did he look back. They would be coming for him, this he knew. But not yet.

Unmolested, he left Brownsville, disappearing into the desert from whence he had come, into the malpais where he had lived as an exile for many years, a harsh and uncompromising land which had been the crucible of his soul.

Chapter 2

Charles Stoneman's house stood to the east of town, on the road that led to Brazos Island and the Gulf of Mexico, so Sam Burkin had to rent a buggy to get there, because he lived in Brownsville, in two small rooms above his law office on the edge of the business district. He traveled armed, a Briggs Single Shot under his coat. The Briggs wasn't much of a weapon, being of .22 caliber, nor very intimidating in appearance, either; but the Briggs was all Burkin had by way of firearms, and he wasn't much of a shootist, anyway. He knew hardly anything about guns—in fact, the reason he was running late for the meeting at Stoneman's was due to the fact that it had taken him an inordinate amount of time to clean and load the pistol, which had been gathering dust for months on the top shelf of his armoire.

It was the day following the killing of Bob Carnacky. Burkin half-expected to be waylaid by bloodthirsty Mexicans wielding machetes as he drove down the road, with the turgid Rio Grande on his right and the dun-colored desert on his left. Normally, he enjoyed the silence and solitude of the desert, for he often traveled this road. But he didn't enjoy the ride today, and was much relieved to arrive at the house in one piece.

The Stoneman residence was a square, two-story brick house built in the federal style—a most incongruous structure in this setting. Stoneman had imported all of the material used in its construction. It was filled with a shipload of fine furniture. This was Stoneman's way—only the best that money could buy. Burkin didn't see anything wrong with that. If a man could afford nice things then he had a perfect right to acquire them, and Burkin wasn't one to envy a wealthy capitalist his material possessions, since he aspired to be one himself someday. No, Burkin wasn't envious of Charles Stoneman's success and wealth; in fact, he admired Stoneman in many respects.

There was only one thing Burkin envied Stoneman for having, and that was Judith.

Arriving at the house, the young lawyer was met at the door by Stoneman's Mexican butler, and Burkin watched the man closely for any indication that the servant's perspective on his place in the grand scheme of things had been altered in any way by the murder of Bob Carnacky. It seemed as though everyone was expecting an armed insurrection by the local Mexican population. As though murder and mayhem were infectious diseases. It was, Burkin mused, an apprehension stemming from guilt. In his birthplace, Maryland's Eastern Shore region, planters lived their whole lives in mortal fear of a slave revolt. You treat badly enough and you have to know that one day they will make you pay the piper.

But the butler was as stoically courteous as always, informing Burkin in broken English that Stoneman and his other guests were already in the study. Burkin had seen the buggies and saddle horses in front of the house, and assumed that the entire leadership of the

Reds and one or two of the Blues was present—almost all of the power and money of Brownsville concentrated in one room, political rivals willing to set aside their differences to make common cause in a crisis.

If there was one occasion when punctuality was called for, this was it, and Burkin made instantly for the doors to Stoneman's study—only to draw up short as he heard his name spoken. He knew that voice. It was the sweetest, most magical voice in the world.

His heart hastened as he turned to see Judith descending the staircase, and for a moment all he could do was gape at her in breathless admiration. Then he remembered the butler, and looked around guiltily, hoping the man hadn't noticed the way he looked at Stoneman's wife. But the Mexican had vanished, and Burkin's long strides brought him to the foot of the stairs, where he clutched Judith's dainty hand and lifted it to his lips.

She laughed softly, delighted by his impulsive gallantry, but drew her hand away quickly with a wary glance in the direction of the study. They could hear voices from the other side of those doors, and Burkin realized he was taking an awful chance. But could a young man so hopelessly in love do otherwise?

"Samuel, I was so awfully worried about you," she whispered. "You're never late."

It was true, thought Burkin. On numerous occasions he and Judith had conspired to meet at remote places—usually an abandoned adobe hut in a remote thicket down by the river—and for these illicit trysts he was never tardy. The memories of those stolen moments made him ache, body and soul, to hold Judith in his arms and experience again the heat of her desire.

"It isn't my safety that concerns me," he replied.

"Has *he* mentioned sending you away until the danger is passed?"

Judith shook her head, and Burkin noticed how the summer sun stealing through the front door's fanlight and sidelights scintillated in the golden ringlets of her hair. Her beauty, he marveled, knew not the slightest imperfection. She was slender of form, full of grace, with flawless white skin and lips as red and soft at the petals of a rose—lips with which he longed to be reacquainted. Her best feature were those bright blue eyes filled with such tenderness when she looked at him.

"He hasn't spoken of it," she replied earnestly, "and I will not leave even if he insists that I go."

"A wife's place is with her husband."

Burkin wanted to ask her if she would leave *with* him. But he had asked the question once before, and he didn't want to cause her more anguish. She was much stronger and more rational than he. She could better endure the torment of those long periods of not seeing one another which often occurred. And she was constantly having to remind him of the folly of their running away together.

"We can only hope this will all blow over in a day or two," said Burkin. "Because as long as Brownsville is up in arms it will be nearly impossible for us to meet. If he is any kind of husband at all, Charles will not let you leave the house without a chaperone, and—"

The doors to the study swung open, and Burkin nearly jumped out of his skin as he whirled, stepped hastily away from the foot of the staircase.

"Samuel!" exclaimed Stoneman. "There you are, at last."

Burkin was certain his expression would betray him. He was blushing furiously.

"I was, um, paying my respects to your wife, Charles."

Stoneman spared Judith a most disinterested glance. "Of course. Where is that blasted Emilio? We need more brandy in here."

"I'll see to that, Charles," said Judith, and Burkin envied her the complete and innocent composure which she had managed.

"Good. Get in here, Samuel. We've got some very important matters to discuss."

Entering Charles Stoneman's study, one might have thought he was in the posh Washington Square town house of a New York aristocrat. Burkin had decided long ago that Stoneman had more books in this one room than could be found in all the rest of Texas. The irony of this was that as far as Burkin knew, Stoneman never read anything but newspapers. At least he had never seen the man with a book. But as for newspapers—well, Stoneman consumed them. He had them shipped to him from as far away as New York. They were brought in on the steamers that plied the Texas coast—the New York *Herald*, the Charleston *Mercury*, the *Picayune* of New Orleans, the *National Intelligencer*, the Washington *Union*. Stoneman was interested in two things, and two things only. Politics and business. These things were the breath of life to him. Without them, Burkin doubted the man would find living worthwhile.

Nonetheless, Stoneman felt obliged to keep a roomful of books. This room was an integral part of his image, with its leather-bound tomes from floor to ceiling, the big maple desk, the massive globe in the corner, the chairs and sofas of shiny black horsehair, the humidor containing Cuban cigars. The study was filled with the blue smoke of those Dosamygos, because nearly every man present had eagerly availed himself of the humidor's contents.

The only man who wasn't smoking was Stephen Powers. He was the sole representative of the Blues. Burkin had expected at least a few more, but of course Powers was the only representative the Blues really needed, for he was the Charles Stoneman of that political machine. He sat in a chair near one of the open windows, a small figure, his broadcloth suit hanging loosely on an emaciated frame, his features pale and pinched and dour, his thinning black hair plastered to his scalp with pomatum. An unprepossessing man, to say the least, but Burkin knew better than to judge this particular book by its cover. Powers had a brilliant mind and a caustic wit as sharp as a rapier. And he was definitely no man's fool. With regard to political machinations, Stephen Powers was a match for Stoneman in every respect. And that was saying something.

"Samuel, I believe you know everyone," said Stoneman, making for the leather chair behind his desk.

Burkin nodded to one and all. Josiah Grindle was present and accounted for, of course, and the rancher Mifflin Kennedy. Turnbull, the spokesman for the merchants and factors was here, and McColley, the burly Scotsman who had fought with Zachary Taylor in the war with Mexico and who now owned a small fleet of merchant ships that carried a fair share of the coastal trade from Matagorda to Tampico.

"You're just in time," Stoneman said. "Mac was about to tell us everything there is to know about

Antonio Caldero. I doubt anyone is more familiar with that fellow's history."

Again Burkin nodded. McColley possessed an encyclopedia of information about Mexico. For the past twelve years he had been doing a brisk trade south of the border, shipping manufactured goods south and bringing gold and silver back. No one knew for certain how rich the tight-fisted Scotsman really was, but he occasionally spoke of buying a small European principality and setting himself up as a potentate, living in a castle with a princess, the daughter of one of those royal houses of which they had so many in the Old World. Burkin had no doubt that the man could afford to make that idle dream a reality if he ever chose to do so.

"Aye," said McColley gruffly, "I know about Caldero. Everyone in Coahuila—nae, make that all of Mexico—knows him. You ask them, they will seldom tell you anything. They'll act dumb on the subject, but they know him, you can read it in their eyes. He stands second only to Jesus Christ in their estimation. The bloody devil."

"They say he's just a bandit," said Burkin. "A cutthroat thief and murderer."

"Depends on who you ask," replied McColley. "To the Mexican, he's a patriot. You see, after the revolution—the one you had here in Texas back in '36—Texans claimed the Rio Grande as their southern boundary. But Mexico had other ideas. Its government claimed their northern boundary was the Nueces. As you probably know, Burkin, legally it was hard to tell who was in the right. The provinces of Coahuila and Texas were governed as a single entity, and had been for quite a while before the revolt. And the Mexicans never granted a single league of land below the Nueces to Anglos.

"So for years the title of this strip of godforsaken real estate was in dispute. But the Mexican government never made a serious attempt to defend it with military force. They were in no condition to fight another war, and the British moneylenders who propped up the government with their pounds sterling discouraged Santa Anna from making good his threat to resume hostilities with the Republic of Texas. For all intents and purposes, the Nueces Strip belonged to Texas by default, if for no other reason.

"But there was one Mexican who wouldn't give up the Strip without a fight. That was one Antonio Caldero."

McColley paused as Judith Stoneman knocked on the study's door and entered bearing a decanter of brandy. All the men seated in the room rose respectfully as she entered. Everyone, Burkin noticed, except Stoneman. Judith greeted each man, but for Burkin and her husband. After the amenities had been attended to, and she had refilled McColley's empty glass, Judith took her leave.

"That's one fine lady you've got there, Charles," said Turnbull. "You're a damned lucky man."

"I suppose so," said Stoneman, with supreme disinterest. "Go ahead, Mac."

McColley took a gulp of brandy, puffed on his Cuban long nine, and nodded curtly. "Caldero waged his private war for nigh on ten years. He made life a living hell—most of the time a bloody *short* living hell—for any American who set foot south of the Nueces. Not even the Texas Rangers could stop him. He didn't quit his plunderin', murderin' ways until the war with Mexico broke out. Then a funny thing happened. You might have thought he'd fight on Santa Anna's side against the United States Army. Santa Anna had plenty of irregular cavalry. Called themselves *Rancheros*. Worse than the bloody Russian Cossacks. Apparently, though, Caldero had no liking for Santa Anna, and he took no part in the war. Lucky for us, since General Taylor's supply lines ran right across the Nueces Strip."

"Some folks say Sam Houston had something to do with all that," remarked Grindle. "That Houston convinced Caldero to keep out of the war. In return, Caldero got his amnesty. One of the first things Houston did as United States senator was see to Caldero's federal pardon."

"The United States government may have pardoned Caldero," said McColley, "but Texas never will."

"It would seem that the pardon was a waste of paper and ink," said Stoneman. "Apparently Caldero is not fully reformed."

"No matter who it was that killed Bob Carnacky," drawled Powers, "you have to assume it was probably justifiable homicide." He smiled crookedly at the shocked expression on Stoneman's face. "Oh, don't pretend outrage, Charles. Your man was one brutal, no-account son of a bitch, and you know it. He was beating a defenseless old man to death and Caldero stopped him. There were witnesses, you know."

"*Mexican* witnesses," said Stoneman. "Hardly reliable, under any circumstances."

"Oh, yes, I forgot. You'll take their vote, but not their testimony."

"I didn't realize you had suddenly become champion of the poor, downtrodden Mexican, Stephen. I haven't seen any *campesinos* invited to your supper table."

"I haven't had any Reds at my table, either," was Powers's quick retort, "but that doesn't mean I don't respect their rights. As for witnesses, I daresay there must have been some Americans who saw what happened. Not that I would expect any of them to come forward in defense of Antonio Caldero." Powers looked straight at Grindle as he spoke.

"I didn't see anything until the deed had been done," said Grindle.

"Of course not. What convenient timing on your part, Josiah."

"Caldero came here looking for trouble," growled McColley. "Maybe he had in mind killing Carnacky from the start. Why else would he show up in Brownsville?"

"Why shouldn't he come here?" asked Powers. "He has been absolved of all his sins. He isn't wanted for any crime that I am aware of. He has a perfect right to visit this fair city."

"He had to know there would be trouble," said Burkin, standing by the window to escape the cigar smoke, and gazing out at the sun-blasted desert. "If what Mr. McColley says is true, few people in these parts are willing to let bygones be bygones where Caldero is concerned."

"So why *did* he come to Brownsville?" asked Turnbull.

The question was left to dangle unanswered in a momentary silence.

Stoneman flicked his ten-dollar cigar out the window as though it were a cheap border-town cheroot.

"What does it matter why he came here? Whether Caldero intended to stir something up or not, that's exactly what he has done. We must expect the worst, even while we hope for the best. By killing Carnacky, Caldero may stir the embers of discontent among our Mexican population. It is our responsibility to arrange for the protection of Brownsville, to maintain law and order, to plan for any eventuality. And we must set aside partisanship to work together in this moment of crisis."

Powers knew that last remark was directed at him. "I doubt we'll have a crisis—unless one is manufactured."

McColley scowled. "What the bloody hell do you mean by that?"

"I mean," replied Powers, smirking, "that there are some who have been looking for any excuse to start another war with Mexico."

"To what avail, sir?" asked Turnbull, with an indignation that Burkin thought was a bit overplayed.

Powers leaned forward, his eyes glinting like diamonds.

"For the purpose of justifying an invasion of our southern neighbor, sir."

"Preposterous," said Turnbull, filling his jowls with air and blowing it out in an explosion with that single word. "I know of no such conspiracy."

"Gentlemen," said Stoneman, playing the mediator, "come now. We must put all this aside and give our undivided attention to the matter at hand. I pray that Stephen is correct, that we have no crisis. But it's better to be safe than sorry. In my opinion we must notify the governor at once, so that he in turn may acquaint the federal government with our plight. I am confident the governor will dispatch a company of Rangers here to keep the peace. And perhaps the federal authorities will see fit to re-garrison Fort Brown. Until that time, however, we're on our own, and it is my humble opinion that we should call out the Brownsville Tigers at once."

Burkin stifled a groan. The Tigers! Hardly an appropriate name for the local militia!

All eyes were suddenly on him, and Burkin was afraid his look of dismay had betrayed his true feelings about Stoneman's suggestion.

"Well, Sam?" asked McColley, impatient as always. "You are, are you not, captain of our militia?"

"Yes, of course. But I think in this case it would be better if we address this to Colonel Jarvis, as he is the commanding officer."

"Jarvis," scoffed McColley. "That drunken old goat."

"That's no way to talk about a military hero," said Powers wryly.

"We all know he broke his leg falling off that stallion last year because he was too besotted to keep to his saddle," said the Scotsman. "It's Burkin here who commands the Tigers, in all but title. So I want to hear from him whether he believes our militia is up to the task."

Burkin coughed and cleared his throat, buying a few precious seconds to think through his dilemma. He could afford to waste no time in self-pity, wondering why the Fates had been so unkind as to arrange for his involvement in the Tigers. He certainly hadn't *wanted* to be captain, having joined the militia only because it was a kind of social club for the young, up and coming men of Brownsville. But the others had elected him to be their captain, and he'd been foolish enough at the time to deem it a great honor. Little did he know!

Like most American militias, the Brownsville Tigers were ill-trained, ill-equipped, and in general ill-prepared for any type of service—much less standing between the good people of Brownsville and an insurrection. The law that required men of sound mind and body between the ages of eighteen and forty-five to serve in a local militia company was honored most often in the breach. Young men signed up because militia duty was fun. It was a lark, a chance to socialize, to dress up in uniforms and participate in parades and other festivities, and it was a perfect way to attract the attention of the young ladies.

As Burkin well knew, the Tigers did not take well to strict discipline—or really any kind of discipline at all. Though he had known next to nothing about proper drilling technique and other martial matters, he had tried at first to take his duty seriously and do his best to mold the Tigers into an effective force—only to discover that the men had elected him their captain precisely because that was the last thing they had expected from him. "Hell, Sam, what is all this soldierin' bunkum?" one man had complained. "If we'd wanted to really learn all this humbug, we would have picked an honest-to-God military man for our captain, not you."

Confronted with this kind of attitude, Burkin soon gave up trying to improve the company.

Now, suddenly, he was overwhelmed by a guilty conscience. How could he explain to Stoneman and McColley and the others that the Brownsville Tigers were a useless bunch of ne'er-do-wells? He had to shoulder at least some of the blame. Yes, Jarvis was partly responsible, he supposed. McColley wasn't far off the mark with his snide comments about the colonel. Jarvis took absolutely no interest in the training of the Tigers. He simply couldn't be bothered, unless it was to ride at the front in a parade. Too busy drinking his sour mash and diddling his young Mexican wife. "I leave it in your capable hands, my boy," Jarvis would tell him. But Burkin had known all along that he was inadequate to the task. And now his inadequacy would be exposed for all the world to see.

"Well, Samuel?" asked Stoneman. "What do you think?"

"I think—I *know*—that the Tigers will do their duty," said Burkin, feeling even guiltier than before for avoiding the unpleasant truth yet again.

"That's the spirit!" exclaimed Turnbull, delighted.

"Excellent," said Stoneman, nodding. "I'm sure Mr. Turnbull here will see to it that your men have an ample supply of ammunition."

"Well, yes," mumbled Turnbull, disconcerted by the thought of profit lost. "Yes, I suppose."

"That's it, then," said Powers, rising abruptly from his chair. "Seeing the Brownsville Tigers patrolling the streets should instill a renewed confidence in the people." He glanced at Burkin with a wry smile twisting the corners of his mouth, and Burkin glanced away, ashamed. "Good day to you gentlemen. Charles, give my farewell and good wishes to your wife."

When Powers was gone, Stoneman rose from his own chair, laughing softly.

"What's so funny?" asked Burkin. He could see nothing even remotely humorous about any aspect of the present situation.

"Stephen is as sharp as a knife, I'll give him that. I suppose there's no fooling him."

"What do you mean?"

"I mean he's altogether correct. This is a golden opportunity for us, Samuel. If we don't have a war by Christmas, I'll be very surprised—and very disappointed."

"Disappointed? You want a war?"

Stoneman glanced at the other men in the room. "Should we tell him?"

"Tell me what?" asked Burkin, thoroughly baffled.

"Aye, tell the man," said McColley. "We know he can be trusted."

Grindle, Kennedy, and Turnbull all nodded in accord.

"We are members of a secret organization known as the Knights of the Golden Circle," Stoneman told Burkin. "The mission of the Knights is the annexation of Mexico by the United States, and the settlement of the controversy over slavery once and for all."

"You expect to settle that controversy by taking Mexico?" asked Burkin. He very nearly asked Stoneman if he were mad. But he refrained, scanning the faces of the four men in the study. They weren't lunatics. They were deadly serious. Burkin had a distinct impression that he would soon wish he had never heard of the Knights of the Golden Circle.

"It is a bold and visionary scheme," said Stoneman. "Have a brandy, Samuel, and help yourself to a cigar. Sit down and I will tell you all about the Knights and what they stand for, and then you will better understand why Carnacky's death is such a boon for us."

It had begun with a man named George Bickley, a Virginian by birth, a doctor by trade who dabbled in history and novel writing. Later, after drifting to Cincinnati, Bickley established a literary periodical, the *West American Review*. But the journal, like his novel-writing, proved a failure. Always keenly interested in fraternal organizations, he eventually created his own, the American Legion, or Knights of the Golden Circle.

Bickley set forth the mission of the KGC in a pamphlet entitled *Rules, Regulations, and Principles of the KGC issued by order of the General President*—the latter exalted post, naturally, being filled by none other than Bickley himself. The Knights, he predicted, would become a powerful, secret, military organization which would free the cotton South from the tyranny of northern commercial and manufacturing tycoons. How was the South to prevent northern Free-Soilers from gaining political dominance over her? How could she protect her culture, her civilization, the finest in the world, from the contamination of northern ideas of industrialization and urbanization and all the evils associated with them? In the South, all white men were equal. But industrialization divided whites into classes—the aristocracy and the laborers. This was a future many southerners like Bickley abhorred. The KGC had the answer. Colonize Mexico. Civilize it. Prepare it for annexation by the United States. And carve from it twenty-five new slave states to add to the Union.

And if the Union rejected annexation, then a Mexico run by the KGC could just as easily be absorbed into a southern Confederacy.

Mexico, said Bickley and his disciples, was an untapped land of plenty. Its annexation would bring untold wealth into the South. The North as well, considering the well-known Yankee avarice of northern merchants and manufacturers. Bickley fully expected northerners to support his plan. Best of all, Mexico would be a perfect place to deposit the four million slaves now contained in the South—those slaves who were the cause of so much discord in the nation these days.

If you were a southerner, the fact that the slave population was four million and growing was cause for grave concern when you added to the calculation the fact that the Free-Soilers were committed to containing slavery within its present limits, even as the abolitionists were seeking to free all the slaves. Pause if you would, said the southerner, and contemplate for a moment what would happen if both the Free-Soiler and the abolitionist had their way. Why, four million Negroes would be set loose upon the South. This would be a social and economic catastrophe of biblical proportions. No Southron, slaveholder or not, would stand by and let such a calamity come to pass.

Whether you wanted to expand the boundaries of slavery because you thought it would flourish in Latin America, or because you wanted to maintain the political balance between North and South, slave and free, in the halls of Congress, or even because you just wanted some place to put all the blacks, it was generally conceded throughout the South that new territories had to be acquired.

That was where the Golden Circle part of the organization's name came in. If you placed Havana, the jewel of the Caribbean, in the center of a circle with a radius of sixteen geographic degrees—about twelve-hundred miles—that circle would include Maryland, Kentucky, part of Missouri, the rest of the South, most of Texas and Old Mexico, all of Central America, the northern tip of South America, and all of the West Indies. This area the KGC envisioned as a great Southern slave empire that would rival in power the Roman Empire of two thousand years ago. This empire would control the world's supply of tobacco, cotton, sugar, and coffee. The organization had already backed filibustering expeditions against Cuba and Nicaragua. These excursions had failed, but the Knights were not discouraged. They just learned from their mistakes. They planned and schemed and organized and propagandized and waited for the right moment.

The Order of the Knights was in many ways as secretive an organization as the Freemasons. It had a constitution, by laws, rules, an elaborate initiation ceremony, and secret signs. The local units were called "castles." There were three degrees of membership. The first was the military degree, the Knights of the Iron Hand. This was the KGC army, ready to take up arms at a moment's notice. "The South, right or wrong," was its credo. The second degree was the financial, the Knights of the True Faith. These were the financiers of the organization. The third degree was the political, the Knights of the Columbian Star. These were the leaders.

It came as no surprise to Burkin that while Grindle was a member of the first degree, and McColley, Kennedy, and Turnbull members of the second, Charles Stoneman was one of only a half dozen Knights in Texas who belonged to the Order of the Columbian Star.

"We have over thirty castles in Texas," Stoneman told him. "We can muster an army of at least five thousand Texans in a fortnight. Why, even some of your Brownsville Tigers are members. And more will come from our sister states in the South."

"I had no idea," confessed Burkin, dumbfounded. "Why didn't you ever say anything about this to me, Charles?"

"You've only been here a year," said Kennedy, the rancher. "Nobody knew anything about you. We weren't sure you could be relied upon."

"I was sure of you from the beginning," said Stoneman. "I knew instinctively that you could be trusted, Samuel. That's why I'm telling you this now, because I am confident you would never betray my trust."

"Of course not," said Burkin woodenly, thinking of Judith. "So what is it that you gentlemen expect of me?"

"Why, nothing," replied Stoneman. "I only thought that you should know, since you will, in effect, be commanding the Tigers, bearing in mind that our old friend, Colonel Jarvis, is perpetually incapacitated by demon rum."

"I see," muttered Burkin. He reconsidered telling these men the truth about their vaunted Brownsville militia. The Tigers were certainly not qualified to be the vanguard of an invasion of Mexico, and Burkin got the feeling that this was exactly what Stoneman and the others had in mind.

"Well, then," said Stoneman. "I believe your first task will be the publication of a notice, calling the militia to arms. I will produce another notice—alerting the citizens that, effective immediately, Brownsville is under martial law, by order of the mayor and city council. Right, Mayor?"

"Quite," said Turnbull, trying to sound officious.

Burkin stared at the merchant. It was easy to forget

that Turnbull was Brownsville's mayor, since Stoneman was the man behind the throne. Turnbull dared not do anything without Stoneman's approval. He was Stoneman's puppet, his rubber stamp.

"Better write a letter to Houston, too," suggested Kennedy.

"Consider it done, Mifflin," said Stoneman.

"Houston? Why Sam Houston?" asked Burkin. "I thought it was Governor Runnels you were going to notify."

"Everybody knows that come December, Sam Houston will be our next governor," said Stoneman. "And he will be particularly interested in what has transpired here. For, as you may know, he has long proposed establishing a protectorate over Mexico. He even offered a resolution to that effect in the United States Senate."

"He's not a Knight of the Golden Circle, is he?" asked Burkin, aghast. "I thought Sam Houston was a Union man. He says he is, often enough."

"He is," said McColley. "He says secessionists are traitors and madmen. But he wants to be president, Old Sam does. Wants it so bloody bad he'd crawl into bed with Lucifer himself if it would help him win the White House."

Stoneman nodded, smiling wryly. "Houston is waiting for an excuse to intervene in Mexico. He's got his reasons, and we've got ours. We'll let him think he's using us. But we'll be using him."

Still somewhat stunned, Burkin took his leave. The Mexican butler saw him out. Burkin was sorry not to have another moment alone with Judith. He had a bad feeling that this business with Caldero and the Tigers and the Knights of the Golden Circle was somehow going to ruin his relationship with Judith Stoneman.

In the buggy on the road back to Brownsville, Burkin gave serious consideration to packing his belongings and booking passage on the next coastal steamer bound for Galveston or New Orleans or Mobile. It didn't matter where, as long as it was far removed from Brownsville, Texas. He wanted no part of this madness. My God, they were going to start a war, for crying out loud! All because Bob Carnacky had gotten his just desserts. *I knew that man was trouble from the moment I had the great misfortune of laying eyes on him.*

But by the time he had reached the outskirts of town, Burkin had made up his mind to stay. He really had no choice in the matter. He couldn't leave without Judith, and Judith wouldn't go away with him, and so he resigned himself to the fact that his addictive desire for another man's wife was going to get him killed.

"God help me," he muttered. "God help me—and the Mexicans."

Chapter 3

"Is that him? Is that really Sam Houston?"

John Henry McAllen couldn't help but smile at his son's excitement. Gideon was sixteen, and usually acted very mature for his age. But this morning he was behaving more like a six-year-old because a living legend was coming to visit.

"That's him."

McAllen knew it was so, even though Houston was a quarter mile away, on the east side of the Brazos River, and the morning sun was in his eyes, to boot. But there could be no mistaking the man, even under these conditions. McAllen knew Sam Houston far too well not to recognize him at a distance.

"It's really Sam Houston? In the flesh?" asked Gideon. "You wouldn't be pulling my leg, would you, sir?"

"No, sir, I would not, knowing how serious you take this."

"I've never met a hero like Sam Houston before."

He is just a man, mused McAllen, *with his share of a man's failings. Great men have great shortcomings.*

Standing on the bluff above the river, McAllen watched Houston lead his saddle horse onto the ferry. Old Jeb was down there, with his son Jethro, who was

Gideon's age; the two of them had been waiting on the other side of the river since before daybreak, for Houston had sent word on ahead that he was due to arrive today.

Watching Houston, McAllen tried to analyze his own reaction to seeing the general again. He was oddly ambivalent about Houston's visit. They were old friends. McAllen had fought with Houston at San Jacinto, on that glorious day when Texas won her independence from Mexico. There had been a time when McAllen would have done anything for Sam Houston, sacrificed everything, even his life, to do the man's bidding. He supposed he would still die for Houston, if necessary, as he would for anyone he considered a friend. But the old sense of blind devotion was gone. In fact, McAllen almost dreaded seeing Houston again, and wondered why he felt that way.

Glancing behind him at Grand Cane, McAllen decided it was in part because he was getting older. He was nearly fifty years of age. Fifty years! A half century! He was still in trim shape, full of vigor, scarcely ever under the weather. His eyesight was good, and he still had all his teeth. There was a lot of gray in his jet black hair these days, and old wounds nagged him when he worked an especially long day. But all in all . . . McAllen idly stroked the scar on his cheek with a thumb. He was in far better shape at fifty than he had any right to expect.

All his life he'd been a warrior. Born in Mississippi, a lawyer by trade, he had captained a Warren County militia company in the Second Seminole War. He and his men had been known as the Black Jacks, on account of the black shell jackets the women of Warren County had made for them. After getting his fill of the Florida swamps, McAllen had come to Texas, and most of the Black Jacks had followed. Together they had served with distinction in the war for Texas independence. After San Jacinto, the new republic had awarded six leagues of land to McAllen—twenty-five thousand acres of prime property along the Brazos. Here McAllen had built his plantation, Grand Cane, successfully cultivating sugar. The Black Jacks, devoted to their captain as well as to one another, had also put down roots. The Republic of Texas had offered land to every man in the company, but McAllen had said no; twenty-five thousand acres was much more than he would ever need, and he parceled the land out evenly among his men. A settlement, also called Grand Cane, had sprung up a few miles from the plantation.

Nowadays, reflected McAllen, there weren't many Black Jacks left. Of the twenty-eight men who had come to Texas with him, only ten remained alive. A. G. Deckard still ran his tavern. Morris Riddle and Cedric Cole were still above snakes. And old Artemus Tice, too, of all the Black Jacks McAllen's closest friend and confidant. But Tice was almost seventy, and his body was becoming frail. *I will see him die,* thought McAllen sadly, *as I've seen so many other friends shed this mortal coil.*

Death had come for so many of the people close to him. Roman and Bessie, house servants who had been like family, were gone now, buried in a plot behind the big house. So was Joshua, son of a runaway slave and a Seminole warrior. Joshua had been like a son to McAllen; a boy caught up in the fury of the swampland war, McAllen had saved his life, and Joshua had repaid him with years of unswerving loyalty. They had been through many a scrape side by side, and McAllen had almost believed the mute half-breed was indestructible. But Joshua had died on that unforgettable day in the Palo Duro Canyon when McAllen had finally found Emily Torrance in the Comanche camp.

"They're almost to this side, now," said Gideon. "Hadn't we ought to get down there to meet them?"

"You run on ahead."

"Yes, sir!"

Gideon took off at a gallop, speeding down the footpath, waving his arms over his head and hollering, "*Hello, Sam Houston! Hello, Sam Houston!*" Slipping and sliding all the way down the face of the bluff, so that McAllen thought *the fool boy is going to break his neck if he isn't careful*, but miraculously the nimble youth kept his balance and made it to the bottom. And down on the ferry the tall, broad-shouldered man in the dusty frock coat and nankeen trousers and wide-brimmed white fur hat looked up and waved back.

McAllen drew a long breath, wondering why his old friend and commanding officer was coming to call. What magnificent scheme had Sam Houston hatched now? President of the Texas republic, governor of the state after annexation in 1845, United States senator almost continually after that—all these Houston had been. And yet McAllen was confident the man's ambition had yet to be satisfied. Sam Houston was a big dreamer and a big doer.

Therein lay the problem. McAllen had realized all of his own dreams. He had Grand Cane, a son, a wife he loved more than he loved life itself. All he wanted was to be left alone. Yes, he was an old warhorse, but he'd put himself out to pasture, and there he wanted to stay. His only desire was to enjoy the life he had made in the few years left to him. But Houston was bound to have something up his sleeve. He almost always did. And John Henry McAllen decided he wanted no part of it, no matter what it was.

Reservations intact, McAllen shrugged the tension out of his shoulders and proceeded down the footpath to greet his Old Chief.

Houston had not visited Grand Cane for years, and he insisted that McAllen give him a quick tour of the plantation. The house had been built at the highest point of the bluff, a two-story structure of hewn cottonwood logs with a roof of thick post oak shingles. Inside, the floors were ash, hand-sawed and planed. Doors, window frames, and interior woodwork were walnut, and the interior walls were plastered. Downstairs, two large rooms flanked a broad hallway. Upstairs were four more spacious rooms. Six walnut columns graced the front porch, running the width of the house. The back gallery connected the house with a stone-walled kitchen. Next to the kitchen stood a cedar-post dairy. Nearby stood the barn, carriage house, and blacksmith's shop. Beyond a row of stately pecans, on the slope to the south, was a row of log cabins, the quarters occupied by McAllen's former slaves. At the base of the slope was the sugar mill, and in the rich bottomland along the river grew the sugarcane.

At the base of the bluff McAllen had built a landing, for here the Brazos was navigable to the coast. It was by riverboat that he shipped his sugar down to the port of Quintana. The cane stood tall in the summer sun. The stalks had been planted in late winter, sprouted in the spring, and in the autumn before the first frost the harvesting would take place. The cane would be ground down, and the juice boiled into crystals, which were then refined in the mill. The syrup would be thickened into molasses.

Now the hands were harvesting the first of this year's two corn crops. The corn provided fodder for the livestock, and came to table in a multitude of forms—as bread, grits, mush, pudding, roasted ears, and whiskey. It was as they watched the hands, working in two gangs, one to pick the ears of corn and the second following behind and using cane knives to hack away the stalks, that Houston turned to McAllen with a bemused expression on his craggy features.

"You freed your slaves some years ago, didn't you, John Henry?"

"I did, General. When I left to get Emily back from the Comanches I made arrangements for Jeb and all the others to be manumitted in the event I never returned."

"But you did return."

"It seemed the fair thing to do, regardless. I gave everyone a section of land and promised to pay wages to everyone who stayed."

"A decision which has caused hard feeling among some of your slaveholding neighbors, I'll warrant."

McAllen nodded. "I can understand their point of view. Makes their own slaves wonder why they're not getting the same kind of deal."

"Not everyone could afford to free their slaves," said Houston, "even if they wanted to. What does a prime field hand bring at auction these days?"

"A thousand dollars at the very least, sir," said Gideon. "Probably more."

"Exactly," said Houston. "A gang of slaves is a big investment."

"It wasn't a question of whether I could afford it or not," said McAllen. "You know what I mean, General. There are some in the South who brand you a Free-Soiler, or worse, an abolitionist."

"And your former slaves?" asked Houston, pointing with his chin at the men and women working in the corn. "How many stayed?"

"All but a very few."

Houston nodded, brows knit above his piercing blue eyes. "Yes, we must be rid of slavery. Mind you, I'm no abolitionist. I don't object to the institution on moral grounds."

"We southerners have a constitutional right to own slaves," blurted Gideon.

Houston chuckled. "I see you've raised your boy to think and speak for himself."

"Yes," said McAllen, with something less than perfect enthusiasm.

"Well, Gideon, we shall have to discuss the issue in more detail. But later. Speaking of Emily, John Henry, I can't wait to meet your lovely bride again."

"I know she is looking forward to seeing you again, sir."

They were on their way to the house when Houston said, "I well remember the chain of events surrounding your wife's capture by the Comanches. That fool Mirabeau Lamar started it all with that debacle at the Council House."

"I've always believed your Indian policy was the wisest," said McAllen. "If we leave them alone they usually return the favor."

"The big raid of 1840—by the Eternal, John Henry, that was a long time ago!"

"Yes, sir, it's been a while."

"I suppose you recollect Antonio Caldero. The role he played in Emily's rescue."

McAllen nodded.

"And I suppose you've heard about what has recently taken place down in Brownsville."

"I've heard," was McAllen's wary concession.

Houston said no more, and they walked on, Gideon following along behind with the general's horse in tow.

A thick hedge of Cherokee roses encircled the main house, and as he passed through the gate set in the hedge, following Houston, McAllen saw Emily emerge onto the broad front porch. She had been watching for them.

"My dear child!" exclaimed Houston, advancing with long strides to take her hand and, bowing in the continental fashion, kissing it lightly. A rather outmoded gallantry, thought McAllen, but he wasn't too surprised; one never knew exactly what to expect where Sam Houston was concerned.

"Welcome to Grand Cane, General," she said, with a sweet smile that could not fail to melt the heart of any man. "It's such a pleasure to see you again."

"It's been entirely too long. By the Eternal, John Henry, the years have not left their mark on her. She is as lovely as ever."

"Yes, I know," said McAllen, and the way he said it made Emily glance at him, surprised and pleased by the earnest, almost reverential tenor of his voice.

Houston was right—Emily hadn't changed much in the nineteen years she had been John Henry McAllen's wife. She was still the willowy, auburn-haired girl he had fallen in love with, and for whom had risked everything to rescue from her Comanche captors.

That had happened in 1840. Mirabeau Bonaparte Lamar had been president of the Republic of Texas, then, succeeding Houston, and Lamar's belligerent Indian policy and saber rattling had resulted in the cold-blooded massacre of forty Comanches who had come in peace to the San Antonio Council House to what they had thought would be the discussion of a peace treaty. The massacre had served to unify the various Comanche bands, placing the young republic in grave peril.

Seeking retribution, the Comanches had struck back that summer, launching the largest Indian raid in Texas history as nearly a thousand warriors descended from the Staked Plains and set the frontier aflame. They moved south, burning farms and villages, killing, raping, and plundering, and they pressed on until they reached the coast and sacked the port of Linnville. On the return home, the raiding party split up into smaller bands, clashing with militia and Texas Rangers. One band had hit Grand Cane, killing several people and abducting Emily Torrance, the ward of one of McAllen's Black Jacks.

The Black Jacks had struck out in hot pursuit, but the Comanches eluded them. Emily's uncle slipped away to continue the search when the others turned back; Yancey Torrance had ventured into the trackless wastes of the hostile Llano Estacado, never to be seen or heard from again.

For more than a year McAllen continued the search for Emily—to no avail. It was then that Houston had intervened with Antonio Caldero on his behalf. Caldero was friend to the Comanche, and he had connections with the Comancheros, the tribe's Mexican allies. With Caldero's help, McAllen had at last found Emily in the Palo Duro encampment of the Quohadi Comanche.

McAllen loved Emily with his whole heart and soul, a much deeper and more profound love than he had ever experienced. He'd been married once before. Leah had been a real beauty. It was that beauty which had beguiled McAllen so—as it beguiled every man who laid eyes on her. But Leah had been unfaithful. She had a need for male attention that no one man could satisfy. McAllen's foolish pride had prevented him from divorcing her—until he'd realized how much Emily meant to him. Only then had he been willing to admit to the failure of his first marriage. Divorcing Leah, he'd set out to save Emily from the Comanches or die trying. The past nineteen years were proof positive that he had made the right choice. He and Emily were made for each other.

"We are lucky fools, John Henry," said Houston. "We both found the mate the Almighty had intended for us. That is something not every man can say."

"And how is Mrs. Houston?" asked Emily. "Well, I hope."

"She and the children are well, though I must confess that my long absences these past twelve years have taken their toll on her. Margaret, for one, was not sorry to see my career as a United States senator come to an end. I missed the births of all my children, save the first." He shook his head. "A poor record, indeed."

"The newspaper said some perfectly awful things

about your vote against the Kansas-Nebraska Bill, General," said Emily.

"They have kicked me as they would a cur dog, Mrs. McAllen. But I cast my vote for the South, the Union, and Texas. That bill was a fraud perpetrated against the South. It was pure humbug, presented by that prince of humbugs, Stephen Douglas. It was never intended to open the door to Kansas for slavery. Those who proposed it knew slavery would never take hold in that territory. Pride blinded my fellow southerners. They loudly proclaimed it was their constitutional right to carry their slaves into *all* the new territories, and the Missouri Compromise be hanged. Little did they know that the Missouri Compromise was their best, their *only*, defense against Free-Soilism. The Kansas-Nebraska Act was a Trojan horse, and now—only now, when it is too late—does the South realize its mistake. I tried to warn them, but they were too busy cursing me to the devil to hear my words. But forgive me. I did not intend to make a speech."

"You are forgiven, General," said Emily, smiling. "I know you two must have a great deal to talk about, so if you'd like to sit out here on the porch I will bring you some refreshments. No strong spirits for you, still, is that right, General?"

"I remain a staunch teetotaler," sighed Houston. "Heaven help me, but I'm even speaking to temperance leagues these days." He shook his head. "If my old Cherokee friends could see me now! They used to call me Oo-Tse-Tee-Ar-dee-tah-Skee. Big Drunk. But Margaret has been a good influence on me. Why, I'll have you know I've even been baptized."

As Emily went back inside, McAllen and Houston repaired to some rocking chairs at the east end of the porch, now shaded from the hot afternoon sun. There they were joined by Gideon, who had stabled Houston's horse. Emily brought them some lemonade, and excused herself again to tend to supper. A pair of spotted hounds came trotting up to sniff their boots and then flop down on the porch near them, panting hard, their tongues lolling.

"I take it your visit is not entirely a social call, General," said McAllen.

"I am ashamed to admit that you are right, as always, John Henry."

"This has something to do with Caldero, I'll wager."

"You'd win that bet. Mark my words, we are going to have stirring times on the border, 'ere long."

"You mean a war? I doubt it. Caldero and I have one thing in common. Our fighting days are behind us, and we know it."

"You misunderstand. I don't mean that Caldero will start a war, though every Texan south of the Nueces is deathly afraid that he'll do just that. No, sir, he won't start it, but we'll have war, nonetheless. We *must*! Or all is lost."

McAllen stared at him. "You mean you *want* a fight?"

"I want to save the Union," said Houston gravely. "It must be preserved. That was General Jackson's creed, and I have adopted it as my own."

Perplexed, McAllen shook his head. "I confess, I don't follow you, General. How could a border war save the Union?"

"Listen, and I will tell you." Houston leaned forward, elbows on knees, the glass of lemonade cupped in his big, rough hands. "It is a complicated tale, but I know whereof I speak."

* * *

McAllen sent Jethro into town to inform Artemus Tice of Houston's arrival, and the physician came out to Grand Cane late in the afternoon with every intention of accepting an invitation to stay for supper. Though he had "dressed for the occasion," Tice could not avoid looking rather seedy; his white linen suit was rumpled and dusty and reeked of chemicals and pipe smoke. He was a small, gray, wizened man, over seventy years of age, wearing a battered stovepipe hat on his head and a pair of spectacles thick as bottle glass on his nose. He used a teak walking stick that sported a staghorn handle—old war wounds and arthritis left him something short of spry. But in spite of his deteriorating condition, Tice's mind remained untrammeled by age.

Tice was McAllen's closest friend and confidant. They had been comrades for nearly thirty years, ever since Tice had forsaken a lucrative practice to accompany the Black Jacks into the living hell of Florida swamps infested with gators, cottonmouths, and hostile Indians. McAllen knew of no man who had more courage or stamina. Every last Black Jack admired and revered Artemus Tice; he'd saved the life, or at least a limb, of nearly every one of them.

No one, however, revered Tice more than Emily. A widower who had never been blessed with a child of his own, Tice treated Emily as he would a daughter, and even before Emily lost her Uncle Yancey and Aunt Mary, she had thought of Tice as an uncle. He had always been the one person she could confide in. She could speak freely and expect understanding and good advice when she needed it. And now that her aunt and uncle were dead, Tice had become even more dear to her heart. Next to her son and husband, Emily loved the old doctor most of all.

By the light of oil lamps they supped in the dining room, with the windows open to let in a cooling night breeze. Emily had gone to great lengths to prepare a frontier-style feast in honor of their guest. There was quail served in gravy with currant jelly, venison marinated in a sauce consisting of onions, parsley, thyme, bay leaves, and cloves added to vinegar and larded with salt pork, in addition to crackling bread and molasses, fresh vegetables from the garden, and loaf cake and coffee for dessert. McAllen produced some claret for Artemus, and had a bit of brandy himself after Houston assured him that it was quite all right to partake in his presence.

"I've more or less lost the hankering," said Houston. "Heaven knows it wasn't easy in the beginning. My old slave, Esau, used to make me orange bitters as a substitute when I had a strong craving for liquor. I soon grew to despise that concoction."

"Is he the one who ran away to Mexico?" asked Gideon.

"He and one other," said Houston, nodding. "I understand one is a barber in Matamoros, and the other joined the Mexican army."

"Many Texas slaves have fled to Mexico," said Gideon. "We should have insisted on their return as part of the treaty that ended the war."

"Frankly, I don't want my two runaways back. They are more trouble then they're worth."

"Some people have called you an abolitionist, sir. Is there any truth to that charge?"

"Gideon!" said Emily sternly.

"No, no, Mrs. McAllen," said Houston. "His is a

fair question, and I am inclined to answer it. No, Gideon, I'm not an abolitionist. I am opposed to the mad fanaticism of men like William Lloyd Garrison. But neither do I approve of the secessionists of the South. Men like William Yancey, who speak of a southern league or confederacy, ought to be committed to the madhouse."

"But if our rights and property are not protected within the Union, we must leave it and make our own way."

"I am a southern man," said Houston gravely. "My wife and children are southern. My home has always been in the South. I have watered southern soil with my blood on more than one occasion. No one has done more for southern interests than I. But I cannot, and will not, countenance talk of dissolution. I cherish every manly sentiment for the South, and I am determined that while I live none of the fraternal bonds which bind it to the Union shall be broken. I wish no prouder epitaph to mark the board or slab that may lie on my tomb than this: 'He loved his country, he was a patriot, he was devoted to the Union.' "

"But the North is trying to destroy slavery," said Gideon, rapid speech betraying his fervor and nervousness. "They prevent us from taking our slaves into the new territories."

"You refer to the new territories where slavery cannot flourish? Nature has fixed slavery's boundaries. It will go where the climate and the soil say it may."

"John C. Calhoun was right to say it is a matter of honor. Of principle rather than practicality. A southern man has the right to go anywhere he wishes, and to take his property with him."

"Calhoun!" Houston grimaced. "Calhoun was a

staunch Union man, too—until he was denied the presidency. Only then did he begin to speak of nullification and secession and other nonsense."

"John C. Calhoun was a great man," said Gideon, red-faced.

"That's enough, Gideon," said Emily. "My apologies, General."

Houston chuckled. "No need for apologies, Mrs. McAllen. I think it's a fine thing that Gideon speaks his mind."

"He can be a hotheaded young man sometimes," said Emily, "and he has been paying heed to the wrong kind of people. This talk of secession—it's pure nonsense."

Houston nodded. "I hope you are right. I believe the majority, both North and South, are as devoted to the Union as you and I. There are extremists on both sides, and we would all do well to ignore their rantings."

"John Adams and John Hancock were branded as extremists, too, when they spoke out against British rule," said Gideon. "I for one refuse to be ruled by northern Free-Soilers and abolitionists."

Emily looked across the table at McAllen, a silent plea for help. He knew what she wanted him to do, and with a sigh he nodded back at her.

"You're excused, Gideon."

Gideon glared at his father, hurt and humiliated, but he said nothing and left the table.

"He has been spending entirely too much time with that Quincy Yates," said Emily.

"A relation of Memucan Yates, by any chance?" asked Houston.

"His son," replied McAllen. "Do you know Memucan?"

"I know of him."

"And he knows all about you," said Tice wryly. "Or so he claims. Says you betrayed Texas and the South with your vote against the Kansas-Nebraska Bill. That you pander to northern interests because you seek to occupy the White House."

"Needless to say, he uses his newspaper to slander and discredit you at every opportunity," said Emily.

"I have become inured to slander," said Houston. "I was attacked when I resigned as governor of Tennessee, and again when I led the army of the Republic of Texas against Santa Anna, and yet again when I was president of the republic for being too easy on the Indians, and once again during my tenure as United States senator. Of necessity I have become somewhat thick-skinned."

Tice raised his glass in a toast. "And may you be slandered as the next governor of the great state of Texas."

"Here, here," said McAllen.

"I wish I could drink to that," said Houston, laughing. "And to the Union, as well. No risk is too great to preserve her."

"He believes he can save the Union by starting a war with Mexico," McAllen told Tice later that evening, as they sat on the front porch, Tice puffing on his pipe and McAllen nursing a glass of brandy. "As soon as he is governor, he'll call out the militia on the pretext that the border with Mexico is threatened. He offered me a brigadier's commission."

"And you turned him down?"

"I did."

"That must have been a difficult thing for you to do, John Henry."

"It was," conceded McAllen. He had never turned Houston down before, and Tice knew how devoted his friend had been over the years to the Old Chief.

Even in a frontier village like Grand Cane, Tice was able to keep abreast of national events, and he tried to put himself in Sam Houston's shoes to get at the motives of what seemed at first blush to be a quixotic scheme.

He knew that Houston's vote against the Kansas-Nebraska Bill had cost him dearly. Even before the vote, many southerners had suspected the hero of San Jacinto of harboring antislavery sentiments, and in the minds of such men antislavery was the same as anti-southern. But Houston had been fearful that the doctrine of popular sovereignty embodied in the Kansas-Nebraska Bill would only exacerbate the quarrel between the sections. "Bleeding Kansas" had demonstrated that such fears were justified.

The issue of slavery had caused a schism in the Democratic Party, and many conservative Unionists, including Houston, had made the mistake of flirting with the new Know-Nothing, or American Party. In fact, Houston's name had been mentioned at the 1856 American Party national convention as a possible presidential candidate. The problem with the Know-Nothings was their zealous nativism, and no party that was so ardently anti-Catholic and anti-immigrant was going to garner enough support to put its man in the White House. Houston had abandoned the short-lived Know-Nothing movement, but like his vote on the Kansas-Nebraska Bill, he had suffered politically for the connection, no matter how brief. The talk these days was that Houston's only hope for the presidency was to run as an independent candidate in 1860, a man of the people, eschewing the caucus and the convention as undemocratic party devices designed to deny the common man his rightful say in the selection of the chief executive.

The upcoming election caused every man devoted to the Union a good deal of concern, and that included Tice. The Democrats were irrevocably split; the northern faction would no doubt nominate Stephen A. Douglas of Illinois as its candidate, even though Douglas was unacceptable to the majority of southerners who had come to realize that the doctrine of popular sovereignty Douglas espoused was of no advantage to them, as he had led them to believe it would be. No, Douglas had pulled the wool over their eyes because he wanted to establish the northwestern territories as quickly as possible, so that a northern transcontinental railroad, with Chicago as its eastern terminus, would seem a viable concept.

Which meant the Southern Democrats would more than likely choose their own presidential candidate—and *that* meant the new Republican Party had a very good chance of putting *its* man in the White House. And if a Free-Soil, antislavery man became president—well, then, Tice figured the southern states would choose to leave the Union. The only question that would remain would be whether the North would let the South go in peace.

The only hope for the Union in that scenario was an independent candidate, or a new Union Party nominee who could appeal to Unionists both North and South. The question remained: Were there enough

Union men to turn the tide in favor of such a candidate? And was Sam Houston the most likely choice for that role?

Upon reflection, Tice could see why Houston might want war with Mexico. The Old Chief was no filibusterer. He had strongly opposed every private expedition against Mexico or Nicaragua or Cuba, and there had been many such excursions in the past ten years. So Tice doubted that Houston sincerely cared about bringing peace to a Mexico torn by civil strife and a political struggle between Juarez and the Constitutionalists and Miramon's Conservatives. Houston had spoken of bestowing—by force, if necessary—the blessings of American institutions on Mexico, but Tice didn't think that was really Houston's top priority.

But a war with Mexico might make Americans set aside their differences, at least for the time being, as they rallied round the flag. And if Sam Houston emerged as the hero of the conflict, it could only enhance his chances of winning the presidency. Once in the President's House, Houston would do everything in his power to prevent the disintegration of the Union.

"Well," said Tice, puffing on his pipe, "I can't say I would mind the general becoming our chief magistrate. Though I doubt even he could keep the South in the Union."

"He thinks he can," said McAllen. "He remembers how Andrew Jackson forced South Carolina to back down from secession in '32."

"But things were different then. South Carolina stood alone. The other southern states were unwilling to back her in her threat to secede from the Union. The cancer of secession has spread quite a lot since then. It's even spread into Texas."

"Houston blames Pierce and Buchanan. He claims our last two presidents have been too weak and vacillating. A strong president, as he would be, could stop the secessionists in their tracks."

"Do you think he's right, John Henry?"

McAllen sighed, gazing moodily out into the summer's night, listening to the crickets and the bullfrogs, the hoot of a distant owl. He brooded over the fragile nature of the serene, insular world he had tried to make for himself. Try as he might, he could not keep the world and all its problems from his doorstep.

"No," he replied, at last. "Things have gotten too far out of hand. We'll have our own civil war before long, Artemus. God help us."

"Then maybe the general's Mexican scheme isn't such a bad idea."

"I want no part of it. Any of it. I just want to be left alone."

"This is something you—none of us—will be able to escape. The Union is at risk, and the general wants to save it."

"So you think I ought to get involved?"

"I'm saying I seriously doubt that you have any choice. It's just a matter of time."

"I'll deal with it then," said McAllen curtly. "And not before."

Tice said no more on the subject. Looking into the future, he could envision one more campaign for the Black Jacks. He was sure of it—as sure as he was of his own mortality. And he was pretty certain that John Henry knew what the future held in store, too. He could protest all he wanted, but it wouldn't change the facts.

Chapter 4

"Don Antonio."

Caldero did not seem to hear the querulous and respectful voice of the Indio house servant as he stood on the balcony with his back to the room in which the man stood. He preferred not to hear it, listening instead to the voice of the wind sweeping across the vast valley of grass from the distant sierra that lay unseen just beyond the curve of the world. All of the land as far as his eyes could see from this vantage point belonged to him. Five-hundred square miles, more or less, all of it inherited from his father. Five-hundred square miles in the province of Coahuila, on the great Plateau del Norte, and more than a hundred miles from the nearest town of any size, which happened to be Brownsville. *You would think,* mused Caldero, with some bitterness, *that here a man could find peace.*

"Don Antonio, they have brought Emilio Patino's body."

Caldero grimaced. "Yes, I know," he said softly. "Tell them I will be down soon."

"Yes, Don Antonio." The servant took his leave, making no sound lest he disturb his *hidalgo*.

Caldero had seen the riders coming from the south,

the body draped over the back of a mule, and he had heard the wailing of the women as the bullet-riddled corpse of Emilio Patino, one of his sheepherders, arrived within the walls of Hacienda Maguey. The women were silent now. They would cleanse the body and dress it and lay it out in the iglesia so that all could pay their last respects to a gentle man who had never harmed anyone. Caldero's presence was required. In a manner of speaking, Emilio was a member of his own family, and to fail to sit with Emilio's widow and children would be unconscionably bad form. He was the *hacendado*, the overlord of all he surveyed, and everyone who lived on Maguey served him. But he served them, as well. He had his responsibilities to each and every one of them, and Antonio Caldero was not one to take his responsibilities lightly. He feared them, too—because his responsibility to Emilio, his family, and all the others who lived here would ultimately require much more of him than simply making an appearance at the church.

The human population of Maguey numbered nearly four hundred. Most of them lived in the *acomodados*, humble adobe dwellings on the outskirts of the *casco*, but within the walls. They either worked in the casco itself or, if they were healthy and male, they became the shepherds of Maguey's many thousands of sheep. If they were healthy young males who also happened to be excellent horsemen, they became the *vaqueros* who tended Caldero's tens of thousands of cattle.

The chapel where Emilio would lay in state the rest of the day and all through the night stood across the plaza from the *casa principal* where Caldero lived with his mother and two daughters. In the morning, the bell in the tower would ring out, calling all those who lived at Maguey to a service presided over by the resident priest. But for now the bell was silent, and in the tower stood an eagle-eyed lookout who scanned the expanse of sere grassland with a field glass, keeping watch for the Anglos who had murdered Emilio and who wanted to kill Caldero and who were lurking out there somewhere on Maguey land.

The *casa principal*, with its thick stone walls and narrow windows and iron filigree, looked something like a fortress, for in the days when Caldero's father was trying to establish this hacienda the Indians—Apaches and Comanches and Yaquis—had often swept through this valley on their raiding sortees. Now an even greater foe lay out there somewhere beyond the summer haze. The Americans.

Diagonally across the plaza were the houses of the priest, the clerk, and the *mayordomo*. Also near the plaza was the coach house, the stables, the storerooms, and the granaries. Behind the *casa principal* was the school. Caldero kept a schoolmaster on the year around, paying him twelve pesos a month, which was a very good wage for a schoolteacher in Mexico. All of the Maguey children attended school whenever possible. On this the hacendado insisted.

In addition, there was the *tienda de raya*, a community store, near the plaza. Caldero paid wages in cash as well as credit at the store, for this was the only place where the people of Maguey could purchase chocolate, tobacco, sugar, rice, cheese, and other luxuries. Despite this monopoly, Caldero made certain that the prices charged at the *tienda de raya* were the same as or less than would be charged in any other store. Caldero also provided each person at Maguey a weekly allowance of maize which, with beans and mutton, made up the basic diet of the campesino and his family. Besides the small garden plots available to any and all, there were two orchards near the *casco* which produced pears, peaches, plums, figs, blackberries, and grapes.

The principal work of the hacienda was tending to the sheep and cattle, or the maize and the orchards. In March and again in August, sheep were sheared for their wool, and once a year a certain number of the stock were slaughtered for meat and tallow. The tallow was wrapped in sheepskins for sale to the mines at nearby Zacatecas.

All of this was now at risk because he had killed the Brownsville sheriff.

Caldero shook his head. No, that wasn't precisely true. It was at risk because the Americans had seized Texas and then had taken the land between the Nueces River and the Rio Grande—that disputed strip of land which Caldero had fought for ten years to keep out of their hands. And now, of course, the Americans had their eyes on Mexico. They were never satisfied. They claimed it was their "manifest destiny" to own the entire continent, from the Darien isthmus to the Hudson Bay. They said it was their mission, their duty, to spread the blessings of their social and political institutions over all the land, to bring these blessings to the benighted peoples of other, less fortunate lands.

Brooding, Caldero reminded himself that he had tried to warn the government. The Americans, he had said, must be held at bay, north of the Nueces.

But Mexico City had refused to heed his warning, forcing Caldero to fight a losing battle, at best a delaying action, virtually alone.

And now? Now he would have to fight yet again.

As before, he would be alone. Because the Conservatives in power and Juarez's rebel Constitutionalists were waging a bloody civil war in the provinces south of here, leaving the northern regions undefended, and giving the Americans the perfect excuse to interfere in Mexican affairs.

Caldero drew a long, discouraged breath. All of the people here at Maguey depended on him for their protection. It had always been so, back even in his father's day. It was his duty to defend them from Indians, bandits, and Americans. This was their home. Without Maguey there would be no place for them. They would perish. He did not care about Maguey for himself. He wasn't really concerned about his own life. But he had a responsibility to these people. So he would have to avenge Emilio Patino's death. He would have to fight and kill the Americans.

He would have to wage war.

The vaqueros found him in the chapel, kneeling before the casket that held the mortal remains of Emilio Patino. He sensed their presence, even though they did not venture but a few feet inside the door, for they did not wish to intrude. So they stood there with *sombreros* in hand, and their spurs jingling against the worn planks of the chapel floor as they shifted their weight from one leg to the other, as uncomfortable as children in the presence of death.

Caldero crossed himself and rose, turning to the pew where Emilio's widow sat, flanked by her three children. He whispered his condolences to the woman, who was still and stone-faced and staring straight ahead, and then he wiped the tears from the cheeks of the sheepherder's eight-year-old daughter. The tears angered him. He looked across the chapel at the vaqueros with his dark eyes blazing. The vaquero named Refugio nodded, because Refugio had been Caldero's *segundo* for years now, had been indeed almost as a son to the hidalgo, and he knew what Caldero was thinking.

When Caldero left the chapel, Refugio and the other vaqueros—the three Maguey riders who had brought the body of Emilio Patino to the *casco*—followed him out. It would not do to speak of vengeance within the walls of a church.

"Tell me," said Caldero curtly, not turning to face the vaqueros, keeping his back to them and seeming to take an inordinate measure of interest in the brassy summer sky. Refugio looked up and saw the trio of turkey vultures high overhead, describing large circles in the Coahuilan sky.

"There were many of them, hidalgo," said Refugio. "A hundred, maybe more. They slaughtered many of the sheep in Emilio's herd. They did not kill Emilio right away. They tortured him. I think they must have been trying to make him tell how to find the *casco*. He told them it was to the south, because that is the direction they rode. Lizamo and Manchaca are following them."

"A hundred, you say."

"*Si, hidalgo*. Maybe a little more." Again Refugio thought he knew what Caldero was thinking as he continued to watch the graceful flight of the carrion eaters. He was thinking that there would be a lot of work for the vultures to do when the murder of Emilio, the defenseless Maguey sheepherder, was avenged.

"Get all the others together," said Caldero, turning

finally to look solemnly at each of the vaqueros in turn. "We will ride in one hour."

"Si, hidalgo!" Refugio was pleased. As he had confidently predicted to the others, Caldero would not wait for Emilio's murderers to find and attack the *casco*. No, he would track the Americans down and fight them far removed from Maguey's innocent women and children.

Seeing the delight on Refugio's face, and on the features of the other vaqueros, Caldero shook his head. About one-hundred vaqueros lived and worked on Maguey, but a good many of them were absent from the *casco*, residing for months at a time at outposts a day's ride or more away. Refugio would be able to collect perhaps forty or fifty of his comrades in an hour's time. But fifty would be enough. Caldero was certain that he could defeat a hundred or more Americans with fifty such men as these.

Vaqueros like Refugio were the best and boldest horsemen in the world. They were in some ways like overgrown children, wild and exuberant and afraid of nothing. They lived life to its fullest and expected to die young. Their pastimes, such as the sport of "tailing the bull," were dangerous—no other kind of hobby could hold their interest. A vaquero caught a bull by its tail, passed the tail under his right leg, turned it around the pommel of his saddle and then, wheeling his horse sharply at right angles, flipped the bull. All too often horse and man or both was impaled on the horns of the infuriated bull.

These men were Maguey's soldiers. They were good shots and deadly with the knife. Comanches and Apaches and bandits were their foes, so they had to be tough, cunning, and ruthless to survive. Quite in contrast were the Maguey sheepherders like poor Emilio, who were no less brave but were generally older family men who did not take so cavalier an attitude toward death.

Caldero entered the *casa principal,* told the Indio house servant to fetch his guns, and went out into the patio where he expected to find his mother.

As usual, Dona Petra was sitting in the shade, wearing the black she had worn every day since the death of her beloved husband. She did not read and she did not knit. She did not do much of anything but sit and relive fond memories. Sitting near her was Caldero's oldest daughter, Teresa. Every time he looked at Teresa Caldero he was painfully reminded of her mother. Teresa was slim and beautiful and a mirror image of the wife Caldero had lost many years ago but still loved so deeply that he often lay awake at night haunted by dreams of her. Teresa was reading a book, and when she looked up and smiled at him Caldero was dazzled with memories of his own.

Lifting the veil from her deeply lined face, Dona Petra also smiled at Caldero as he approached, but hers was a tremulous and knowing smile, for though she seldom ventured out of the house these days she was nonetheless cognizant of all that went on at Maguey. She had her sources of information in the platoon of house servants Caldero kept to attend to her every need. He had no doubt she already knew that Emilio's body had been recovered and brought to the *casco*, and that he was going now in search of the sheepherder's killers.

Kneeling beside her chair, Caldero took his mother's gnarled, spotted hands in his own and told her he was leaving, and why.

She nodded. "This is your destiny, my son. I knew this would happen the day you rode into Brownsville. You cannot escape the purpose for which God placed you upon this earth."

"It is not a destiny I would choose for myself," replied Caldero, thinking about the woman who had accosted him on the Brownsville street moments after he'd shot Carnacky. *You will protect us*, she had said. *This was destined to happen.*

"You have a strong sense of what is right and what is wrong," said Dona Petra. "Your father did, as well. He fought for what he thought was right all his life, and so have you. I am proud of you."

Caldero smiled bitterly. "I am called a bandit and a murderer."

"By your enemies. But your people look up to you. You are their champion."

"I am tired of the fighting and of the killing. I just want to be left alone."

She shook her head sadly. "It is not meant to be, my dear Antonio. Now go. Do not worry about me. I have learned to accept the tragedies of life. And do not worry about your daughters. They must learn to accept them. If you die, die knowing that your family is proud of you because you will have shed your blood for your people. Who can do more?"

Sam Burkin was scared. He was disgusted, too. So disgusted with his fate that his fear was overshadowed by an impotent fury working like acid on his soul.

He sat, hot, hungry, thirsty, and covered with dust on a rock in the scant shade of a scrawny ironwood tree at the bottom of a *barranca*, wondering where the hell he was and what the hell he was doing there.

The rest of the Brownsville Tigers were scattered like trash up and down the sandy, rock-strewn bottom of the ravine. It was the middle of the afternoon and so hot that a breath seemed to sear the lining of Burkin's lungs. He felt as though he were suffocating. He couldn't seem to draw a deep breath. Fondly he remembered his New England birthplace. Never before had he really missed his home, but he missed it terribly at this moment. Quiet, peaceful, civilized New England. *This* country wasn't worth inhabiting. It was useless, unless you were a scorpion or a rattlesnake. Why in God's name did Stoneman and the Knights of the Golden Circle want this wasteland in the first place? The humane thing to do would be to invite the Mexicans north and leave this land to the devil. Only Satan could truly appreciate it. A horrible place to live—and a worse place to die.

They had been lucky to find the spring—a trickle of brackish water leaking out of a crevice between some boulders here at the bottom of the barranca. It was the only piece of luck Burkin could remember having for at least a year. That was why they had stopped so early in the day, to let the men and horses drink. And no one was in a big hurry to move out. The saddle-weary Tigers sat or lay in what shade they could find or manufacture using their blankets or their horses to block out the sun. Some of them slept, too exhausted to worry about whether they would ever wake up again. A few anxiously scanned the rim of the barranca. They hadn't seen a living soul in two days and yet everyone sensed that danger was near. They were deep in enemy country. No one made a lot of noise. Leaving Brownsville, the Tigers had been boisterous, in high spirits, and confident of glory. They weren't very confident or boisterous now, mused Burkin.

Two men were walking toward him—Massey and Rouett, the former a clerk in his father's store, the latter a recent immigrant who worked in the tanning yard. Burkin knew Massey would do all the talking; the lanky pale-haired youth was a spokesman for the Tigers rank and file. All Rouett knew how to do was glower. An Alsatian, he didn't speak English any better than he seemed to understand it.

"Most of the boys think we ought to turn around and head for home, Sam," said Massey.

"That's Captain Burkin to you."

Massey grinned. "Get off your high horse, Sam. Admit it, we're lost. And we haven't got a prayer of finding Caldero."

"Yes, we're lost. Too bad we haven't stumbled across another helpless old man to torture. Maybe then we could find out where we are."

Massey gave him an odd look. "What's got into you, Sam? He was just a lousy old greaser."

"*Ja,*" said Rouett, nodding gravely.

"Well, that old greaser outsmarted you," said Burkin. "He outsmarted us all. I don't know where Caldero's place is, but it sure as hell isn't *south*, like the old man said."

"No." Massey stubbornly shook his head. "He was telling the truth. I was fixin' to cut off his third finger when he talked. Now, if he'd been lying he would have lied right up front and saved those other two fingers."

Burkin stared at Massey in disbelief. The man described his torture of an innocent old man with as much emotion as if he were describing how he went about wringing a chicken's neck. The human capacity for senseless brutality was perfectly reflected in this man, mused Burkin. How could a store clerk be so completely transformed into a sadistic butcher in such a short span of time—unless savagery of this kind was second nature? Massey's conscience was clear. He didn't think of the old sheepherder as a human being. He and a few of his cronies had snuffed out the Mexican's life as easily as they would roll a gnat between two fingers.

"You're incredibly thick-headed, Massey," said Burkin. "The old man knew you were going to kill him. Why would he care if he kept all his fingers, you idiot? He played it the way he did so that we'd be convinced he was telling the truth. It was the bravest act I have ever witnessed—and the fact that I stood by and witnessed it and didn't try to stop you was the most cowardly thing I have ever done."

"I don't believe what you're saying," said Massey, truculent—he deeply resented being called an idiot. "We just missed Caldero's place somehow, and that's all there is to it. The old greaser was telling the truth. I'd stake my life on it."

"*Ja,*" said Rouett, glaring at Burkin.

"Fine." Burkin made a disdainful gesture. "Have it your own way. But we're not turning back."

"We're all out of rations," protested Massey. "And if we hadn't stumbled on this spring we'd be out of water by now, too. What do you think we're gonna find out here? What are we going to do?"

"I don't know. But one thing we're not going to do is turn back."

"You don't know." Massey snorted in disgust. "You're the captain, aren't you? You're supposed to know."

Burkin laughed. "Oh, so now you want me to be a *real* leader, is that it? You elected me because you thought I wouldn't—make that *couldn't*—force you boys to toe the mark. You didn't want a captain with military experience because you just wanted to play at being soldiers. Well, that's just too damned bad. I'm the captain and I say we're not going back."

"You're touched," decided Massey. "The sun's fried the brains in your head."

"*Ja*," agreed Rouett.

"Shut up," Burkin growled at the Alsatian. "If I had any brains I wouldn't be in this predicament. But no, I had to join the militia, because that's what a man does if he wants to get ahead in a new place, make the right friends and the best connections. Don't feel too badly, Massey. You're not the only idiot here."

"Maybe we'll just un-elect you," threatened Massey.

"Go ahead. But as long as I'm the captain we're not going back before we've done what we set out to do. I don't think we ought to be here. From the beginning I knew it was a mistake. But again, I'm a coward, so I didn't air my honest opinion. So be it. We stick until we find Caldero. We'll stay here until morning. The horses need rest. At daybreak we'll turn around and ride north. I'm betting Caldero's hacienda is in that direction."

Massey looked at Rouett and shook his head. The Alsatian shrugged his bulky shoulders. With nothing more to say, they turned and walked away.

Burkin wasn't sorry to see them go. He wanted to be alone with his misery, and to try to sort out the reasons for his obstinate determination to go through with a task he had no stomach for. It would be so easy to admit failure and go back to Brownsville empty-handed. That would be best for all concerned, since it was still possible that this whole miserable business would just blow over. Yes, best for all concerned—except Samuel Burkin.

Because, in some convoluted way he hadn't bothered trying to sort out, he figured that if he failed in this he would be doomed to always play second fiddle to Charles Stoneman. On the other hand, if he captured Antonio Caldero he would be the biggest man in Brownsville. Bigger even than Stoneman. And that would most certainly prove advantageous in his ongoing campaign to win Judith away from her husband. Exactly how, he wasn't sure. But she would never give up the life Stoneman had made for her unless Burkin was in a position to offer her more and to protect her from her husband. Because Stoneman would try to destroy them both. But if he was the man who brought Caldero to justice he would be too big of a man for Stoneman to destroy.

Justice? Who was he kidding? Antonio Caldero would find nothing even remotely resembling justice in a Texas courtroom. Bob Carnacky being gunned down by a member of the race he had treated with such brutal contempt for so many years—now *that* was justice.

An odd sizzling sound, immediately followed by a puff of dust an arm's length away from Burkin's booted feet startled him. Then came a sharp *crack!* that echoed through the barranca. Burkin noticed Massey and Rouett—they had whirled around and stood there looking at him, not sure what had happened. He stared back at them, befuddled and unmoving. In fact, it seemed that every Brownsville Tiger in the ravine was frozen in place.

And then Burkin watched the side of Rouett's head explode in a mist of blood and bone fragments; in the next instant the Alsatian's body hit the ground as though an invisible giant fist had picked him up off his feet and slammed him down. Splattered with Rouett's blood and brains, Massey began shouting an incoherent and unnecessary warning and took off running. Only then did a stupefied Burkin realize what was going on. The hot stillness of the desert was shattered by a crashing volley of rifle fire, and as one the Tigers were galvanized into action, some diving for cover, even though there was precious little of that, and others lunging for their weapons or their spooked horses. As he grabbed for the reins of his own horse, which was tethered to the wind-twisted and heat-stunted ironwood shading him, Burkin fired a quick glance at the rim of the barranca, saw dark shapes moving among the rocks up there, and the muzzle flashes by the dozen. As fear put a lump big enough to choke on in his throat, Sam Burkin concluded that he no longer had to worry about finding Antonio Caldero.

Burkin got the vague impression that Tigers were falling all around him, slain in the deadly hail of bullets from the rifles of the men who occupied both sides of the barranca. The ravine had become a death trap, and Burkin experienced a short-lived burst of irritation when he thought about the sentries he had posted up there on the rim. At least he had remembered to do that much. But those men had failed to sound the alarm. Then it occurred to him that, in all likelihood, this failure was because those men were dead.

It also occurred to him that his first concern in this situation ought to be for his command. A real military man would heroically brave death in a valiant attempt to rally his troops—or at least organize an effective fighting withdrawal from the ravine. But Burkin would have none of that. It was every man for himself.

As he grabbed his horse's reins, the spooked mount yanked sharply away, snapping the limb of the ironwood to which it was tied, and Burkin almost lost his grip on the leathers. Backstepping, the horse pulled him off his feet. He scrambled up, lunged for the saddle. Snorting in fear, the wild-eyed animal shied away. Burkin swore profusely at it and cursed its mother, fell down a second time, got up again, grabbed the saddle horn and tried to fit boot into stirrup. But now the horse was running, and Burkin had to give up on the stirrup, clutching at the pommel and racing along beside the galloping horse until his legs got all tangled up and he was dragged for several anxious seconds.

Suddenly the horse uttered an unnerving shriek and went down, and Burkin finally surrendered his desperate grip on the saddle. Somehow, sprawling over the horse, he avoided its flailing hooves. Huddled on the ground and using the animal's body for cover, he realized that his rifle was still in its scabbard, and since the horse had fallen on its left side the rifle was within reach. The good people of Brownsville had provided him with the weapon, being of the opinion that the leader of their proud militia ought not to go into battle armed only with a .22 caliber Briggs peashooter. The rifle was a Warner revolving carbine, and Burkin thought it rather odd in design, as it had a six-shot cylinder just like a pistol, into which you inserted the percussion cartridges. It was .40 caliber, with a twenty-four-inch barrel and a walnut stock with a crescent butt plate. He had fired it only twice, shooting at game, and missing both times and after that he'd given up so as not to embarrass himself further in front of his men.

Bullets were thudding into the horse, and all Burkin wanted to do was dig a hole in the ground and crawl into it. But he was going to have to fight his way out—he knew that now. So he dragged the carbine from its hard leather boot and looked around for something to shoot at. Only then did he see the vaqueros, a half dozen of them, galloping toward him, yelling like wild Indians and shooting off their pistols.

Laying the Warner's barrel across the neck of the fallen horse, Burkin drew a bead and fired. Powder smoke stung his eyes. When he could see again the vaqueros were almost upon him. Obviously he had missed. The bitter taste of fear nearly gagged him as he worked the carbine's lever, rotating the cylinder and firing again in haste. This time one of the Mexicans tumbled out of his saddle. Burkin had no time to congratulate himself. The vaqueros were on him, the ground quivering beneath the thundering hooves of their horses.

As they swept past, one of the Mexicans fired down at him at point-blank range. The bullet hit Burkin like a fist. He writhed at the searing pain. As the others rode on, the vaquero who had shot him checked and turned his desert mustang, intent on finishing the job. Burkin momentarily forgot all about his gunshot wound. Sitting up, he brought the crescent stock to shoulder and fired. The hammer fell, but the carbine failed to discharge. He hadn't worked the lever to rotate the cylinder! With a strangled cry Burkin fumbled with the lever action, knowing he wasn't going to be fast enough—the Mexican was drawing a bead on him.

But the vaquero didn't get off a shot. A look of surprise on his lean, sun-darkened face, the Mexican slumped forward and slipped out of the saddle. Burkin had no idea where the killing shot had come from. The mustang shied away from the dead man but did not bolt. Burkin saw his chance. Scrambling to his feet, he ran to the horse and grabbed at the reins. Miracle of miracles, the horse stood its ground. At least one of God's creatures, thought Burkin, was keeping its wits in this maelstrom of death and noise and confusion.

As he hoisted himself into the saddle, Burkin remembered his wound, and with remembrance came the pain, accompanied by a wave of nausea. Squeezing his eyes shut, he doubled, face buried in the mustang's mane, sucking air through clenched teeth. He groped at his left side, where the pain originated, below the ribs, and gasped in shock as he realized that his shirt was soaked with blood. Raising the shirt, he took a quick look at the wound. The bullet had torn through the flesh, passing completely through without damaging any vital organs. That bullet would probably not kill him. The next one might, though. It was time to get moving.

The battle seemed to have forgotten him, moving farther down the barranca, past the spring. The Tigers—those left standing—were bunched together now and trying to make a stand. Burkin couldn't really tell how they were doing because of all the dust and gunsmoke. The way was open for him to make good his escape. He could see no one at the northern end of the deep ravine, the direction from which the mounted vaqueros had come.

But he just couldn't bring himself to go. Now that the initial burst of panic was gone, he could approach the subject of running away a bit more rationally, and as appealing as it was to his sense of self-preservation, pride reared its ugly head. If he deserted the others he would never be able to look Judith in the eyes again. He would never be Stoneman's equal. And, worst of all, he would despise himself for the rest of his life.

Once again Sam Burkin found himself in the role of Fate's plaything. He really had no choice.

Quite sensibly, the mustang had been drifting northward, away from the din of battle. Burkin heeled the horse around. Drawing the Briggs pistol, he kicked the animal into a gallop and charged back into the fray, thinking that it was a shame Stoneman and Judith couldn't see him at this moment, at his most gallant—especially since they were never going to see him again.

The Tigers had made their stand behind some rocks and dead horses, surrounded on all sides by the vaqueros, some of whom remained on the rim of the barranca, firing down into the melee, though profiting less than they had at the outset, for the fog of the battle obscured their vision. Others had worked their way down the steep flanks of the ravine to close with their enemy, but by doing so they exposed themselves to the Tigers' fire. As Burkin galloped past, one of the Mexicans scrambled to the top of a rock outcropping and leaped at him, intent on dragging him from the saddle, but Burkin shot him in midair at point-blank range, and rode on.

An instant later the mustang stumbled and fell, shot several times, and Burkin lost the pistol in his clumsy, painful fall, gasping as the pain in his side was exacerbated by the impact with the ground. Dazed and bleeding, he sat there for a moment, only dimly aware of his surroundings—until someone grabbed him and he began to fight, lashing out with his fists. His assailant cursed as one of Burkin's blows landed, and only then did Burkin realize it was Massey. The lanky store clerk and murderer of innocent old men was helping him to his feet, and guiding him into the midst of the remaining Tigers.

"I thought you had run out on us, Captain," said Massey, setting him down with his back to a blood-splattered rock, right next to a dead Brownsville Tiger. Burkin stared at the dead man's face, trying to remember the fellow's name. Funny, but he couldn't recall. It did not, however, escape him that Massey had called him Captain and not Sam.

"If I'd had a lick of sense I would have," he replied. "Get me a gun."

Massey grinned. His angular features were covered with pale Coahuilan dust and dark smudges of gunpowder. He thrust a rifle into Burkin's hands.

"Here, take this one. I'll get another. There are plenty more lying around. They may kill us all, Captain, but we'll make them pay a steep price for the privilege."

With that Massey was gone, eager as he was to enter the fray again, and Burkin couldn't help admiring the man's courage, even if he was a cold-blooded killer. He glanced around him at the tight knot of Brownsville Tigers who were fighting as fiercely as their namesake, and he suddenly felt proud to be associated with them.

A bullet ricocheted off the face of the rock against which he was resting. Burkin hardly flinched. Quite calmly he raised the rifle and fired at dimly-seen movement on the rim of the barranca. He kept firing, and when the rifle was empty he took another from the lifeless hand of a fallen comrade and kept shooting.

Then he realized that there was nothing left to shoot at. The Mexicans had vanished, leaving their dead behind. Burkin couldn't believe it—couldn't believe they had driven off the enemy and that he was still among the living.

"I reckon they've had enough," said Massey, in amazement. "What do we do now, Captain?"

"Take a couple of men and make sure they're gone. The rest of us will see to the dead and wounded."

"And then what?"

Burkin nodded. "Then we go home."

He had gotten what he'd come to Mexico for. He would go home a hero, with several dozen witnesses to his heroism. He no longer needed Antonio Caldero.

And besides, he had a hunch Brownsville would hear from Caldero again.

Not far away, just beyond the rim of the barranca, the Maguey vaqueros gathered around their leader. Caldero was reloading his weapons, and he spared the mounted men scarcely a glance. He knew that a dozen of his vaqueros had perished in the fight, and nearly as many again had suffered wounds. The deaths saddened him, but he had learned not to dwell on such things. He had the deaths of many men on his conscience. Twelve more would not break his will or undermine his resolve. The warrior's fatalistic philosophy was nothing new to him. How easy it was to slip back into old ways, to accept the cost in lives of a worthy cause. For the time being, at least, Maguey was safe. The Americans would run back to Brownsville. Of this Caldero was certain. So twelve of his young vaqueros had given their lives to buy time for the people of the hacienda. Blood for time. This was one of warfare's principal calculations, a measurement Caldero could make with a reasonable amount of objectivity.

When he had finished reloading, and swung into the saddle, Caldero turned to Refugio.

"Go back to Maguey," he said. "Take the seriously wounded with you. Send word to the outposts. Bring all the men who can fight together and ride for Brownsville. I will meet you there."

"Leave Maguey undefended, hidalgo?"

Caldero nodded. "We will keep the Americans too busy to even think about Maguey. We will take the fight to them. We are going to capture Brownsville."

Even in the shadows of the dying day, Caldero could see the faces of Refugio and the other vaqueros brighten when they heard his words. They had seen their comrades fall, but their taste for adventure, and their dedication to Maguey and to Caldero had in no way been diminished.

While Refugio rode for Maguey, Caldero and the others easily eluded the Americans sent out to scout the area, and the following morning, when Sam Burkin and the Brownsville Tigers, having buried their dead, left the barranca and turned northeast for the Rio Grande and home, Caldero and twenty vaqueros followed.

Chapter 5

John Henry McAllen had found that as he grew older the years he'd spent in grueling military campaigns came back to haunt him. The war against the Seminoles, waged in the Florida swamps, had been particularly rigorous. He had abused his body for months at a time with little sleep, bad food, and several bouts with dysentery and malaria—not to mention a number of wounds received in combat. Shortly thereafter he had participated in the Texas revolution, and while he had managed to avoid adding to his battle scars in that conflict, the food had been just as bad and the opportunities for sleep just as scarce.

In addition, he and the Black Jacks had engaged in a number of excursions against the Comanches. The most sustained and arduous of these pursuits had been the time he'd searched for Emily, twice venturing deep into the Llano Estacado, or Staked Plains, to find the woman he loved.

Even though he had lived a relatively peaceful life for more than a dozen years now, those violent days had taken their toll. McAllen had always taken his health for granted, but now, to his dismay, he was finding out he had limitations in terms of physical endurance where he'd had none before.

Still, he insisted on working hard at Grand Cane. Not that his labor was necessary to keep the plantation going; he had plenty of help. But it was not in his nature to sit back and supervise—he felt compelled to work long hours at a variety of tasks. When time came to cut the sugarcane he was there wielding a cane knife alongside the others. He would spend days from dawn to dusk in the mill. He would be there with ax in hand when fences were mended or another acre of land was being cleared. He would walk the rows of man-high corn, gunnysack on his hip, pulling the ears from the stalk when it came time to harvest that crop. There was always something that needed doing at Grand Cane, and McAllen was incapable of sitting in a porch chair or in the saddle watching others sweat.

But he hadn't the strength or the stamina of his younger days, and when the workday was done he would be bone-tired. Emily kept after him to work less and relax more. She was worried he might work himself into an early grave, and in her opinion he was in a state of denial, refusing to concede that middle age had finally caught up with him. Of course he disagreed; hard work was good for a person, he would say. And often he would add that his son Gideon ought to try it.

"That boy acts like a rich planter's son," he would complain. "All he wants to do is hunt and fish go to the horse races and cockfights. He only wants what Grand Cane can give him. He doesn't realize he has to give back. You have to work for what you get in life. It isn't handed to you on a silver platter. And if it is you don't appreciate it, and ultimately you will lose it."

"He's just a boy, John Henry."

"This will all belong to him one day, and if he thinks he won't have to work to keep it he is in for a rude awakening."

Something about Gideon kept the discontent simmering inside McAllen. He loved his son, but he didn't understand him. As a young boy Gideon had constantly been underfoot, wanting to help his father do everything. A few years ago, though, Gideon had changed. It seemed to McAllen as though the change had been wrought overnight. And it wasn't for the better. Nowadays Gideon was just plain lazy. Spent entirely too much time with Quincy Yates. The two of them fancied themselves a pair of dashing young cavaliers, getting into all kinds of trouble. The cold hard truth was that Gideon had become an embarrassment and McAllen was at a loss as to how to deal with the situation.

So it was that when he returned to the big house late in the day, after twelve hours of unremitting labor, to find Emily sitting in a rocking chair on the front porch, her brow furrowed with concern, McAllen immediately assumed that whatever vexed his wife had something to do with their son. With a sigh he settled his stiff, aching frame into another chair and glanced at the orange coattails of the vanishing sun above the western horizon.

"What's the matter, dear?" he asked.

"Have you seen Gideon today?"

"No, but then I don't usually, when there's work to be done. Why do you ask?"

"He has been away from the house since daybreak."

"Running with that Quincy Yates, no doubt. He'll be back in time for supper."

"Somehow I don't think so."

He gave her a long look, alarmed by the way she said it, so sad and yet so calm. "Why do you say that?"

Emily shrugged. "Gideon hasn't been the same since General Houston left."

"I hadn't noticed a change in him."

Now it was her turn to give him a long look, and McAllen knew exactly what she was thinking.

"Of course," he added, "I never see much of him."

"I'm just afraid he will run off and do something foolish. And Quincy is a bad influence. Not that I place the blame on the Yates boy. Gideon feels as though he must prove himself. And that's our fault."

"My fault, you mean," said McAllen, defensive.

"You can't help who you are, John Henry. Gideon loves you. He looks up to you and wants to be like you."

"Is there harm in that? I am his father, after all."

"But he thinks he has to be a fighter to win your approval, a soldier just like you."

"He's just a boy. All lads want to be soldiers."

Emily sighed. John Henry could be thick-headed when it suited him.

"This goes beyond a boy's dreams of adventure and glory," she said. "Gideon wants your praise. And you must admit, John Henry, that you seldom praise him for being who he is. So he wants to be someone else. Something he's not."

McAllen ran his thumb along the scar on his cheek. A Seminole warrior had put it there nearly thirty years ago. For a moment he said nothing.

Emily just waited. She knew her husband well enough to know that he would not respond with angry denials, as many other men might. One of the things she loved about John Henry was knowing she could be open and honest with him. She blamed herself for not having spoken to him about this sooner, because she had wanted to spare him. But now she was afraid that in trying to spare her husband she had lost her son.

"You're quite right, as always," McAllen said at last, gazing into the gray twilight. "Gideon and I have grown apart these last few years. I should have done something about it. I just didn't know *what* to do."

Emily reached out to put her hand over his. "The two of you just need to spend more time together."

"Of course." He stood up quickly.

"Where are you going?"

"Into town. I'd better find him."

"Don't be too cross with him."

McAllen glanced at her, surprised. "Am I that way?"

"Sometimes. Not often. You're a good, decent man, John Henry. The best man I've ever met. You allow everyone their shortcomings—except for Gideon."

He bent down and kissed her on the lips and Emily responded with all her heart and soul.

"We'll be back before long."

She nodded, smiling, trying to mask her dread. She wasn't sure where that dread came from, or what exactly she feared might take place. But something was terribly wrong, or about to be. Something that would be not easily set right. She had an instinct about such things . . .

The town of Grand Cane had grown by leaps and bounds since its founding nearly twenty-five years ago.

Originally populated almost entirely by Black Jacks and their families, a small and remote outpost on the rim of the frontier, it now boasted a population of more than two hundred and fifty. And no longer was this the rim of the frontier. The threat of Indian raids had been removed, and so of late the settlers had come in droves. Most were decent folk. A few were not so decent. McAllen put Memucan Yates in the latter category.

Like McAllen, Yates had been born and bred in Mississippi, but that was all the two men had in common. Yates was a journalist. He fought his battles with the pen and not the sword, and he could be as aggressive and ruthless as the most heartless warrior. He likened his printer's ink to the blood of his enemies. The Brazos *Intelligencer* was known throughout Texas as one of the most vitriolic of partisan newspapers. This was a notoriety McAllen for one thought Grand Cane could do without.

Yates was a southern rights man, a secessionist who had supported Hardin Runnels in the 1857 gubernatorial campaign and who continued to do so now, as Runnels sought to defeat Sam Houston and win reelection. Yates and the Brazos *Intelligencer* espoused reopening the African slave trade and immediate withdrawal of the southern slave states from the Union. This divorce from the "unfaithful Yankee harridan" must incorporate an equal division of the territories, and if the North refused, Yates urged southerners to take what was rightfully theirs by force of arms.

Arriving in Grand Cane, McAllen went immediately to the dogtrot cabin where Yates lived and worked. He and his son lived on one side of the cabin while the office of the Brazos *Intelligencer* was housed in the other. The editor's wife, it was said, had divorced him back in Mississippi—they claimed that was why Memucan Yates had headed west—and sight unseen McAllen credited the woman with having abundant good sense. He found Yates in the office, setting type in preparation for tomorrow's edition of the weekly.

"Captain McAllen!" exclaimed Yates. "What an unexpected pleasure. Come to compliment me on the many kind words I wrote about your recent houseguest?"

McAllen knew he was kidding—Memucan Yates had never said anything complimentary about Sam Houston, whom he considered a tool of northern Free-Soilers and a traitor to his native South.

"Sorry, but I make it a point never to read your newspaper, Yates. I don't have the time to waste."

Yates smiled. He was a tall, angular man, with a mane of unkempt iron-gray hair and skin creased and yellow like old parchment. A hook of a nose jutted out over a pinched mouth. His spine was bowed—McAllen supposed this was the result of a lifetime spent bent over a desk or typecase. The cluttered office, with the printing press as its centerpiece, was brightened by the mustard yellow light of several oil lamps. Yates wore a long canvas apron smeared with printer's ink. In fact, McAllen thought the brimstone stench of ink was nearly overpowering.

"You might find this edition of interest," said Yates, gesturing at the press. "Dire reports have just come from the south. Texans have been slaughtered by that renegade, Antonio Caldero."

"And where did this slaughter occur? South of the river, no doubt."

Yates eyes narrowed into suspicious slits. "The

Brownsville militia was authorized to pursue Caldero into Mexico after he murdered Sheriff Carnacky."

McAllen's smile was wintry. "Militia against Caldero? That was a fool's game. In ten years of trying, the Texas Rangers couldn't get the better of that man. A half-trained bunch of Sunday soldiers weren't going to get the job done."

"I'll quote you on that, Captain. Hardly a proper sentiment with regards to brave, patriotic men who only sought justice."

"Justice?" McAllen laughed bitterly. "They wanted a war and now they've got one. I suppose you want war, too, don't you, Yates? War as an excuse to invade the northern provinces of Mexico? To extend the blessings of American institutions? Particularly the blessing of the peculiar institution of slavery."

"We are all well aware that you are an abolitionist at heart, sir. Which makes you a traitor to the South, in my book."

McAllen's eyes blazed. But Yates stood his ground. Personal safety had never concerned him. His was the courage of conviction.

"I am Southern-born, Yates," rasped McAllen. "That does not deny me the right to stand for the Union against the connivances of men who are willing to tear this nation apart for the sake of personal advancement."

Yates snorted. "I seek no aggrandizement, only the truth. My mission is to encourage those who have the courage to stand against northern tyranny and defend their Constitutional rights."

McAllen glanced at the printing press—and fought a sudden urge to turn it into a pile of rubbish with his bare hands. Yates he thought of as a serpent, and the press was the serpent's fangs by which the poison of secession and states' rights—or were those one in the same?—was being injected into the hearts and minds of the community. Specifically, the heart and mind of an impressionable young man by the name of Gideon McAllen.

The thought occurred to McAllen that he'd never had any luck with newspaper editors. There had been a man named Singletary, editor of an Austin weekly, who had made his life a living hell by publicizing the indiscretions of Leah, his first wife. This Singletary had done because McAllen had been a Houston man, and Singletary had been a zealous supporter of Mirabeau Bonaparte Lamar. Singletary had died a violent death, though not by McAllen's hand. Not that he hadn't thought about it. Now here was Yates, another journalistic thorn in his side. But McAllen reminded himself of the purpose of his visit.

"I didn't come here to argue politics with you," he said curtly. "I am looking for my son."

With an expression of spiteful triumph, Yates said, "You'll not find him here, I assure you. He and Quincy left a few hours ago, bound for the border."

McAllen's blood felt like it had frozen in his veins.

"You're lying," he gasped.

"Am I?"

McAllen took a threatening step forward, fists clenched. "By God if this is true I'll hold you personally responsible, Yates."

"Me?" Yates chuckled. "If you want to lay the blame where it truly belongs, you need look no further than yourself, Captain."

The rage left McAllen as quickly as it had come. He realized that Yates was right. This was just what

Emily had been telling him. He blamed Yates—and the editor's ne'er-do-well son, besides—for filling Gideon's gullible head with all sorts of nonsense about southern rights and honor, but he could not abdicate the responsibility for his own actions, by which he had driven his son into their sphere of influence. Gideon was rebelling against his father and everything his father stood for—and he was doing it, ironically, not out of political conviction but because he loved his father so much. He'd been hurt by his father's indifference, and was striking back the only way he knew how. The guilt McAllen experienced at that moment nearly brought him to his knees.

"I suppose you have given them your blessing," he said, his words like acid. "I suppose you won't care if your son dies for some misbegotten cause."

Yates turned quickly away to bend over his typecase. "A father cannot deny a son his independence, any more than the North can deny the South her rights."

McAllen thought he could detect a note of anxiety in the editor's voice. Memucan Yates was a liar and a troublemaker, but he was also a father, and he was no less concerned for Quincy's welfare than McAllen was for his own son's safety.

Turning to leave, McAllen paused at the door. "It's odd, but in this instance you and Sam Houston are after the same thing. You both want war with Mexico."

"Politics makes for strange bedfellows, don't you know?"

"You're all mad," decided McAllen, and walked out.

He dreaded having to tell Emily about her son—

dreaded it more than anything he had ever had to do. She would be devastated. All he could give her to alleviate the pain would be his solemn vow. He would go after his son and bring him back. Artemus Tice had been right, as usual. He had no choice but to become involved in this lunacy. Against his will he was being drawn into a web of intrigue and violence. So be it. But he was still determined to avoid at all costs what he most feared—a confrontation with Antonio Caldero. One of them would surely have to die. McAllen didn't want to be put in that position. He owed no man a greater debt than Caldero. Without Caldero's help he probably never would have been able to rescue Emily from her Comanche abductors.

Only one thing could make him fight Caldero. Not the pursuit of justice. Not the welfare of Texas. Not even the wishes of Sam Houston. Only the life of his own son. *That* John Henry McAllen put above all other considerations—including Caldero's life, or even his own.

Gideon McAllen was besieged by self-doubt that night. He and Quincy Yates had made good time, and Gideon calculated that Grand Cane lay thirty miles behind them. But now he was homesick. Worse than that, his conscience was bothering him. By now his parents suspected that something was wrong. No doubt his mother was sick with worry. *I should have left a note*, he decided, gazing morosely into the small fire they had built for the purpose of heating up some coffee and roasting the prairie chicken Quincy had killed on the trail.

Problem was, leaving had been a spur of the moment thing. As he rode away from Grand Cane plantation that morning he'd entertained no thoughts of running off to Mexico. But obviously Quincy had been planning to do just that for some time. It was thanks to Quincy that they had blankets and provisions and weapons.

"Have you heard about the goings-on down south?" Quincy had asked him. "I'm headed for Mexico. You want to come along?"

Caught off-guard, Gideon hadn't known exactly what to say. "Well, I . . . I don't know . . . I . . ."

"Oh, come on," said Quincy, laughing, a fierce pleasure lighting up his rakishly handsome features. "We'll have a grand old time of it. Guns, gold, and glory in Mexico. Not to mention more dark-eyed senoritas than you could shake a stick at."

"What exactly are you planning to do, Quince?"

"Why, ride for Brownsville, of course. I'm sure hundreds of men from all over are making tracks down there to hit a lick for the honor of these United States."

"Stop pulling my leg. You don't care about the honor of the United States any more than your father does."

They were strolling along the west bank of the Brazos—Quincy had taken him down to the river as soon as he'd arrived at the Yates cabin because he wanted their talk to be private. Now and then Quincy would bend over and scoop up a stick and lob it into the green waters of the Brazos. That was the way with Quincy; he never could be still. Always had to be doing something, always in perpetual motion. That was one of the things Gideon liked about him. Quincy never failed to dream up some kind of adventure for them. Only this time he'd outdone himself. Mexico, of all places!

"No, I reckon I don't much care about that," admitted Quincy at last, shooting a sidelong look in Gideon's direction. "But I thought you might. Your father being Captain McAllen and all."

Gideon's cheeks felt a little warm. "Just because he's my father doesn't mean I have to agree with him."

"My father says the time is coming when men will have to make a choice. Will they stand with Texas or with the Union?"

Gideon found it rather strange that Memucan Yates was so devoted to Texas. At least he claimed to be—even though he'd only lived in Texas for a few years. Compare that to *his* father; John Henry McAllen had risked his life for Texas independence. He had fought wild Comanches at least a dozen times in defense of the frontier. So why was it that Memucan Yates seemed to be more committed to Texas than his father?

"Yes, sir, you've got me pegged," said Quincy, chuckling. "I'm going to Brownsville for the fun of it. We'll have a grand old time down there. So what do you say? Are you with me, Gideon?"

"I don't know." Gideon desperately needed more time to think.

Quincy poked him in the ribs. "You know you want to go. So what's the problem? Are you afraid your father might whup you?"

"I'm not afraid of him."

"Good. Then it's settled. You're always complaining because your father doesn't respect you or your opinions. Well, here is your chance to show him that you're a man with a mind of your own."

"Your father doesn't mind you going?"

Quincy chunked another stick into the river and watched the strong current carry it away. "Not in the slightest."

"So when were you planning to go?"

"Right now. Today. I've already got the guns and the ammunition and enough supplies to get us to where we're going."

In the beginning it had seemed to Gideon like a magnificent lark, and he'd been excited by the prospect—for the first few miles. Then second thoughts began to creep up on him. The doubt and the guilt assailed him mercilessly. Was he really behaving like a man, with a mind and a will of his own? Or was he acting like an irresponsible kid who couldn't be trusted? And his poor mother! He loved her so. How could he so blatantly disregard her feelings? He realized he was doing this to get back at his father. But his mother was the one he would really be hurting.

Countless times he nearly turned back. But he was afraid of what Quincy might say if he did. And then there was that dark desire to prove himself to his father, no matter the cost. This more than anything else drove him on. At least one McAllen would fight for Texas and the South and the way of life that Gideon found so beguiling. He would prove himself to be a true southern cavalier. Gallant and brave and proven in battle, he could then stand toe to toe with his father. He would earn John Henry McAllen's respect.

John Henry McAllen left Grand Cane at daybreak the next morning. Though he was reluctant to leave

Emily, in another respect he was very much relieved to be going away. Though she had taken the news about Gideon very bravely—McAllen couldn't shake the feeling that she had known, somehow, that her son had run away from home—and there were no histrionics, no bitter recriminations, he couldn't escape the guilt he imposed upon himself. Emily didn't blame him, but he blamed himself every time he looked at her and saw the grief and concern behind her courageous front.

He rode his best horse, a gray hunter sired by Escatawpa, the legendary stallion that had carried him through all of the campaigns of his early years. He wore his pair of Colt Patersons. The .31 caliber, five shot percussion pistols were by no means the latest thing in handgun design. Bigger caliber six-shooters were available these days. But McAllen remained loyal to the old Patersons. They had never failed him.

He wore his famous black jacket, too. The distinctive shell jackets that the women of Warren County, Mississippi, had made for him and the men who followed him into battle against the Seminoles nearly thirty years ago had been covered with glory by those who wore them. Not only the Seminoles, but also Mexican soldiers and Comanche raiders had learned to dread the sight of the black jackets.

But McAllen wasn't hoping to intimidate anyone with the jacket. Over the years he had become rather superstitious with regards to that particular item of clothing. Though he would never admit it to anyone, not even Emily, he had come to believe that as long as he wore the jacket he would always come home when the campaign was over.

In spite of the earliness of the hour, Emily was up

and dressed and there to see him off. While beyond the hedge of Cherokee rose Old Jeb stood by with the gray hunter saddled and ready, McAllen embraced his wife on the front porch. She kissed him and softly implored him to return to her safe and soon, making no mention of Gideon, knowing she did not need to admonish him concerning the importance of his mission. John Henry had given his solemn oath that he would bring Gideon back, and she found solace in the fact that he always kept his word.

"I'll take care of things while you gone, suh," Old Jeb assured him.

In the saddle, McAllen nodded. "I know you will." Jeb's assurances were wholly unnecessary; McAllen trusted the man with the well-being of his wife and his plantation. Both would be safe as long as Jeb was alive.

With a long look back at the porch where Emily stood, pretty as a picture in a pale blue muslin dress, McAllen committed the image to memory, knowing not how long it would have to sustain him. It might be a matter of weeks, or even months, before he saw her again, because he'd made up his mind not to return empty-handed.

Riding due south, he calculated how long it would take him to reach Brownsville on horseback and made a swift decision—he would make for the coast and hope to book passage for himself and the gray hunter on a coastal steamer bound for Brownsville. He would not leave the hunter behind. If he had to venture into Mexico he wanted the best possible horse beneath his saddle, and there were none better in Texas.

Of course, with any luck he might be able to catch up with Gideon long before that—or, at the very least, reach Brownsville before his son. Whether Gideon and Quincy Yates planned to make the entire journey overland or, like he, had ideas of a quicker sea passage, McAllen had no way of knowing. The main thing was to find Gideon at Brownsville or earlier, before the boy went into Mexico with another ill-conceived expedition to corner Antonio Caldero.

But when he did find his prodigal son—then what? What would he say or do? Should he try to reason with the boy? Or should he hogtie him and haul him back home like a stray calf? McAllen wasn't sure what the best course of action would be. According to Emily, he needed to start treating Gideon like a young man, and show some respect for the boy's opinions and feelings. On the other hand, it would be a mistake to be too lenient. McAllen wondered what his own father would have done had he run away from home and placed himself in harm's way. But this proved a fruitless mental exercise, for he realized that his father had all along shown him the respect he had thus far failed to show Gideon. McAllen bitterly rebuked himself for being so blind. Perhaps the first thing to do when he saw Gideon again was apologize. And then, if Gideon refused to listen to reason and return to Grand Cane voluntarily—well, then, McAllen could always give him a good whipping and drag him back.

Finally, McAllen stopped anguishing over what the future held in store. He could only cross the bridge when he came to it. Or, in this case, *build* the bridge. A bridge between a misguided son and his mule-headed father.

At some point that afternoon—McAllen couldn't say at precisely what moment—he became aware that he was being followed. There was no sign of any pursuit, but his instincts had been honed by all those years on the war trail, and he relied upon them. This was good country for a tracker who wanted to remain concealed. Though rolling prairie, it was liberally dotted with stands, or "islands," of trees. A man who knew what he was doing could get right up on his prey before having to reveal himself. And it soon became apparent that the person or persons following him knew exactly what they were doing.

He decided to circle back around and try to get a look at them. Riding hard, and keeping as much as possible to the prairie's low places, he found a good vantage point in a stand of trees he had passed only moments before. There he settled down to wait, clearing his mind of all idle speculation.

He didn't have long to wait.

There were six of them, and McAllen recognized every one. They all wore their black jackets. Artemus Tice was in the lead, and riding with him was Morris Riddle, the farmer, Will Parton, fire and brimstone preacher and shepherd of Grand Cane's souls, Cedric Cole, the sharpshooter who ran the ferry, Lon Mayhew, a wagoner who was the best shot in the bunch next to Cole, and that was saying something, and Buford Doss, a farmer like Riddle who had taken a Mexican wife and spoke the south-of-the-border lingo like a native—he'd say he had to do it to get anything out of his spouse, who stubbornly refused to try to master the English language.

McAllen watched them pass, a hundred yards away, riding single file and right on his trail. These men had honed their tracking skills by hunting elusive Seminoles through black-water swamps, so following someone across the Texas prairie was in their case no hill for a stepper. He waited until they had gone by his position, and then broke cover. Startled, Tice and the other wheeled their ponies around and reached for pistol or rifle; recognizing McAllen, they urged their horses forward and gathered around him, wearing sheepish expressions.

"What are you boys doing out here?" asked McAllen.

"I'm assuming that is a rhetorical question," said Tice. "You know perfectly well what we're doing and why. Right after you left, Emily sent Jethro into town to tell me what happened."

"How come you didn't fetch us yourself, Cap'n?" asked Cole.

"This is a personal affair, and it's for me to handle alone."

The Black Jacks exchanged looks. McAllen's response had been brusque, and he thought that perhaps he had hurt their feelings.

"When those road agents shot and killed my boy a few years back," said Mayhew, "you said you'd help me run the jackals down if it took the rest of your born days. Didn't take nearly that long, as it turned out, but you were right there with me from start to finish."

"And when the Comanches killed Mary Torrance and stole Emily away," said Parton, "we took after those heathens, every last one of us."

"What they are trying to say, John Henry," said Tice, "is that one Black Jack's personal problem is a problem for us all. You wouldn't let one of us go off alone like you're doing."

"I let Yancey go off alone."

Tice shook his head. He was well aware that McAllen was still haunted by his decision to let Emily's uncle continue after her Comanche abductors even while the rest of the Black Jacks had to turn back.

"You had no choice there," said the physician. "This isn't at all the same sort of thing, and you know it. We're not letting you go down to Mexico and tangle with Caldero all by your lonesome."

"And if I make it an order?"

"We'll have to disobey that order, Captain," said Buford Doss. "It'll be the first time, I reckon. But there's a first time for everything."

McAllen shook his head. "I have no intention of tangling with Antonio Caldero."

"Might not be your choice to make," said Doss.

"So what's it going to be, John Henry?" asked Tice. "Do we ride along with you to Brownsville—or just meet you there?"

McAllen had to smile. "So you old coons are bound and determined to get yourselves killed? I'd have thought at your age you'd have better sense. Come on, then, we've got some miles to go."

Morris Riddle let out a whoop of joy. "One last campaign for the Black Jacks, eh boys?"

Chapter 6

Wrapped tightly in bandages and laid up in bed, Sam Burkin was very nearly at his wit's end. Back in Brownsville for the better part of a fortnight, he had been called upon by everybody who was anybody. Everybody, that is, except the person he most wanted to see—Judith Stoneman. The others had come visiting in order to congratulate him on his heroics; Massey and the rest of the survivors of the disastrous clash with Antonio Caldero had described how their captain, though an avenue of escape had been open to him, had chosen to rejoin his command and fight it out with the Mexican marauders, if need be to the death. No one seemed to pay much attention to the fact that they had failed in their mission. Caldero remained at large. The Tigers had been badly whipped. And yet Burkin had somehow come out of it all smelling like a rose.

The Mexican leader had even emerged victorious in a second skirmish with the Americans. Burkin had all the information in hand. A newspaperman from New Orleans had accompanied the second American expedition, and had written about its trials and tribulations. The article had been intended for publication in New Orleans, but someone—Burkin was inclined to believe it had been Stephen Powers—had gotten his hands on it and produced it in broadside form for distribution in Brownsville.

When news arrived that Caldero and his men were camped only a few days away—and on the American side of the Rio Grande, to boot—Colonel Jarvis had buckled on his sword and, temporarily eschewing the use of strong spirits and the comfort of his wife's velvet arms, declared his intention to sally forth and redeem the honor of the Brownsville Tigers. What Burkin found truly remarkable was that there were men foolish enough to rally around Jarvis and put their lives in his hands. About eighty men had marched out to meet Caldero, taking with them two small cannon, Fort Brown's entire complement of artillery.

It was a perfectly insane thing to do, of course. United States regulars were reportedly on their way to the border, as were the Texas Rangers. The wisest course would have been to wait for reinforcements. But the honor of Brownsville demanded a rematch with Caldero. The expedition's fate was committed to posterity by the wry and witty correspondent from the Crescent City.

The broadside read:

> After a little drilling, they marched under the command of Colonel Jarvis who, it is said, accomplished a feat he had never before managed, namely staying firm in his saddle for more than a quarter of an hour. They took with them two pieces of brass artillery, and I believe they meant to do some mischief. Now, mind, I will not state it positively, but I think the facts are that Jarvis got as far as Mr. Glavaecke's ranch, situated about three miles from here, in four days; and proceeding on at the same rate they got at last to

> Santa Rita, seven miles from Brownsville, in a week; and there, sure enough, they found the enemy, or perhaps more properly speaking, the enemy found them.
>
> A halt was called. Jarvis and his men made a firm stand. Much discussion ensued, and much difference of opinion prevailed, and Jarvis discovered to his dismay that the entire force was comprised of colonels, captains, or majors. I say much difference of opinion prevailed, chiefly on the subject of the propriety of fighting after dinner.
>
> The colonel, mounted on a beautiful white steed, in vain reiterated the words of command, 'Come along, boys!' The boys, however, would not budge. As I said, they made a firm stand—at a respectful distance from the enemy's lines, or where they suspected the line to be, as only a few Mexicans could be seen, dodging in and out of the chaparral.
>
> Quite by accident some shooting commenced. Jarvis's men made a desperate charge—for home—leaving their cannon in the possession of the enemy, and though it had taken them a week to get to Santa Rosa they made much better time in getting back. I was personally acquainted with one of the men in this famous expedition who, though a cripple, has since declared to me that he got home on that occasion in less than forty minutes!

The newspaperman's whimsy was not much appreciated in Brownsville, and he, too, had beat a hasty retreat home to New Orleans. Charles Stoneman, for one, was outraged by the printing and distribution of the broadside. Stephen Powers, said Stoneman—for Charles was also certain Powers was behind the broadside—ought to be charged with treason, for the broadside served only to add to the distress of the people of Brownsville, lowering their morale and contributing to a growing panic.

Burkin found it all rather amusing, though in Stoneman's presence he evinced stern disapproval of the broadside. Fortunately, no lives had been lost, and only a few men had suffered injuries, acquired for the most part in the undignified haste of their retreat. Humiliated, poor Jarvis sought succor once more in the bottle. Burkin felt a little sorry for him; the old incompetent fool had meant well.

As for Caldero, no one knew at this point where he would strike next. The people of Brownsville were barricading their streets and boarding up their homes. Caldero was intercepting the mail, but after reading it he would reseal the letters, hang the mail bag in a tree, and send word into town where it could be recovered. When his men took ninety of Mifflin Kennedy's beefs, Caldero pinned a due bill to the rancher's door. And now, apparently, he had sent a proclamation to Charles Stoneman, and Stoneman was calling for all of Brownsville to assemble this afternoon. Everyone was expected to be at the open-air town meeting to be held in the main square—except for Burkin and the other Tigers who were still recuperating from their wounds. Burkin had no intention of going. He had other plans—plans involving Judith.

His burning desire to see her had brought him to the brink of indiscretion, and beyond. He had paid a young lad known about town as a reliable messenger to deliver a letter to the Stoneman residence this morning. A letter addressed to Judith. A dangerous and desperate act, but Burkin thought he had trimmed down the odds a little by waiting until this morning to send the letter, knowing that Charles Stoneman would be meeting with other leaders of the Reds for a breakfast discussion prior to the town gathering—a discussion scheduled to take place in the room above Grindle's saloon.

Still, there was a chance that something could go wrong, some unforeseen circumstance that would betray him, and Judith, as well. But if that happened then Judith herself would have to bear some of the blame. She could have come to see him. She could have at least sent a message. Even if she had come with Charles, who visited often, Burkin would have understood. Why hadn't she come? He was going out of his mind, imagining all sorts of possible scenarios. She certainly owed him an explanation. He had to know what was going on. So he had asked—no, make that insisted—that she meet him at their customary rendezvous at one o'clock this afternoon. One o'clock. The scheduled time for the town meeting called by Charles Stoneman to get under way. The meeting which Charles would preside over, and which would probably run all afternoon.

It was not yet eleven in the morning, but Burkin simply could not lie still a moment longer. Slowly, gingerly, he got up, and experienced only a minor twinge of pain in his side where the bullet had struck him. That was encouraging. Making his way to the window, he remembered the doctor's warning. Three weeks of strict bed confinement, else he ran the risk of reopening the wound. He'd lost a great deal of blood; he was in a very weakened condition, and further bleeding could be dangerous.

The trek back to Brownsville, more so than the wound itself, had nearly done him in—a nightmarish ordeal across the malpais. Blessedly, he could recall precious little of the journey, since most of the time he'd been delirious with fever. At some point along the way, Massey had cauterized his wound with a knife heated white-hot over a campfire's flames. Massey, the natural-born torturer, had tortured him, but to save his life, not destroy it. He hadn't bled to death, thanks to Massey. But the doctor had told him he was lucky to be alive.

Parting the curtains on the window, Burkin looked down at the Brownsville street. He lived in a two-room flat above his office, on a side street at the edge of the business district, which encircled the main square. This had been all that he could afford. Not exactly in the mainstream of Brownsville affairs. Of course now that would all change. Everybody knew him now. He was a hero. *Still,* he thought, *I would trade my new status for a single kiss from Judith.*

A tapping on the door startled him and he jumped, wincing at the lance of pain in his side, and then shuffling with bated breath to the door, throwing it open, and breathing again when he recognized the freckled face of the messenger boy, who stood in the stairwell that separated his two private upstairs rooms.

"I come right in like you told me to," said the boy.

"Yes, yes. Is there anyone downstairs in my office? Did anyone see you come in?"

"Nary a soul, Mr. Burkin, I promise."

Burkin ushered the lad into the room and closed the door. "Did you deliver the letter, just like I said?"

"Yes, sir. I give it right to Mrs. Stoneman herself."

Burkin could detect a glimmer of curiosity in the boy's eyes. The kid wasn't dumb. He had to suspect that something a little underhanded was going on here.

"There is a twenty dollar gold piece on the table over there," said Burkin. "It's all yours."

The boy scooped up the double eagle, bit it, gazed in awe at it, turned the coin this way and that to watch how the sunlight streaming through the window glanced off its burnished sides.

"Holy cow, Mr. Burkin! I ain't never even touched one of these before, much less had one for my very own!"

"Just remember, you must tell no one about the errand you've run for me today. We have a verbal agreement."

"Yes, sir. My lips are sealed."

"A verbal agreement," repeated Burkin, ominously wagging a finger at the boy. "If you break your word I will have you thrown in jail. You know I can do that, too."

"I promise I won't tell a livin's soul."

"Did she say anything? Mrs. Stoneman, I mean."

"No, sir."

"You waited until she'd read the letter, didn't you? I told you to wait."

The boy nodded. "I done just like you told me. I waited."

"And she said nothing? Absolutely nothing?"

"No, sir. Well, she did thank me. But that's all."

Burkin sighed. "Run along, then."

As the boy left, Burkin agonized over whether he had handled him correctly. Perhaps he should have made light of the whole affair. Given the lad a dollar instead of a double eagle and refrained from making him swear his eternal silence. Like as not the boy wouldn't have thought anything about it, and wouldn't have mentioned the errand to anyone else, regarding the matter of no importance.

But Burkin decided he couldn't take that chance. And so he had resorted to bribery and intimidation.

He began to dress, having to remind himself to go slow, to curb his impatience, and when in his haste to see Judith again he forgot to go slowly enough, the sudden breathtaking stabs of pain served to remind him. The pain was getting worse now that he had been standing for a while. Wondering whether Judith would be there at the rendezvous, the abandoned adobe down near the river, was pure agony. And the knowledge that it wasn't safe for her if she *did* heed his summons was agony, too. He was putting her life in jeopardy. There was no telling where Caldero's vaqueros would show up next. Burkin shuddered to think what those half-civilized Mexicans would do to Judith if she fell into their clutches. But the die was cast. The deed done. There was no going back. He despised himself for giving in to the overwhelming desire that now consumed him to the point that he would risk anything to see, touch, taste, possess Judith again.

It took him an infuriatingly long time to get dressed. When at last he was done he made his way downstairs and outside. Keeping to the alleys like a sneak thief, trying to remain unnoticed and regretting for once his newfound celebrity, he took a circuitous route to the livery. There he rented a horse and buggy. The livery man gave him an odd look, but asked no questions. *Perhaps,* thought Burkin, *he can tell I am in no mood to answer stupid questions*. Or maybe he was just one of those rare and wonderful people who knew how to mind their own business.

Not until he was leaving Brownsville, again by a

back route that avoided the main thoroughfares and took him through the Mexican section, did Burkin realize that he was bleeding. Not much, just enough to spot his shirt with blood. But that didn't deter him. Nothing would prevent him from seeing Judith this afternoon. *I must be mad*, he decided. *That is the only way to rationalize what I'm doing.*

He felt every bump, shake, and rattle of the buggy as he drove the five miles to the adobe. There didn't seem to be another soul abroad in the desert. No one else was foolhardy enough to venture out of Brownsville. The town was under siege. Caldero didn't have to post a cordon of armed men around it to accomplish that. Just the knowledge that he was out here, somewhere, was enough. Charles Stoneman had the war he so ardently desired. *Well, Charles, how do you like it now? Next time maybe you'll be more careful what you ask for.*

When Burkin reached the place where he had to turn off the road, he was forced to go very slowly. This was rough traveling, and he didn't want to crack an axle and strand himself. A few hundred yards from the road, he left the horse and buggy in a dry gulch and went the rest of the way on foot. It was nearly one o'clock by his timepiece. The sun had reached its zenith. The heat was a hammer trying to pound him to his knees. He pressed resolutely on, nauseated, dizzy, his face beaded with cold sweat. Staying to the gulch, he entered a thicket of catclaw and mesquite. To his right, somewhere in the brush, a rattlesnake gave its warning. A moment later he could see the adobe. He prayed to God she would be there, even though he knew he had no business asking God to serve as his accomplice in sin.

A familiar sorrel horse was tethered to the remnant of a corral overgrown with weeds. Burkin's heart sang with joy. He rushed forward. Judith was standing on the bank of the shimmering river, gazing across at Mexico, and when she heard him she turned, as pretty as an angel in a pale blue skirt and yellow muslin chemise that set off the gold in her hair.

Burkin pulled up short a few feet away from her.

"You came," he said.

"Of course."

"You shouldn't be standing out here in the open like this."

She laughed softly. "Don't be silly. There isn't anyone for miles around."

"These days you can't be too sure."

"Are you concerned for my safety, Samuel?"

"Of course I am." Then he remembered that it was his message that had brought her out here where danger lurked behind every rock and cactus. "But I had to see you, Judith. I couldn't stand another day not seeing you."

She seemed pleased. "You silly, impetuous man."

"Judith . . ." He moved to take her in his arms, but she pushed him away, gently, almost playfully.

"You're bleeding, Samuel."

He looked down at his shirt. The splotch of reddish-brown blood had spread. Funny, but he no longer felt any pain. Just a tingling numbness in his side.

"You don't want to get blood all over my dress, do you?" she asked. "Now how would I explain *that* away? Come." She took his hand and led him, as though he were a little boy, to the adobe.

Part of the roof thatching had blown away long ago, and there was some debris on the hardpack floor. A rickety trestle table was the only furnishing. In the corner were two blankets, rolled up and tied in an oilcloth slicker. He had brought those blankets on the occasion of their second meeting here, and had left them for future meetings. Burkin reminded himself to shake them out this time before using them, in case of scorpions. But Judith didn't want to bother with the blankets. She unbuttoned her chemise, and then the camisole beneath, taking her time, smiling faintly as she watched him watch. Burkin stared, the way a man dying of thirst stares at a mirage, as she stepped out of her skirt and then her petticoat. Finally she stood there, naked but for the open camisole, and Burkin admired the flare of her alabaster-white hips, her narrow waist, her flat stomach, the sweet valley between her taut breasts as she raised her arms to undo her hair, which fell in an amber cascade to her shoulders.

"Now you can get me bloody," she said in a husky voice, and Burkin stumbled forward.

When their fevered joining was done and their passion spent, Burkin rolled off Judith and lay beside her like a dead man, on his back in the dust, feeling weak and dizzy. He gazed up at a patch of blue sky that could be seen through the hole in the adobe's roof, and wondered why he didn't feel deliriously happy, as he usually did after he and Judith had made love. The answer was simple enough. His physical need for her had been momentarily satisfied, but too many questions remained regarding Judith's recent actions to permit Burkin any peace of mind. He wanted to possess her fully, completely, and forever. For now all he could do was possess her for a few moments, and then she was no longer his.

"Why didn't you come to see me?" he asked.

She rolled over on her side and ran her fingers through the sweat-matted hair on his chest.

"I couldn't. Charles wouldn't allow it."

Burkin's heart lurched in his chest. "You mean he suspects something between us?"

"No, silly. The thought hasn't even entered his mind. He won't let me go to Brownsville until this business with Caldero is resolved. He says he is a prime target if there *is* an insurrection, and that makes me a target, too."

"At least he is demonstrating a little concern for your safety," said Burkin dryly. "Most of the time he acts like you don't even exist. Why in heaven's name did you ever marry him, Judith? You can't love him. You know he doesn't really love you."

"He loves me in his own way. The only way he knows. And I married him for a very good reason. My family wanted me to. The Stonemans of New York are very well-to-do, you know. I was of marrying age, and he was as good as any and better than some when it came to husband material. And I didn't really mind. I am accustomed to having nice things. It doesn't really bother me that Charles doesn't love me."

"Yes, it does. Or you wouldn't be here with me now."

"Charles needs me. He has to have the best of everything. The best food, the best clothes, the best house. And the best wife."

Burkin laughed. "The best wife wouldn't be lying here with a man who wasn't her husband, would she?"

It was a rather cruel comment to make, and Burkin

immediately regretted having said it, but Judith wasn't even fazed. "That's why he must never know," she said, matter-of-factly.

"I'm of half a mind to tell him, just the same."

"No, you won't. Because if you do you will never see me again."

He sat up and looked at her, scowling.

"You're never going to leave him, are you?"

"I never said I would, Samuel."

"You're perfectly content with the way things are."

"We both have to be."

"What if I had a lot of money? Could give you all the nice things you've come to expect out of life?"

"My family has a number of business concerns in New York that are built on Stoneman money. I won't jeopardize that. Besides, I like you just the way you are."

Burkin knew he shouldn't say what he was going to say next, but he couldn't stop himself.

"What if something were to happen to Charles? What if he dies? I don't suppose you'd remain the widow in black weeds for the rest of your life."

She gazed earnestly into his eyes. "I really don't look my best in black."

Confused and discontented, Burkin shook his head. "Sometimes I just don't understand you, Judith. I've been going out of my mind these past weeks, wanting to be with you. I guess you don't feel the same way."

Judith stood up and held out her arms, and he took her hands and stood up, too. Her slender body was covered with dirt and smears of blood—his blood—and for some reason that excited him. She put his hand on one of her breasts and smiled.

"Some things simply can't be helped. We must

make the best of what we have. You have me, Samuel. I give myself to you in a way I don't to Charles. You will have to be satisfied with that." She curled her arms around his neck, pressing her body against him as she kissed his lips, and Burkin felt the heat of renewed passion rising up within him. She laughed softly. "Oh, we'd better not do it again. Look at you. You're bleeding. I'm going down to the river to clean up." And before he could form the words of warning, she was gone.

"Judith! Wait!"

But she pretended not to hear him. Standing in the adobe's doorway, he watched her run down to the riverside, her yellow hair flowing, and she knelt in the shallows to cup the water in her hands and splash it on her body. She made a terribly beautiful and arousing picture, and Burkin cast prudence aside and walked down to join her, kneeling behind her and wrapping his arms around her. Playfully she splashed his face with water, trying to squirm out of his grasp. They wrestled in the cool, murky shallows, their play quickly turning serious, and then Burkin took her again, in a way he had never done before, from behind, and there was nothing very gentle about it, but Judith didn't seem to mind at all. She arched her glistening back and her soft cries pierced his mind and urged him on to greater exertions, and when it was over they lay sprawled on the bank like shipwreck survivors. The heat of the sun coupled with sheer exhaustion made Burkin doze off. He came to with a start, realized Judith no longer lay beside him, and got up to stumble wearily to the adobe.

She was dressed, and trying to put her hair back up, and she looked none the worse for wear.

"I really must be getting back before I'm missed," she said.

"No one knows you're gone?"

"No one. And I want to keep it that way. Besides, Charles may be home soon."

"I doubt it."

She smiled sweetly. "You'd better get back to town and have a doctor take a look at you."

He glanced at the tight wrap of bandages around his midsection. They were damp and soiled and stained with blood, but he couldn't have cared less.

"When will I get to see you again?"

"When this is all over, I suppose," she said, with an infuriating ambivalence, "and everything is back to normal."

Burkin groaned. "We can't go on like this, Judith."

"Of course we can." She stepped closer and kissed the downturned corner of his mouth. "We *must*," she whispered, and then she left the adobe.

Burkin stood there, feeling empty as he listened to the diminishing sound of her horse and she rode away. Stiff and aching and listless, he got dressed—and it was at that moment, as he glanced through the doorway, that he saw the lone rider, sitting his horse across the wide, shimmering river, and Burkin's heart seemed to leap into his throat.

The horseman was at least a hundred and fifty yards away, and Burkin could tell very little about him, except that by his garb he was clearly a Mexican. And though the man's wide sombrero cast his features into shadow, Burkin got the distinct impression that the rider was looking right into the adobe, could see him, and was watching every move he made.

In a panic, Burkin lunged for cover, forgetting that

his trousers were still down around his knees, and falling very painfully as a consequence of this oversight. He looked around for a weapon, something, anything with which he could defend himself, and cursing himself for an idiot because in his all-consuming haste to see Judith he'd left his little Briggs single-shot pistol back in Brownsville. He strained to hear the sound of a horse splashing across the river—the Rio Grande was shallow enough to ford at will at almost any point. Surely the horseman was one of Caldero's cutthroats, and Burkin fully expected him to cross over and take this opportunity to kill a lone gringo.

The seconds crawled by, and Burkin heard nothing to indicate that the rider was coming for him. Mustering up a little courage, he crawled to the doorway and peered around the edge.

The rider had vanished.

Maybe he didn't see me, Burkin told himself. But it was no use trying to fool himself. Of course he'd been seen. In fact, he had no doubt the Mexican had been there for some time. Why, he had probably seen the shameless coupling in the shallows! Burkin felt his cheeks get hot with shame. What in heaven's name had possessed him to make love to Judith out in the open for God and everybody to see? I *have well and truly taken leave of my senses.*

He sat there with his back against the wall for over an hour, watching the dusty beams of sunlight that slanted through the hole in the roof creep across the hardpack floor and up the far wall. The appearance of the horseman had completely unnerved him, and it took that long to summon the wherewithal to get up and moving again. *So much for Brownsville's hero!*

At last he finished dressing, checked the far bank

of the river again, and finally left the adobe, plunging into the thicket, locating the dry gulch and following it back to the buggy, and all the while his skin crawled, and he expected the Mexican to jump him at any moment. The horse in its traces looked none too happy about having been left to stand all afternoon in the hot desert sun. Burkin was so relieved to see the animal that he mumbled an abject apology, which the horse answered with a cynical whicker.

On the road back to Brownsville, Burkin tried to figure out what he would say to explain himself should he run into anyone, particularly Charles Stoneman, who would take this route to return home. According to his timepiece, Burkin had been away from town for more than five hours. The town meeting had probably concluded long ago. In all that time someone might have come calling at the law office to see how he was doing. It was truly amazing how popular he had become, virtually overnight. How would he explain his absence if someone had come to pay him a visit and found his rooms empty? Burkin couldn't come up with a suitable answer. Images of Judith kept distracting him—her eyes, her mouth, her breasts, the flare of her hips . . .

The lateness of his return, the cause of such intense and prolonged anxiety, actually proved a boon, for the twilight of day's end helped to conceal his entrance into town, so that by some small miracle he managed to return the horse and buggy to the livery and make his way home without being noticed, as far as he could tell. The streets of Brownsville were quiet. It was supper time. That reminded Burkin—he was weak with hunger. He couldn't remember when he'd last eaten. Yesterday, or perhaps the day before. This was what

Judith Stoneman was doing to him. He hadn't been able to sleep or eat. He'd risked his reputation at the very least—and quite possibly his life—just to be with her. He almost hated her for the power she possessed over him.

Once again in his quarters, he gingerly removed the bloodstained bandages, wrapping them in his travel-worn clothes and hiding the bundle under his bed. He had indeed reopened the wound, and was debating whether to go directly to the doctor when he heard the door to the street open and the voices of two men downstairs, followed by boot heels thumping on the stairs. He stood there, frozen, listening.

"Samuel? Are you awake?"

It was Stoneman.

I've been found out, thought Burkin, and he was petrified with guilt and shame and fear, so that he was just standing there, naked as a jaybird, when Stoneman and the rancher, Mifflin Kennedy, walked in.

The smile on Stoneman's face vanished when he saw Burkin.

"Good God, man. You're bleeding."

"I took a hard fall," Burkin replied, and he marveled at how easily he could manufacture a lie, with such dexterity, and at an instant's notice. All that agonizing over excuses had been for naught.

"I'll fetch the doctor," said Kennedy, and was gone, thundering down the stairs.

"Sit down, Samuel. Sit down." Stoneman helped him to a chair, swept a quilt from the bed, and covered Burkin with it.

"No need to fuss over me," said Burkin. "I'll be fine."

"We missed you at the town meeting."

"I was trying to get dressed and go when I hurt myself. I . . . I must have knocked myself out."

"You're a good man, Samuel," said Stoneman, pleased that Burkin had made such an effort. "I've come because I thought you would be interested in hearing the proclamation that Caldero has issued." Brandishing a folded piece of brittle, yellowed paper, Stoneman unfolded it and read, wearing a smile that to Burkin seemed a little forced. The message was brief and to the point. Caldero began by cataloging the sufferings of his people under American governance. They had been robbed of their property, incarcerated without trial, hunted down, and even murdered by men with avarice in their hearts and "the black entrails of vultures." Burkin thought that last was a nice touch. Very Latin. Caldero went on to urge his people to take heart. If the Lord enabled him to fight against their enemies he would break the chains of their slavery. He did not wish to make war on the whole town of Brownsville. Some of the Americans were decent people who treated their Mexican neighbors with respect. But he had sufficient artillery to batter down every house in the town, and he would do so unless his enemies were delivered into his hands.

There Stoneman paused and glanced at Burkin. "His list of enemies follows. My name is at the top. I suppose that means I'd better be careful."

"Do you think he'll actually do it? Use those cannon he captured to bombard this town?"

Stoneman moved to the window. "Who knows? That man is capable of anything. But if he does, he hasn't enough ammunition to do much damage."

"What are you going to do, Charles?"

"In spite of his threat, I believe it is safer in

Brownsville than at my home. So I'm staying here in town for the time being."

"And what of Judith?"

"I've just sent twenty men to bring her safely in."

"Sounds to me as though we'd better get some help, and soon."

"We'll get help. Have you heard the news about Jarvis? He was found dead today, a knife between his ribs. They are looking for his wife. She's disappeared. She was a Mexican, you know."

"My God," said Burkin, shocked. "But how do you know she killed the colonel?"

Stoneman shrugged. "She's a Mexican, isn't she? Also, one of the street patrols shot and killed a Mexican boy they spotted lurking behind Mahlon Webley's house."

Burkin made no response. Poor Mexican youths often hunted for discarded food and other items behind the homes of Brownsville's wealthy residents. Everyone knew that. The trigger-happy members of the street patrol—possibly Brownsville Tigers—had no doubt executed a lad guilty of nothing more sinister than wanting to fill an empty belly. Burkin didn't fail to notice that Stoneman was unmoved by the tragic circumstances of the boy's death. *No doubt*, Burkin thought bitterly, *he would say that it is always the case that innocent people lose their lives in war.*

Kennedy returned with the doctor in tow, and Stoneman tarried until Burkin had been tended to, and then he and Kennedy prepared to leave.

"You'd better keep a sharp eye out, Charles," advised Burkin. "You could get killed."

"Nothing is going to happen to me, Samuel, but thanks for your concern."

Standing at the window, Burkin watched Stoneman and the rancher leave his law office and turn up the street. A movement in the shadows on the far side of the thoroughfare captured Burkin's attention. This was a man, rising from the place where he had been sitting, at the corner of a darkened building. Burkin couldn't see him very well in the evening's gloom, but by his plain clothes and serape it was obvious he was a Mexican. As Stoneman and Kennedy proceeded down the street, the man moved in that direction, as well, staying as much as possible to the shadows.

Burkin's smile was grim. Stoneman had wanted war—but he just might get more than he bargained for. Perhaps, like poor old Colonel Jarvis, an assassin's knife between the ribs.

And that would leave Judith a widow who by her very nature would not be inclined to wear a widow's weeds for long.

Chapter 7

In Gideon's opinion, the most expeditious route to Brownsville was to make straight for Quintana or some other port, there to book passage on a coastal steamer. Though in his spur-of-the-moment departure he hadn't brought any money of his own, Quincy Yates had a little—enough, Gideon thought, to purchase a sea passage for them and their horses.

But Quincy was opposed to the idea, chiefly because he was afraid Gideon's father might make an effort to intercept his son, and would no doubt assume that they intended to travel by sea. Quincy reminded Gideon that John Henry McAllen's factor conducted his business in Quintana, and through him McAllen had connections in every Texas port. They might well find Quintana on the lookout for them. Gideon replied that he doubted very much that his father would go to any great lengths to stop him. "He would, if it was your mother's wish," countered Quincy, and with that Gideon could hardly argue.

Their only recourse, then, was the overland route, a rigorous ordeal under the best of circumstances, and particularly grueling at the height of summer. The region known as the Nueces Strip was a notorious wasteland fit, as far as Gideon was concerned, only for the cactus and the sagebrush, the rattlesnake and the scorpion. To attempt a crossing in the middle of summer was to court disaster. But regardless of his reservations, Gideon pressed on. He had much to prove, to himself and to his father, and he simply could not turn back, no matter what. In this case, discretion was *not* the better part of valor.

The days took on a monotonous regularity. They would get an early start and make as many miles as they could before the furnace sun reached its zenith, then they would stop and, if fortune smiled, spend several hours in a piece of shade, resting their horses and their own saddle-weary bodies before mounting up in the late afternoon for several more hours on the trail. After nightfall they would make camp, usually in an arroyo or a thicket in order to conceal their campfire.

What started out as an adventurous lark turned into a grim test of endurance. Quincy's high spirits, which had been greatly in evidence the first few days, quickly deserted him, so that soon they might go all day without a word passed between them. Each left the other alone with his misery. Eventually Gideon began to wonder if Quincy lacked the resolve to see this through. It had been a damn-fool idea, Quincy would say. His father probably needed his help with the newspaper. And so their roles were reversed, with Gideon the resolute advocate of the endeavor, and Quincy the reluctant participant. Gideon would remind his friend of the gold and the glory awaiting them on the border—not to mention all those dark-eyed senoritas. Besides, they had come too far to turn back now.

On the tenth day of their trek, the question of turning back became moot. For four days now they had failed to find a water source. Locating the occasional spring or creek in the Nueces Strip required familiarity with the region, something that neither of them possessed. All they could depend on was blind luck, and so far they'd had none of that. Gideon considered berating Quincy for failing to take into account the shortage of water in south Texas during the summer months, but decided it really wasn't worth the effort. He hadn't thought of it, either. By the tenth day they and their horses had been without water for nearly thirty-six hours. There was no way they could turn back now. The only recourse left open to them was to press on. If they didn't find water in the next day or two . . . Gideon didn't want to think about that.

But they were spared the final ignominy of leaving their bones to bleach in the trackless desert, for on the afternoon of the eleventh day they stumbled upon a spring seeping out of a rock outcropping. Only after he had partaken of the brackish water did it occur to Gideon that it might be alkaline. He'd heard tales of men and horses going stark raving mad, and even dying, after drinking bad water on the trail. Not that it mattered. If they didn't drink this water they were food for the buzzards anyway.

As it turned out, the water was good, and they spent the rest of the day at the spring, stretched out in the shade cast by their horses. Gideon felt too weak and fatigued to move, or even think. He dozed, waking with a start, only to drift off again, and the process repeated itself several times. The third or fourth time that he came to—he couldn't be sure—he realized it was dark. Night had fallen. The sky was crowded with stars. The horses were nervous. They smelled something not to their liking, a scent of danger carried on the wind. Gideon noticed that Quincy was sleeping soundly, and decided not to wake him. It was probably just a coyote lurking upwind that caused the discontent of the horses. He found the brittle remains of a couple of dead sagebrush and made a small fire, intent on cooking up some coffee.

The aroma of the coffee roused Quincy. Sitting with Gideon around the fire and watching his friend set the pan aside to let the coffee grounds settle, he looked long and hard at Gideon and said, "I guess we ought to have tried to get passage on a ship, after all."

Gideon laughed. He could afford to, now that they weren't going to die.

"It's a tad late for that now, Quince."

Quincy smiled, relieved that Gideon was in a good frame of mind. "How far you reckon until Brownsville?"

Gideon shook his head. "It can't be more than two or three days." He had nothing concrete on which to base this assessment. More than anything it was wishful thinking.

"Maybe this wasn't such a good idea after all," admitted Quincy glumly.

"When we get to Brownsville you can take a ship back to Quintana, if you want."

Quincy lapsed into ashamed silence. Gideon retrieved their two tin cups from his saddlebags and sat on his heels to pour the coffee. Suddenly a horse snorted, Quincy yelped "Christ!" and Gideon jerked his head around to see a man emerge from the night, advancing on them with a pistol in his hand.

"Make a move and it might be your last," the man said, his voice raspy and full of menace.

Gideon reacted without conscious thought, slinging the pan of coffee at the man and lunging forward in the next instant. Hot coffee in his face staggered the intruder, and Gideon hit him low, at the knees, knocking him backward. The man's pistol, a Walker Colt, went off, and Gideon flinched as the big hand cannon made a sound like close thunder, but the barrel was pointed skyward, and before the man could recover, Gideon was straddling him and had his hunting knife, a cheap piece of work that Quincy had provided him at the outset of their journey, at the stranger's throat. The caress of steel against his Adam's apple froze the man.

"Use that pigsticker or put it away before you make me mad," he growled, disgusted.

"Be quiet!" snapped Gideon.

"Aint a smart thing to do, killin' a Texas Ranger," came a disembodied voice from the darkness, and Gideon looked up to see a second man appear in the throw of the firelight. He wore a long coat and carried a Volcanic Lever-Action rifle cradled like a baby in his arms.

"Well, Mase," drawled the man who had just spoken, "either he aims to give you a close shave or a new smile."

"He's just a kid," replied Mase. "Don't know no better."

"Are you really a Texas Ranger?" Gideon asked him.

"Swear on a Bible, if I owned one."

"Maybe you ought to take up preachin' or some other peaceable occupation," suggested the second man wryly. "To let a stripling get the better of you . . ." He shook his head. "Might be you're gettin' too slow and careless for this kind of work, Mase."

Gideon took the knife away from Mase's throat,

got up, and extended a hand to help the Ranger to his feet.

"Sorry," he said. "I thought you might be a road agent, or one of Caldero's Mexicans."

Mase accepted the assistance and the apology. Standing, he wiped coffee grounds off his face with a sleeve and holstered the Walker Colt.

"Everybody makes mistakes," he said. "Name's Mase Williams. That feller yonder is Captain Tobias."

"I'm Gideon McAllen. And this is my friend, Quincy Yates."

Quincy was still sitting by the fire, so startled that he hadn't been able to move. Now he got to his feet, started to say something, and then changed his mind and just nodded. He wasn't sure he could trust his voice not to crack.

"McAllen? You say your name's McAllen?" asked Tobias, moving closer to get a better look at Gideon. He was a tall lean man with streaks of gray in his hair above the ears, and eyes as black as coal.

"Yes, sir."

"Your pa happen to be John Henry McAllen, of down Brazoria way, by any chance?"

"Yes, sir."

Tobias smirked at Mase. "Must run in the blood."

"What's that?" asked Mase.

"McAllen hatred for Texas Rangers."

"I don't know what you're talking about," said Gideon. He wasn't sure he liked the none-too-friendly way Tobias was looking at him.

"I'll tell you all about it, son. My company's camped two miles west of here. We come over to fill the canteens in this here spring. Reckon the least we can do is share our coffee with you, seein' as how you were kind enough to share yours with Mase."

"We're bound for Brownsville," said Quincy.

"Is that so. Don't you just love a coincidence? So are we. You can ride with us."

Gideon glanced at Quincy, who shrugged. There was something to be said for joining up with a company of Texas Rangers as far as safe travel was concerned. And even though Gideon's intuition warned him that he might be better off keeping his distance from this man, Tobias, he didn't argue. It would avail him nothing to decline the captain's invitation. It wasn't really an invitation, anyway.

Gideon was surprised to find only ten men in the Ranger camp. When Tobias had said a company he'd just assumed the man meant a hundred riders, or at least fifty. Was this all the state of Texas intended to send to Brownsville in the way of reinforcements? He'd heard that the Rangers were the best fighters the world have ever known, and these men certainly looked capable enough to live up to the Ranger motto of "one fight, one Ranger." But Quincy had told him that reports reaching his father had put Antonio Caldero's forces as high as several hundred men and growing daily, as disaffected Mexicans flocked to his banner. Caldero had crushed the Brownsville militia. True, the Brownsville Tigers were not of the same caliber as Tobias and his men, but still—twelve men hardly seemed sufficient.

Gideon knew the history of the Rangers as well as any Texan. The corps had been created by resolution in 1835, during the fight for independence from a dictatorial Mexico. It called for sixty men whose assignment was to guard the frontier. Their primary function was to deal with Indian raids. Later it was decided to increase the size of the corps to three companies of fifty-six men each. The volunteers were required to provide their own horses and weapons.

Their first exploit was against the Mexicans rather than the Indians. A company scouting along the Gulf Coast captured five Mexican sailors who had come ashore from a sloop laden with supplies—provisions destined for Santa Anna's army, which the captain was trying to locate. Using the captured boat to reach the supply ship, the Rangers boarded the vessel and seized her. Two more sloops arrived, and the Rangers decoyed their officers aboard the captured vessel now in their hands; in this way they took all three ships, along with twenty-five thousand dollars' worth of supplies that Santa Anna badly needed—all without the loss of a single man.

It was during the republic's existence, in the years between 1836 and 1845, that the Rangers really came into their own—except when Sam Houston was president. Houston went to great lengths to make peace with all the Indian tribes of Texas. He was inclined to do so by his past relations with the Cherokees, among whom he had lived on two separate occasions. He respected the red man as few of his kind did. But he was also forced to do all in his power to keep the peace on the frontier because the young republic's treasury was chronically empty, and Houston knew that Texas could ill afford to pay for a long conflict with the Indians.

Houston's successor, Mirabeau Bonaparte Lamar, was of an entirely different state of mind. Lamar hated Indians, and he loved war. In his opinion, the Indians were nothing more or less than obstacles to Texas expansion. He dreamed of a great empire stretching to the Pacific Ocean. But the tribes were in the way. So they had to be removed or exterminated. The white man and the red man could not live together in peace and harmony, he said, because nature forbade it. The only policy to pursue, therefore, was "to push a rigorous war against them, pursuing them to their hiding places without mitigation or compassion."

No force was better suited to this task than the Texas Rangers.

Eight companies of Rangers were provided for by legislative appropriation. The sum of one million dollars was set aside for the protection of the frontier. This seemed like a large sum of money for the time, but war was expensive, and Lamar had to make it last. While at first he favored a regular military establishment for the Texas republic, he soon found out that the Rangers were not only the most effective Indian fighters but also the most economical.

Confronted by Lamar's hostility, the Indians—primarily the Comanche bands—stepped up their raids along the frontier, marked roughly by the Colorado River in the 1840s. Their depredations became so severe and frequent that cannon had to be placed around the new capital at Austin just in case the Comanches were bold enough to attack the seat of Texas government. Farms were burned, travelers waylaid, farmers ambushed in their fields, and occasionally a woman or child was abducted. The Comanches made life very precarious for the hardy settlers trying to put down roots along the upper reaches of the Colorado, Trinity, and Brazos rivers.

To make matters worse, the Mexican government

was known to be circulating agents among the Indians, men who incited the tribes to continue their attacks on Texas, to destroy their homes and disrupt their commerce. There was talk of an alliance between the Indians and the Mexican army which, it was promised, would someday soon march across the Rio Grande and reclaim Mexico's lost northern province. Concrete evidence of this plot was provided by the journal of a Mexican spy named Pedro Julian Miracle, who was killed by a group of Red River settlers. As a consequence, Texan hearts were hardened against the Indians. Lamar's policy of extermination or expulsion gained support. And the Rangers were given wide latitude in the way they waged war against the red men.

Then came the debacle of the Council House. Lamar sent word to the various Comanche bands that peace might be possible, but only if the Indians demonstrated their good faith by releasing all of their white prisoners. It was arranged that a meeting would take place in the Council House at San Antonio. Perhaps the Comanches should have known better than to attend that meeting. But they were at war with tribes to the west, and earnestly desired a peaceful resolution to their conflict with the Texans. A number of chiefs appeared in San Antonio. Feelings ran high, a crowd of Texan onlookers became hostile, the Comanches became alarmed, sharp words were spoken, and then gunshots rang out. When the smoke cleared, thirty five Comanches lay dead, including many principal chiefs, as well as three women and two children. From that moment on, vengeful Comanches swore a fight to the death.

Gideon was familiar with the details of the Council House fight. His father had been in San Antonio at the time, sent there by Houston to keep an eye on things. Houston didn't trust Lamar, and he had no liking for the Texas Rangers, either. John Henry McAllen was of like mind. Both men were convinced that the Rangers were cold-blooded killers and inveterate Indian haters who were excessive in their zeal. Much was made of Indian depredations, of their raping, torturing, and murdering civilians. But the Rangers responded in kind. They made no finer distinction between warrior and squaw, adult and infant. They raped and murdered Indian women. They butchered defenseless Indian children, operating under the brutal premise that nits made lice.

So said Houston and McAllen, anyway. But others made the case that one had to fight fire with fire. Yes, the Rangers were at times merciless, conceded their defenders. But then, they had to be. You could not make civilized war on barbarous heathens. The rules of war could not apply in a contest with the savage Comanche horde.

Gideon had not given the matter much thought. In his lifetime the frontier had been pushed westward from Grand Cane as more and more settlers emigrated to Texas; finding the prime land to the east already claimed, they moved west in spite of the danger. The result was that the Comanche scourge, once so prevalent as far east as the Brazos, ceased to be a concern at least until one ventured a hundred miles or more west of the Colorado River. One thing was certain: the Comanches had not been vanquished in nearly twenty years of unremitting conflict, despite the best efforts of the Rangers, and perhaps because of those efforts the fierce warlords of the Staked Plains remained the white man's implacable enemy.

The Rangers Gideon saw encamped that night a few miles from the spring were all cut from the same cloth—lean, fit, and taciturn, physically and mentally hardened, with bright keen eyes in sun-darkened faces. These men seldom spoke, and smiled even less often. Every one carried a minimum of a knife, a pair of pistols, and a rifle. They had that unmistakable look of born hunters and killers of men.

"Mase and I found these greenhorn kids down by the spring," Tobias told his fellow Rangers. "They're going to Brownsville. Reckon if they don't come along with us they won't ever get there."

The critical scrutiny of the Rangers made Gideon intensely uncomfortable. Obviously he and Quincy were greenhorns; an experienced traveler would have known better than to have made camp too near a spring, exposing one's self to unwanted intrusion by wolf, panther, Comanche, bandit—or Texas Ranger. Of course, the fact that they had made that cardinal error had proven fortunate in this case. Or had it? Gideon couldn't decide if it was good luck or bad that he and Quincy had fallen in with these men.

The other Rangers accepted their captain's pronouncement with a signal lack of enthusiasm. Gideon could tell they didn't give a damn whether two green kids made it to Brownsville or not. And Gideon seriously doubted that Tobias really cared, either. Maybe it was just that Tobias understood how difficult it would be to explain why a company of Rangers, theoretically charged with the responsibility of protecting the lives and property of Texans, left a pair of young men to an uncertain fate.

"At least he doesn't hold it against you that your father is John Henry McAllen," Quincy whispered to

Gideon as they spread their blankets a respectful distance from where the Rangers were bedded down. "Everybody knows there is a lot of bad blood between your father and the Rangers."

Gideon just nodded. Yes, Quincy was quite right, everyone knew. A long-standing feud had existed for many years between the Texas Rangers and McAllen and his Black Jacks. It was impossible to point to any one thing by itself that was the source of the animosity. The Rangers resented the Black Jacks because there were many who said that no finer fighter force than McAllen's Mississippians existed. At least, that had been the case fifteen, twenty years ago. Then, too, McAllen hated the Rangers for their brutality in slaughtering innocent Indian women and children. But Gideon thought the real bone of contention was the fact that the Rangers had been obstacles in his father's path during those long months when John Henry McAllen turned the world upside down looking for his beloved Emily when she'd been a captive of the Quohadi Comanches.

Gideon should have slept well that night. He hadn't slept much at all since leaving Grand Cane, and here he was as safe as a man could be on the frontier, surrounded by Texas Rangers. But sleep eluded him. His mind was troubled and restless. He didn't feel at ease. In fact, he felt as though he had jumped from the frying pan into the fire.

The next morning, Mase Williams offered Gideon and Quincy some coffee and hardtack. The other Rangers had gone about their Spartan breakfast without giving even a thought to sharing the victuals with their unwanted guests. Mase seemed genuinely friendly, which was all the more remarkable, in Gideon's opinion, because this was the man he had bested the night before, and Mase had taken some pretty merciless ribbing for that from his comrades. Mase was no doubt a proud man, so why didn't he hold a grudge?

Gideon and his friend gratefully accepted Mase's offer, but they scarcely had time to wolf down the hardtack and gulp the coffee before the Rangers were saddled up and ready to ride. Mounted, Captain Tobias loomed over them, biting a chew off a pigtail of tobacco, and advising them to hurry the hell up. "Throw those henskins on your ponies, boys, or we'll leave you behind for the buzzards."

They traveled hard and fast all day, dismounting at regular intervals during the hottest part of the day to walk their horses, wiry desert mustangs every bit as resilient as the men who rode them. Gideon and Quincy were exhausted. So were their mounts. Gideon decided these Rangers and their scrawny horses could probably keep moving at this pace for a week, day and night, without respite. That came from chasing fast-moving Comanche raiders, he supposed. In a single day they covered more ground than he and Quincy had managed in two, maybe three days. *Another twenty-four hours at this pace*, he thought, *and my horse and I are both finished.*

But the following day was not a full one, because noon found them in the vicinity of Brownsville.

For some miles Gideon had been hearing something that sounded like distant thunder. But there wasn't a cloud in the sky. Gideon could hardly remember what a cloud looked like, for that matter. One needed only to look at this desolate wasteland to realize that rain was a very unusual event in these parts. So what was the explanation for that occasional booming noise in the distance?

Paused on high ground where they could see the town of Brownsville laid out before them, with the shimmering ribbon of the Rio Grande snaking through the dun-colored desert just beyond, they saw a puff of smoke from south of the river, followed by a geyser of debris erupting from one of Brownsville's structures. Gideon knew then that someone was firing a cannon into the town. It had to be the Mexicans. Caldero was attacking Brownsville!

He glanced at Tobias, expecting the Ranger captain to order a gallant charge into action. Instead, Tobias just sat his horse and watched, looking quite amused—and in no hurry to ride to the rescue.

"Looks like Caldero's got himself a new toy," he drawled.

"I make it to be two artillery pieces, Captain," said Mase.

"Reckon we'll have to take them away from those Mescans 'fore they accidentally hit something and hurt somebody. Come on, boys, they've gone and started the dance without us."

They rode into a town that appeared at first glance to be completely deserted. No one ventured out into the open with cannonballs shrieking in every five minutes or so. Tobias and the Rangers seemed in no rush to seek cover. Gideon was as nervous as a cat on a hot stove, but he did his best to hide it. The Rangers thought little enough of him as it stood now, without him giving them cause to treat him with any more disdain.

But it was Quincy who broke under the strain. They heard an odd whistling sound, getting louder in a hurry, and then Tobias, as laconic as before, said, "Here comes another one of Caldero's calling cards, I reckon," and Quincy almost fell on his head as he leaped from the saddle, pasty-faced. He let go of his reins and dived for cover beneath the raised porch of the nearest building. Gideon had the presence of mind to catch up the dragging reins before Quincy's horse could make up its mind which way to run, and then, with the whistling becoming an ear-piercing shriek, the shot hit on the next street over with a dull explosion, a spot marked a moment later by a plume of dust and smoke.

Tobias and his men checked their ponies and waited for Quincy to crawl out from under the porch.

"Boy, you see any other yellow dogs up under there?" asked Tobias.

"You're all lunatics," muttered Quincy. "Raving lunatics, that's what you are."

"When your time comes," said Tobias, "you can crawl and whimper all you want to, but it won't make a lick of difference, so you might as well stand tall and take what's coming like a man."

As he handed the sulking Quincy the reins to his horse, Gideon noticed that Tobias was shooting a quick, approving glance in his direction.

Riding on, they reached the main thoroughfare, and two men emerged from a building to stand under a wooden sign identifying the place as Grindle's saloon. Tobias steered his mustang over to them and the others followed.

"My name is Charles Stoneman," said one of the men on the saloon's boardwalk. "This is Josiah Grindle."

"Captain Tobias, Texas Rangers."

Stoneman looked relieved, and then puzzled—as he counted the horsemen. "Where are the rest of your men, Captain?"

"This is the whole shebang."

Stoneman looked at Grindle, then back at Tobias, perturbed. "I guess the governor fails to comprehend the serious nature of our situation down here."

"If he didn't think it was serious he wouldn't have sent us."

"Caldero is said to have several hundred men under his command."

"I doubt that. And most of the men he does have are probably Mescan dirt farmers. I reckon ten to one odds are still pretty good—for us, eh, boys?"

Gideon heard that godawful whistling sound again. Gripping his saddlehorn so tightly that his knuckles turned white, he listened as the whistle grew into a shriek, this time louder than ever before. The explosion was very, very close—close enough to rattle the saloon's front window and make the horses nervous.

"Gentlemen," said Grindle nervously, "come on in and have a drink on the house."

"Reckon we'll get on across the river and find those cannon first," said Tobias. "You can buy us each a bottle when we get back."

"I have received word that a company of United States dragoons has landed at Port Isabel and will be here by tomorrow morning at the latest," said Stoneman. "I suggest you wait for them, Captain, before crossing into Mexico and engaging the enemy."

"Texas Rangers don't need the help of a bunch of blue-leg horse soldiers," said Tobias contemptuously. "You folks get on back inside where it's safe. We'll silence those big guns for you, don't worry."

Grindle tugged on Stoneman's sleeve. "Come on, Charles. Leave them to it. They know what they're doing, I guess."

Stoneman nodded. "Good luck to you, Captain." Obviously it was his opinion that Tobias would need much more than luck to come back and claim his drink on the house, but he wasn't going to stand out here and argue.

Once Stoneman and Grindle had gone back inside, Tobias shifted in the saddle and looked across at Gideon.

"You and your friend want to go hide with them, or ride with us?"

His pride wounded, Gideon was quick to answer. "I'm coming with you. How about it, Quincy?"

Quincy had shamed himself once before in front of these men. He could not do so again.

"I'm game," he said, unconvincingly.

Tobias nodded. "You boys have come a fur piece to see some action, and now you're gonna get your chance. Come on, if you're lookin' for glory."

They crossed the Rio Grande in search of the two cannon, but when they found the site where the Mexicans had placed the artillery pieces to bombard Brownsville, the little brass six pounders and their crews had vanished, leaving tracks that headed south, deeper into the Coahuilan desert. Gideon hadn't caught a glimpse of the enemy since crossing the river, and apparently none of the sharper-eyed Rangers had, either, but no one doubted that they were being watched.

"Those greasers are damned cowards," sneered

Tobias. "Least they could've done was stand their ground and fight it out like men."

Gideon could tell that Tobias and his men had been aching for a fight, and were now deeply disappointed. On the other hand, he was vastly relieved. Brownsville was no longer being pounded, so they had accomplished what they'd set out to do, and Gideon was ready to get back to town. The hair on the back of his neck was standing on end. They were being watched, and he expected the Mexicans who were out there, lurking in the chaparral, to start sniping at them at any moment.

So he was both startled and dismayed when Tobias announced that they were going after the cannon.

"We can make better time than they will," he said, "and with any luck we'll catch up to 'em before nightfall."

"I don't think that's a good idea, Captain," said Mase. "They might be leading us straight into a bushwhackin'. We don't know where Caldero is or how many men he's got. We ought to do a bit of scouting first."

Tobias scowled. "If we let them cannon go, the Mescans will just bring 'em right back up again and start lobbin' shot into town like they done before. I ain't inclined to play cat and mouse. We come across the river to capture some artillery and by God that's what I aim to do."

Gideon was disappointed when Mase just shrugged; he'd hoped Williams would press the issue and somehow bring Tobias to his senses. But Mase had made his point and he wasn't going to argue about it.

They pressed on after the cannon, and with every mile deeper into Mexico they rode, the less likely it seemed to Gideon that he would get back alive. He was not at all happy with Quincy Yates for talking him into this mad escapade, or with himself for *letting* his friend talk him into it. Worst of all, Quincy had lost every ounce of enthusiasm for this venture—and had acted like a coward, to boot.

The broiling sun slipped slowly down the western sky, and their shadows grew longer. Gideon had decided that neither he nor his horse could make another mile when Tobias abruptly called a halt. A hand resting on the butt of his belt pistol, the Ranger captain suspiciously scanned the horizon.

"I smell trouble comin'," he said flatly.

The Rangers had already filled their hands with rifle or revolver.

A shot rang out.

On pivoting horses, the Rangers sought the source of the gunfire. Gideon was sure it had come from somewhere to his left. But he couldn't see anything out of the ordinary. A second shot, and suddenly a dozen riders were silhouetted against the setting sun on a low rise to his right.

"Gideon!" gasped Quincy. "I . . . I've been hit."

Gideon turned to see his friend slide out of the saddle and hit the ground limp as a rag doll.

"There they are!" shouted Tobias. "Come on, boys! Let's give 'em their medicine!"

He kicked his mustang into a gallop and the rest of the Texas Rangers followed, charging straight at the Mexicans.

Chapter 8

Gideon forgot all about Tobias and the Texas Rangers when he saw Quincy Yates fall. Horrified, he leaped from his own saddle to reach his friend's side. Quincy was lying facedown, and Gideon rolled him over gently. His blood ran cold. The front of Quincy's shirt was soaked with blood. His features were ashen, and a pink froth was beginning to leak from the corner of his mouth. Gideon knew then that Quincy's lungs had been punctured by the bullet. Knew, as well, that there was no hope for him. Quincy was going to die, drowning in his own blood. This couldn't be happening. This had to be a bad dream. Gideon had the urge to run away. The last thing he wanted to do was stay here and watch his friend fight a losing battle for life. But he *had* to stay—he cradled Quincy's head in his arms. Quincy's eyes fluttered open and he managed a smile.

"Found the glory . . . didn't I?" he wheezed, and with a strangling cough he began his final struggle. Gideon's eyes burned with tears as he held Quincy tight—held him until he felt his friend give up the fight and go limp in his arms.

The sound of gun thunder intruded on Gideon's grief, and he remembered then where he was and what was happening. He glanced at the melee of riders silhouetted against the blood-red sun, but that scene did not hold his attention for long as he realized that both his horse and Quincy's had wandered off. He did not even consider for a moment joining the Rangers in their fight. His only thought now was escape. The enemy was all around him. His only ally now was the darkness. Perhaps he could hide in the brush until nightfall, and then elude the Mexicans. And after that? He would be alone, on foot, without food or water, and armed only with the knife and pistol he carried in his belt. What were his chances of getting out of Mexico alive, much less of getting home? He didn't even want to think about that.

"Good-bye, Quincy," he said, choking on emotion, as he let go of his friend and in a crouching run made for a thicket of catclaw a few yards away.

He reached cover in the nick of time, for a pair of Mexican horsemen galloped up to the place where Quincy's body lay. Scarcely daring to breathe or move, Gideon watched them in the fast-fading light. One of the men dismounted and nudged Quincy with the toe of his boot. Then he said something to his comrade, who remained mounted and looking westward, where a few scattered gunshots still rang out. The first vaquero took Quincy's pistol and stuck it in his own belt. He examined Quincy's knife and then tossed it away. And then he turned Quincy's pockets inside out. Gideon was outraged. The bastard was robbing the dead. Only there wasn't anything to steal. Quincy's poke was in his saddlebags, strapped to an errant horse. Disappointed, the vaquero stood up and looked around. He looked right at Gideon's hiding place in the catclaw. But the darkness was deepening, and he didn't see Gideon. He bounded with remarkable agility back into his saddle, and he and his companion galloped west.

Gideon put his head down on his arms and began to breathe again. He trembled from fear and fatigue. His plan was to wait, for hours if need be, until he was certain that the Mexicans were long gone. Then he would locate the North Star in the night sky and head for home.

Not that he expected to make it. But a person had to try.

The charge of the Texas Rangers had caught the Maguey vaqueros by surprise. Leaving two dead men behind, Tobias and the others made a break for the open country. In the brief melee several vaqueros were slain, and several more, including Refugio, sustained wounds. Refugio was the leader of the twenty Maguey riders who had ambushed the Rangers, and while his wound was not mortal, it temporarily incapacitated him, leaving the others leaderless. That fact, coupled with the coming of night, resulted in the failure of the Mexicans to pursue Tobias and his men.

Refugio had expected his ambush to lead to fear and confusion among the Americans, making them easy prey. He remembered how the Brownsville militia, trapped in the barranca, had reacted several weeks earlier. But the Rangers were not the Brownsville Tigers. They'd struck back, quickly and savagely, the way a wounded scorpion responds to a threatening presence. Their segundo having fallen in battle, the vaqueros were not inclined to contest the retreat of the Rangers.

When it became clear that there would be no pursuit, Tobias called a halt to count heads. It was then that Mase Williams expressed his desire to go back.

"We left those two boys to fend for themselves, Captain."

"They're both dead," replied Tobias curtly. "Forget them."

"That Yates boy might be dead. But McAllen was still above snakes when I saw him last. We'd go back for one of our own."

"He's not one of us."

"Was a mistake to bring them with us in the first place."

Tobias glowered at Mase. "You scared of John Henry McAllen, by any chance? Is that what's eatin' you?"

"There'll be hell to pay."

"Do I look worried?"

"Way I see it, you wanted something to happen to that McAllen kid. That's why you dragged him along with us. That your way of gettin' back at his father?"

"You're too smart for your own good sometimes, Mase."

Mase shrugged. "So what's it all about, Captain?"

Tobias bit off a chew from a pigtail of tobacco. "John Henry McAllen killed a friend of mine, a Ranger by the name of Eli Wingate. It happened back nearly twenty years. I rode with Captain Wingate. We were chasin' the Quohadi Comanch' and had tracked them clean to their camp in the canyon of the Palo Duro. McAllen was already there. He was after that Torrance gal the Comanches had taken prisoner. She's his wife now." Tobias shook his head. "Imagine that. Marryin' a woman who'd probably been taken by every Comanche buck with a hankerin'. It ain't right or proper, if you ask me."

"Way I hear it, the feud between McAllen and Wingate was personal."

"McAllen killed my captain. Now I've killed McAllen's son. I'd say that makes us even."

Mase Williams shook his head. "God help you when McAllen finds out about this."

Tobias spat a stream of tobacco juice. "I'm shakin' in my boots," he sneered. "Now, let's ride. If we keep movin' through the night we ought to be in Brownsville by sunrise. I could use that free drink."

Gideon had thought he could make it back to the Rio Grande in one day, but he was wrong.

He wasn't sure, but he figured he'd come twenty or so miles into Mexico with Captain Tobias and the Texas Rangers prior to the ambush. That night he left the ambush site, making sure that he had obliterated his tracks, using some brush to extinguish his footprints until he was several hundred yards away from the place where Quincy Yates lay dead. This was in case the Mexicans came back. He steered his course by the North Star, the way his father had taught him. But he didn't get very far in the darkness. When the moon set he decided to stop after walking right into a low-lying patch of prickly pear and then disturbing a rattler. He never saw the deadly diamondback, but the telltale sound of the serpent's warning was close enough to make his blood run cold. Sitting on a rock, hugging his knees against his chest, he waited for the dawn.

It was the longest night of his life. Alone in the terrifying vastness of the desert, he listened to the distant wailing of coyotes and grieved for Quincy. No one was around to see so he wept unabashedly, and prayed fervently and wished he was home. So much for guns and glory and dark-eyed senoritas! Poor Quince. Poor Memucan Yates. The man had lost his only son. What an awful blow that would be. Gideon could just imagine what it would do to his own mother if he suffered the same fate as Quincy. His mother *and* his father, too. Gideon had sometimes regretted not having a little brother, for selfish reasons of his own. Now he regretted it more than ever, but not for himself. That way at least his parents would have had *someone* to cling to if anything happened to him.

At last the dawn came and Gideon set out, determined to reach Texas before day's end—resolving not to spend another night alone in the desert if he could help it. But in a few hours he was exhausted. The sun sapped the strength from his body. He had no food, no water. He eventually reconciled himself to the fact that he wouldn't make it to Texas in one day, and perhaps not at all. Now he had to fight an inner battle. His opponent was despair—despair the likes of which he had never experienced. By mid-afternoon the only thing that kept him going was the thought of his mother and father; he had to spare them the agony that Memucan Yates was doomed to suffer. To God he prayed for deliverance—not for himself, really, but for the sake of his parents. How did it go? That psalm David had written? Something about the valley of the shadow of death. Gideon felt himself to be in that valley. In that shadow. He stared Death in the face.

And then, as the shadows of evening lengthened and the day came to a close, he heard a dog barking. Throughout the ordeal of that hellish day his horizons had been steadily shrinking. At first he'd looked far to the north, searching for the shimmering waters of the Rio Grande. But now he saw only the ground directly in front of him; no longer concerned with finding the river, or even eluding capture, he concentrated solely on that little piece of Mexico he had to conquer with his next step. One step and then another, and each one the supreme test of his endurance. Hearing the dog gave him a glimmer of hope. Where there was a dog, there would usually be humans nearby. Stumbling to a low rise, he spotted a small adobe hut below. A pen made of dead acacia stalks held a flock of sheep, about forty or fifty in number. A black-and-white dog stood before the hut like Horatio guarding the bridge, barking even more furiously now that Gideon was in plain sight. A man emerged from the hut, an old man wearing a straw hat and ragged clothes and sandals on his feet. He looked at Gideon, but did not budge from the doorway.

Gideon staggered forward, waving at the man, hoping that by waving he could make the man understand that he meant no harm, that he was friendly. He was afraid the man would turn back inside and fetch a weapon, perhaps a gun. *Then I will have to shoot him,* thought Gideon. *I will shoot him and the dog if I have to.* But the man did not move from the doorway.

Gideon paused thirty feet shy of the hut. The dog had worked itself into a perfect frenzy by now, dancing forward and then backwards and then sideways with fangs bared, barking incessantly.

"Water," croaked Gideon. "All I need is water."

The old man's face was deeply lined. He looked at least a century old. The sunken eyes, black as night, were impassive. He didn't seem to be afraid, more curious than anything. And apparently he didn't understand a word Gideon was saying. What was the Spanish word for water? Gideon knew it—he just couldn't remember it. His head was throbbing and he couldn't think.

In desperation, he sank to his knees and held his arms out away from his sides, hoping that by adopting this posture he could make the old man see that he meant no harm. But the old man still did nothing. The dog, however, reached a new level of frenzy, and Gideon thought, despairing, that the dog was going to attack him and he would have to shoot it, and then he would probably have to shoot the man next *and I think I might anyway because the old fool just can't get it through his thick skull that I mean no harm I mean what's wrong with him can't he see I need help for God's sake?*

And then the girl came out of the hut and saw him and spoke sharply to the dog, and her voice worked wonders because the canine's belligerence vanished in a heartbeat and it went to her with tail wagging. She turned next to the old man and spoke briefly to him, and he nodded and disappeared inside, taking the dog with him. Gideon got to his feet as she approached, a willowy girl about his age, and he realized that she was rather pretty in spite of the smudges of dirt on her face, and prettier still when she smiled at him—a smile that almost brought tears to Gideon's eyes because this was the first time in what seemed like ages that anybody had smiled at him.

She held out her hand. "Come, you are safe here."

"You speak English," he gasped. "How?"

"Yes. But come with me. You need water and food and rest. We will talk later."

Gideon took her hand and the tension fled his body like an exorcised demon. Somehow he knew without the slightest doubt that he could trust this girl. He would live, after all. It was a miracle that he had found this place—this wisp of a girl. God had intervened and spared him.

He didn't make it to the adobe hut; a few steps from the door, he was suddenly overwhelmed with dizziness. The world tilted sharply under his feet and then tilted just as sharply the other way, like the deck of a ship caught in a tempest, and Gideon lost his balance, and even as he fell, mumbling an apology, he kept a tight grip on the girl's hand, refusing to let go of his salvation.

Long before he was even halfway to Brownsville, John Henry McAllen began to wonder if God Almighty was punishing him.

Reaching the coast at the port of Quintana, McAllen and the Black Jacks thought themselves fortunate to find a coastal steamer bound for Port Isabel and points south. The ship was the *Inferno*, one of a fleet of such vessels owned by the Scot merchant, McColley. Loaded with textiles, pots and pans, and other goods bound for the south-of-the-border market, the *Inferno* would return laden with Mexican gold and silver, much of which would wind up in McColley's coffers. Since he had room to spare, the steamer's skipper took all seven men and their horses aboard, charging them two dollars apiece for the passage, with a dollar extra for each horse. This money he would be allowed to pocket. The fare suited McAllen and the others. In fact, price was no object for McAllen;

he would have bowed without complaint to usury if it would get him to Brownsville quickly.

But the *Inferno* turned out not to be a quick means of transport to their destination. The second day out of Quintana, a boiler exploded, killing one man and seriously injuring two other members of the crew, keeping Dr. Tice busy for the duration of the trip. There was no hope of repairing the damage to the engine room at sea, and the skipper debated whether to return to Quintana under sail. McColley expected his ship captains to keep to a strict schedule, and the *Inferno*'s skipper had to calculate how long it would take to repair the boiler in port to the time it would take to sail to Port Isabel, where another boiler might be had. After anguishing over this decision for half a day, the captain opted for a return to Quintana. Sails were hoist, but there was not a breath of wind for the canvas to capture, and for the better part of two more days the steamer lay doggo, several miles off the coast, unable to proceed.

McAllen fumed. He was trapped aboard the steamer as it wallowed in the greasy swell between a merciless sky. He and his comrades could get ashore by means of the *Inferno*'s dingy, but there was no way to transport their horses to dry land. He and the others discussed their options. They could go ashore without their horses and hope to locate suitable remounts, but this stretch of coast was sparsely populated, and there were no guarantees that this plan would work. McAllen decided not to leave the horses. With that resolved, all that was left was to wait and pray for a breeze. That gave Will Parton yet another day to try converting the steamer's crew, a "godless collection of scoundrels and rogues," according to the preacher.

Cedric Cole and Lon Mayhew used the fins of sharks circling the ship for practice. Buford Doss wrote letters to his wife; he wrote a letter every day and never tried to post them.

Finally the wind picked up and the sails filled out and the *Inferno* began to move. The steamer was no clipper ship, and progress was slow. The prevailing winds were from the east, and the skipper changed his mind about beating his way back to Quintana. They headed down the coast instead, and even though the winds were steady, it took the better part of a week to reach Port Isabel. As he disembarked, McAllen knew he had lost whatever advantage he might have gained by taking the sea route.

A road connected Port Isabel with the town of Brownsville, following the course of the Rio Grande and passing near Fort Brown, the outpost constructed by Zachary Taylor's forces during the Mexican War. McAllen was surprised to see signs of life in the fort—sentries on the adobe walls and the Stars and Stripes hanging limply from the flagpole in the hot and breathless summer air. He'd been under the impression that the fort had stood abandoned for many years.

As they passed the stronghold, an officer galloped out to intercept them. He introduced himself as Captain Donaldson, commanding the company of dragoons dispatched to the area by the War Department at the request of the Texas governor.

Donaldson wanted to know who they were, where they came from, and what purpose they had for coming to the valley. When McAllen answered every query, and made it clear that the sole reason for his presence was to find an errant son, Donaldson's demeanor became more amiable.

"Please forgive my impertinence, Captain McAllen," he said. "We've had several bands of armed civilians passing through, and most of them are here looking for a fight. My orders are to do everything possible, consistent with maintaining the honor of the United States and the sovereignty of her soil, to prevent this outbreak from escalating into full-scale war. I've got patrols all along the Rio Grande for the purpose of keeping the Mexicans on their side of the river—and our people on this side."

"I have no intentions of crossing the river into Mexico," assured McAllen.

Donaldson nodded. "I have heard of you, sir, and of your volunteers, so I know I can rely on you. You are free to proceed—with my earnest best wishes for the success of your mission."

McAllen thanked him and rode on.

Reaching Brownsville, he saw ample evidence to verify what Donaldson had said about armed bands of civilians. The sidewalks were thick with them. They stood in idle groups, watching the comings and goings and waiting for something—anything—to happen. McAllen could understand the army captain's concern. These men were restless and bored. They'd come looking for trouble, and if they didn't get some coming their way pretty soon they would make a little of their own.

He split the Black Jacks into three groups. Tice and Cole, and Parton and Riddle, would search the town for Gideon, or news of him. McAllen intended to do likewise, alone, while Mayhew and Doss would watch over the horses. At sundown they would meet up again.

It didn't take long for word to spread that McAllen and the Black Jacks were in town. An hour into his search, McAllen was approached by a man who claimed he'd been sent by Stephen Powers, and said that Powers requested the honor of a call.

"Does this have anything to do with my son?" asked McAllen.

"I couldn't rightly say, Captain. Mr. Powers didn't tell me anything else."

McAllen nodded and told the man to lead the way.

Powers was waiting in an office at the bank he owned. It was a nicely furnished room, with darkly paneled walls and velvet upholstered chairs and a Regency desk so huge it made the wizened man who sat behind it look like a very small child. Wearing the dirt and grime of many days away from home and hearth, McAllen was reluctant to sit on anything, but he occupied a chair at his host's insistence. He declined, however, Powers's offer of a cigar or a drink. Until he knew what Powers wanted from him he wasn't going to accept his hospitality.

"It is a real pleasure to at last make your acquaintance, Captain," said Powers. "I've heard a great deal about you over the years."

"I've heard about you, too, sir."

"Knowing what I do about you, I was surprised to hear you had come to Brownsville during our present difficulties."

"Why is that?"

"This is a bad business, frankly, and the men who started it, and who hope to profit by it, are not of the same political bent as you or I. But perhaps I am being overly presumptuous. I am told you are a Union man."

"That's true, I suppose."

"The men of whom I speak are states' righters and secessionists, for the most part."

McAllen leaned forward. "I really don't care what they are. All I'm here for is to locate my son, Gideon."

"Oh?" Powers blinked, elbows planted on the arms of his chair and his hands clasped in front of his face. "Your son is here in Brownsville?"

"He's either here or on his way."

"For what reason, if you don't mind my asking?"

McAllen grimaced. "He's come to fight. To prove himself in battle. And I'm here to stop him before he gets himself killed." He stood up. "My apologies, sir. I only answered your summons on the chance that you might have had information concerning Gideon's whereabouts. Frankly, I don't have the time or the desire to discuss any other matter."

"I want to save lives, Captain McAllen, and I think you can help me do that. All I ask is a moment of your time."

McAllen hesitated, then sat down again. "I would appreciate it if you'd make this brief."

"Thank you. I understand you are acquainted with Antonio Caldero."

"We've met."

"On one occasion he did you a favor, isn't that so?"

"That's true."

"What do you think of him?"

McAllen shrugged. He wasn't really interested in Caldero, or Powers, or whatever it was that Powers had in mind. "He's not a man to be trifled with."

"So you respect him."

"I guess you could say that."

"And how does he feel about you?"

"Why don't you ask him?"

Powers smiled. "I would like for you to ask him."

"What?"

"Do you think you could get to him? See him, talk to him? Tell him that the greatest service he could provide for his country would be to disband his army and turn himself in. Because if he does not, sir, we *will* have war, and at the very least Mexico's northern provinces will become new slave states loyal to a southern confederacy."

"Take a step back, Mr. Powers. You're getting too far ahead of me."

"Have you heard of the Knights of the Golden Circle, Captain?"

"I've heard of them, but I couldn't tell you much about them."

"Because the KGC is a secret organization, much like the Freemasons. Only their reason for being is rather more sinister, I'm afraid. Their mission is to create a southern slave empire. Mexico is not their first target. There have been expeditions launched at Cuba and Nicaragua. Fortunately, those have failed. But the Knights are not easily discouraged. I'm sure you've seen many armed men on our streets today. I venture to guess that quite a few of them are members of the KGC."

"Is Captain Donaldson aware of this?"

"He suspects, I'm sure."

McAllen shook his head. "Then let the army handle it. I want no part of this, Mr. Powers. Besides, Caldero would be a fool to give himself up. He'd be dead before he even got to trial for killing that sheriff. And

I know one thing about Caldero—he's certainly no fool."

It was Powers's turn to lean forward. "What if I could guarantee him a trial, and a good lawyer?"

"A *fair* trial?"

"That could be arranged."

"No lawyer could represent him and hope to stay in Texas."

Powers flashed a crafty smile. "I think I know one who could be persuaded to do it."

McAllen again got to his feet. "Mr. Powers, I admire your desire for peace. But I really can't help you. I must find my son and take him home to his mother."

Powers stood and extended a hand. McAllen took it, and found the man's grip surprisingly strong for someone who looked so physically weak. He got the impression that this unprepossessing man might be easily underestimated, and that to do so would be a grave mistake.

"If there is anything I can do to assist you in your quest, Captain McAllen, do not hesitate to call upon me again."

McAllen was grateful for the offer—and grateful, too, that Powers had the good grace to take no for an answer and drop the matter of Antonio Caldero.

Stepping out of the bank, McAllen realized it was nearly sundown. Anxiously he scanned the street, hoping against hope that he would spot Gideon. Maybe he had beaten his son to Brownsville after all. He clung to that hope even as he tried to ignore apprehensions that something had happened to Gideon en route. Perhaps Tice and the others had some good news for him. He turned in the direction of their appointed rendezvous.

As he crossed the mouth of an alley, someone spoke his name and he turned, peering into the deepening shadows of the alley to see a man standing there with a pistol in his hand.

"You're John Henry McAllen of Grand Cane, aren't you?"

McAllen wondered if an acknowledgment would seal his death warrant. He didn't know this man, but he had many enemies . . .

"I am," he said.

The man took a cautious step closer, the gun held steady. McAllen noticed that the hammer wasn't cocked.

"Name's Mase Williams," said the man. "I mean no harm. Just want to talk."

"If you want that, why don't you put the gun away?"

"Not just yet. I've got a lot of livin' I want to do, Captain. I ain't ready for a dirt nap."

"Then what do you want?" snapped McAllen. "I'm in a hurry."

"Heard you were in town. Figured you were here looking for your boy. I know about him. Seen him."

"Is he well?"

"Don't rightly know if he's dead or alive. Don't even know where he is, exactly. But I can tell you this. He's somewhere in Mexico. And if he's still above snakes, he's in a mess of trouble."

McAllen remained fiercely stoic. "You'd better tell me everything you know."

When McAllen failed to appear at the appointed time and place, Artemus Tice and the other Black Jacks began to worry. Since indecision was not a Black

Jack trait, they promptly split up again into three groups of two men each and set out to search different parts of Brownsville. This time they took their horses with them.

Tice was accompanied by the laconic Cedric Cole. He knew that if shots were fired the others would hurry to the sound of the guns. Brownsville was a place where a man could get into a lot of trouble in very little time. Apart from the heavily armed idlers, patrols sanctioned by the town government roamed the streets. Tice had heard they were a trigger-happy bunch. Their orders were to keep a lookout for a possible insurrection by the Mexican population. There weren't any Mexicans on the street, Tice noticed. They were prisoners in their own homes.

Approaching Grindle's saloon, Tice decided to check inside. Most of Brownsville's businesses had been closed down for the duration of the crisis, and those that weren't usually locked their doors early, so there were not a lot of public places to check. He left Cole outside to watch the horses. That included McAllen's gray hunter, which Tice had taken responsibility for in its master's absence.

"I must be living right," said Tice as he walked up to the table in a corner where McAllen sat alone with bottle and shot glass. "I've never found you this easy before, John Henry. Did you find out anything about Gideon?"

McAllen looked up at him and Tice felt a cold shudder run down his spine when he saw his friend's expression.

"Is the boy dead?" asked Tice flatly.

"Could be," rasped McAllen.

Tice pulled out a chair and sat down. With trembling

hands he peeled the wire frame spectacles off his ears and rubbed dust off the lenses onto the sleeve of his black shell jacket.

"Tell me what happened, John Henry."

"He and Quincy Yates fell in with some Texas Rangers. For some reason they rode into Mexico with the Rangers, looking for the cannon Caldero had been using to shell the town. They rode into an ambush three days ago."

McAllen faltered, picked up the bottle, poured himself another tall shot of cheap whiskey, and knocked it back in one gulp.

"Who told you this?" asked Tice.

"One of the Rangers. He said he was sorry it happened."

"Did he see Gideon die?"

"No. Last he saw of of him, my son was alive."

"I don't have much good to say about Rangers, but it isn't like them to leave one of their own behind."

"Gideon wasn't one of them. He shouldn't have been there in the first place."

"Where did the ambush take place?"

"About twenty miles due south."

"Well, what are we waiting for? We cross the Rio Grande under cover of night, we might get lucky and slip past any scouts Caldero's posted. You know he must be watching the comings and goings."

McAllen reached out and clutched Tice's arm.

"Artemus, I'm going alone this time and I want no argument from any of you."

"No way any of us will let you go into Mexico by yourself, John Henry. You know that."

"Apart from you and Will, the others have family. Folks that depend on them. And Emily will need you more than ever if anything happens to me. You know there isn't much chance of coming back from Mexico."

Tice adamantly shook his head. "I'm going, and there is absolutely nothing you can do short of killing me that will prevent that. As for the others, I won't speak for them. Let them decide for themselves. Tell them you want them to go home. But don't make it an order, John Henry. It would break their hearts to have to disobey an order from you."

McAllen studied Tice's words, staring morosely into his empty glass. He knew that Tice didn't insist on going for his sake only, but also for Emily's. The old physician would do everything in his power to make certain McAllen returned safe and sound to his wife. And right now McAllen didn't much care about living. Odds were that Gideon was dead. But he wouldn't rest until he knew for certain his son's fate, and had the body in his possession. As for Tice, he couldn't return to Grand Cane and look his surrogate daughter in the eye and tell her he'd let her husband go into Mexico by himself. McAllen understood this.

"When do we go?" asked Tice.

"The moon will set in about an hour, by my reckoning. Best time to cross the river."

"I'll go round up the others."

McAllen followed him outside. He'd bought the bottle, and took it along with him, and tossed it to Cedric Cole, who caught it by the neck, smiled gratefully, and indulged in a long swig.

"What's the occasion?" asked Cole, gasping at the whiskey's fire.

"I'm going across the border into Mexico to find Gideon," replied McAllen. "I think you should go home to your wife, Cedric."

"You know," drawled Cole, after a moment's thoughtful silence, "I've never been to Mexico before. Always wanted to see what it was like."

While McAllen and Tice went in search of Buford Doss and Will Parton, Cole went in the opposite direction to locate Lon Mayhew and Morris Riddle. Before long all the Black Jacks were reunited in Brownsville's town square. It was there that McAllen told them everything he knew, and what his intentions were. As Tice had predicted, they all opted to go with their captain.

As they were about to mount up, a half dozen riders galloped into the square. McAllen recognized one of them as Mase Williams. He assumed the others were Rangers, as well.

"I'm Tobias," said one of the riders. "Captain, Texas Rangers. I'm looking for one John Henry McAllen."

McAllen stepped forward. "You've found him."

There wasn't anything remotely friendly about the Ranger captain's cold smile. "Since Mase told you about your kid, I figured you might be wantin' to see me. Well, here I am."

"I don't have the time right now, Tobias."

"Make the time. You got a bone to pick with me, start to pickin'."

McAllen glanced at the other Rangers. Obviously they had come here looking for a fight. All except Mase Williams, who clearly didn't like this confrontation at all.

"I'm going out to find my son," said McAllen flatly. "For your sake, he'd better still be alive."

"I don't cotton to threats," snarled Tobias.

McAllen grabbed one of the Ranger captain's stirrups and pulled up on it, hard and fast—so hard and fast that Tobias couldn't catch himself and came out of the saddle and hit the ground on the other side of his horse. McAllen slapped the mustang's withers and the animal jumped out of the way. Tobias was scrambling to his feet. McAllen was aware of pistols being drawn by every man present, heard the deadly clatter of hammers being cocked. But his attention was focused on Tobias, who was drawing his own six-shooter. McAllen kicked it out of his grasp, knocked Tobias down again. As Tobias started to get up, cursing, he froze when he saw the Colt Paterson in McAllen's hand.

"And I don't like looking up at you," said McAllen. "It's not polite to stay in the saddle when you're talking to a man afoot," said Morris Riddle.

Tobias slowly got up and brushed himself off. He picked up his gun, moving slowly now, and holstered it. Then he scanned the faces of the Black Jacks and smirked. "Look at you. A bunch of has-beens, going off to Mexico to die." He turned to the Rangers. "Put the iron away, boys. We'll let Caldero kill these old codgers for us."

Turning to his horse, Tobias mounted up and rode away without a backward glance. The Rangers followed him.

"Texas Rangers," said Lon Mayhew, and spat. "Good for nothin'."

"Forget them," said McAllen. "Let's get moving."

A few minutes later they were crossing the Rio Grande, and as their horses splashed through the shallows, Will Parton cheerfully quoted scripture.

" 'Yea, though I walk through the valley of the shadow of death I will fear no evil . . .' "

Chapter 9

She told him her name was Maura. Maura O'Quinn Perez. Her father was an Irish mining engineer who had come to Mexico a few years before the war with the United States. His wife had come with him, but she had so disliked Mexico that within a year's time she had returned to her native Ireland. O'Quinn had not been all that sorry to see her go. Quite the contrary, in fact. They simply did not get along. She had not been able to bear him any sons, which was his heart's desire. But he was Catholic, and divorce was out of the question.

Then he had met Maura's mother, who worked in a mining town—doing what, Maura did not say. They fell in love. When Maura was born, O'Quinn was beside himself with joy. He discovered that a daughter filled him with as much joy and wonder as a son ever could. Maura was the apple of her father's eye. From him she learned to speak English. But when she was six years old her mother died. Maura didn't tell Gideon how it had happened. Only that her death had a profound effect on O'Quinn. He became involved in the civil war that was even now raging in Mexico. Currently he fought with Benito Juarez and the Constitutionalists. He used his expertise with explosives to blow up bridges and railroad tracks, making it extremely difficult for Miramon's generals to conduct their military campaigns against the rebels.

To place Maura out of harm's way, O'Quinn had brought her here, to stay with her grandfather. Ramon Perez was a sheepherder. He had always been. Here he had been born, here he would die, doing the only thing he knew how to do, the same thing that his father had done before him. At first Gideon felt sorry for her. Raised in far better surroundings, doted on by her loving father, who as an engineer was well-to-do by Mexican standards, Maura had been thrust into a world of abject poverty. She wore a plain dress, tattered at the hem and mended many times by her own deft hand. There were no shoes for her feet. Her meals consisted of mutton and bread made from the maize for which Ramon traded the wool he garnered from his flock. She had no books to read and no friends her age to talk to. And yet she did not complain. She didn't seem to mind at all. Gideon was soon to learn that Maura O'Quinn Perez was one of those people who knew how to adapt to situations and to make the most out of what life doled out.

Gideon was dismayed to learn that Ramon Perez was loosely affiliated with the Hacienda del Maguey—Antonio Caldero's home. Ramon was allowed to trade at Caldero's *tienda de raya,* exchanging his wool for a few staples, including a portion of the maize from Caldero's fields. He agreed to trade or sell his wool only to Caldero, and no one else. In exchange he was guaranteed protection by the Maguey hidalgo. In this day and time, Maura explained, no peon could survive in the lawless northern provinces unless he lived in or near a village—or enjoyed the protection of a powerful *hacendado*.

It wasn't really necessary for Gideon to explain how he had come to be in Mexico. Maura knew all about the war the Americans were waging on Caldero. That was how she described it—the Americans were the aggressors, while Caldero was merely trying to defend his homeland. But Gideon went ahead and told her about leaving home with his friend, falling in with the Texas Rangers, and following Captain Tobias into disaster. Now, though, all he wanted to do was go home. He didn't want to make war on Antonio Caldero. He had come looking for guns, glory, and gold, to prove himself, and all he'd found were guns—and death. Could Maura see her way clear to helping him get home? She said that she would try. But would her grandfather feel obligated to turn him in to Caldero? Maura spoke earnestly with her *abuelo* on this score, and then gave Gideon assurances that he would be safe in their home.

She could not, however, guarantee his safety in the *malpais*. The border was fifteen miles away—Gideon had veered off his due-north course during the day; ironically, this had taken him in the direction of Maguey, the last place in Mexico he would want to go. Antonio Caldero's *casco*, Maura told him, was but a day's ride to the west.

"If I could just get across the river," said Gideon.

"To go from here to the river will be very dangerous," she replied, and Gideon could detect that faint and incongruous brogue of hers. "Maguey vaqueros are everywhere. You would be safer to stay here until the war is over."

Gideon shook his head. "Who knows how long that will take? And what if Caldero's men were to come here?"

"You do not understand the way of things here. My grandfather is under the hidalgo's protection. The vaqueros would not enter this house to search it without permission from the hidalgo. If they come here it is for water from the well that my grandfather helped his father dig sixty years ago. It is the best water in all of Coahuila. Yes, they may come here, but if they do you only have to stay inside, out of sight, and you will come to no harm. Even if they were to find out you were here they would have to go back to Maguey and ask the hidalgo's permission to come in and get you."

Gideon sighed. He believed Maura, and he was not indisposed to staying here with her until everything blew over, but what about his poor mother? He told Maura that his mother would be worried sick about him, and she would fear the worst if much more time passed without hearing from him. Even if he stayed for a short while he would somehow have to let her know he was alive and well.

"Then you must write her a letter," said Maura. "I will take it across the river, to someone I know, who can be trusted to deliver it into your mother's hands."

"Who would that be?"

"The wife of a peddler. She is Mexican. He used to come across the river all the time, driving a wagon covered with pots and pans—you could hear him coming for miles. Always he passed this way, and several times his wife would ride with him. She will make sure your letter reaches your home."

"But isn't it dangerous for you to try to cross the river?"

"The Maguey vaqueros know me, and will not hurt me."

Gideon thought about Tobias and the Rangers. Not

exactly gentlemen, that crew. With the possible exception of Mase Williams, who seemed decent enough, the Rangers were not the kind of men who would merely tip their hats to a Mexican girl and then ride on, leaving her unmolested. They were notorious in some circles for the treatment they gave Indian women. Now that they were fighting Mexicans, maybe they would think it was okay to rape, torture, or murder a girl like Maura.

"It isn't Caldero's men on this side of the river that I'm worried about," he told her. "I hear a lot of men, some of them riffraff, have come down here for a piece of this fight. All that will matter to them is that you're Mexican."

"Riffraff? What does this mean?"

Gideon smiled. "Bad men. Men who wouldn't think twice about hurting you."

"I am not afraid."

"I can see that," he said, impressed by her courage. "Then you must write your letter, and stay here with us until it is safe for you to go home."

"Yes, all right. If I can get a letter to my mother, I will stay."

"I am glad."

Gideon was, too.

Artemus Tice had been on the trail with John Henry McAllen for thirty years. He had been there with McAllen during the latter's darkest hours—when a Black Jack comrade lost his life in battle, when the future of the Texas independence movement had looked most bleak, when McAllen had been forced by circumstances to let Yancey Torrance go off alone into the Comanche-infested Staked Plains, knowing that

Yancey would probably not survive, and during that long and tortuous ordeal when Emily had been a captive of the Quohadi Comanches. The physician knew McAllen better than anyone else, except Emily; he knew his friend was no emotional weakling. Not by a long shot. He'd seen his tough-minded friend weather many a storm that would have broken lesser men, would have driven them, sobbing, to their knees.

But when they spotted the body ravaged by scavengers out in the middle of the Coahuilan desert, at the place where Caldero's men had ambushed Captain Tobias and his Texas Rangers, McAllen was very nearly shattered.

The vultures led them right to the spot. It had been easy enough to follow the tracks made by Tobias and Gideon and Quincy and the Rangers as they headed south in pursuit of Caldero's two artillery pieces. The body had been horribly mutilated by wolves or coyotes and, of course, the ubiquitous turkey vultures. Several of the birds, so bloated from feeding on the corpse that they could not fly away as the Black Jacks approached, were shot. Then it was time for the worst of it—checking the body to ascertain, if possible, the identity of the dead man.

That was when Tice glanced at McAllen and, seeing the inexpressible anguish on his friend's face, experienced an agony of his own. Were these the remains of Gideon McAllen? That question shook McAllen to the core. Though his features were set in a stoic mask, there was no color in his cheeks. Tice thought his friend looked old and haggard at that moment; the vigor, the life, was sucked out of him. *If this is his son,* thought Tice, *I'm not sure he will be able to survive the blow.*

"Stay right there," said Tice, as McAllen began to dismount. "I'll do it."

McAllen bleakly shook his head. The Black Jacks watched him, compassion on every rugged countenance, as he walked slowly, unsteadily, to the body. He stood above it for a moment, gazing at the horror caused by the scavengers. The clothing had been ripped into indistinguishable shreds. One arm had been nearly detached from the torso. The corpse lay belly down, and the side of the face that McAllen could see was a blackened mass of dried blood and torn flesh, with the skull showing through in places. The eyes, of course, were gone. *This isn't Gideon*, McAllen kept telling himself, over and over again. *This isn't my son. It can't be.* But he knew that was just wishful thinking, not conviction. The size and hair color was about right. McAllen choked down rising bile. How could he be sure, one way or the other? There had to be some way . . .

The boots. He was pretty sure those weren't Gideon's boots. *Pretty* sure. Kneeling, he pulled off one of the boots, then the other. Paper fell out of the second boot, and with trembling hands McAllen picked up the paper, unfolded it, and read the contents.

It seemed to Tice as though McAllen remained motionless for a small eternity. The old physician sat his saddle, gripping the pommel so hard his hands hurt. He prayed as he had never prayed before, at least since Emily's abduction. Finally McAllen stood and walked back to the waiting horsemen. He handed the paper to Tice. There were tears in his eyes, something Tice had never seen before. Were they tears of sorrow, or relief? Steeling himself, Tice read the letter.

It had been written by Quincy Yates, addressed to his father, assuring Memucan that all was well, that he and Gideon would soon arrive in Brownsville and please not to worry, they would be home soon.

"It's the Yates boy," Tice told the other Black Jacks.

"Thank God it wasn't Gideon," said Buford Doss.

Tice folded the letter and stuffed it under his dusty black shell jacket. He didn't care much for Memucan Yates's politics, but he felt sorry for the man.

"I'll see to it that Quincy's father gets this."

"Reckon the boy planned to post it once he got to Brownsville," said Morris Riddle. "Wonder how come he didn't?"

"Didn't get the chance, I expect," surmised Will Parton. "I was told the Rangers rode straight through to silence those cannons of Caldero's." He dismounted. "Come on, boys. Let's give him a decent Christian buryin'."

While Cole and Riddle and Doss dug a grave in the hard ground with their knives and hands, Mayhew and Parton collected rocks, which would be piled up on top of Quincy's final resting place to discourage the coyotes from digging him up. Tice watched McAllen take a flask from his saddlebags and down a dose of the whiskey it contained.

"Gideon's still alive, John Henry," he said. "I'm sure of it. I feel it in these old bones of mine."

McAllen swung wearily into the saddle. "We'd better have a look around."

Thankfully they found no other bodies—Tice didn't think he could endure that ordeal again. They did, however, find a great many tracks. Tice couldn't make much sense of them, but McAllen seemed to be able to. The Ranger named Mase Williams had told him in some detail what had transpired here. McAllen pointed out the sign Tobias and his crew had made retreating to the north, and he paid a great deal of attention to the tracks he said marked the route taken by the Maguey riders after the ambush. These were headed in a northwesterly direction. Tice had a pretty good idea what McAllen was thinking, but he didn't say anything.

Returning to the place where the others were burying Quincy Yates, McAllen waited until the job was done, and Will Parton had read from his Bible. Then they all turned to their captain, waiting for the word. They shared the same thoughts, the same questions. Gideon hadn't been found. That meant they weren't going home. This they accepted without complaint. So it was up to McAllen to tell them where they *were* going.

"Tobias left my son behind to die," said McAllen, "and this is where it happened. If Gideon had been killed we would have found him. So he must have been alive when the fight was over. I'd say odds are good that Caldero's men took him prisoner. They headed in that direction. My guess is they're going home. Home to Caldero's hacienda."

He paused and looked at them with the most solemn of expressions on his beard-stubbled and dust-caked face.

"Caldero probably has a hundred men riding for him. These men are a tough breed. They know how to fight. They learned by waging war against the likes of the Comanches, and you know how dangerous that can be. So you might as well turn back here. Go back to Grand Cane."

"Exactly what are you aimin' to do, Captain?" asked Buford Doss.

"I'm going to Caldero's hacienda to find out if my son is there."

"And if he is?"

"I'll bring him out."

"Alone? Against a hundred guns?"

"You're missing the point, Buford."

"Buford always was sort of thick in the head," jibed Riddle.

"That's real funny, coming from you," was Doss's mock-indignant response.

"What John Henry is trying to say," offered Tice, "is that the odds are too high to go in shooting. He's not going to pick a fight. He's going to try to talk Caldero into giving him his son back."

"Sounds like suicide to me," remarked Cole, laconic as usual.

"And what if Caldero ain't inclined to give Gideon up?" asked Mayhew. "Then what are you gonna do, Captain?"

"I promised my wife that I would bring Gideon home, safe and sound. I won't put him at risk."

"So you won't fight, no matter what," said Parton.

"That would be a losing proposition."

The preacher scowled. "What makes you think Caldero won't just fill you full of lead, Captain? On account of how he helped you find Mrs. McAllen when those heathen Comanche had her? Because of that you plan to give yourself up, and then expect him to let you and your boy go free just for old times' sake?"

"I won't be bringing Gideon out of there if Caldero doesn't want me to," said McAllen. "It's as simple as that. I realize this kind of thing cuts against the grain with you men. That's why I'm telling you to turn back now. There is nothing more you can do for me."

It struck Artemus Tice how oddly reminiscent all this was with the occasion some twenty years ago when Yancey Torrance had set out alone to find Emily, having urged McAllen to take the other Black Jacks home to Grand Cane. *They have families that depend on them. Farms and businesses that will fail without them.* This had been Yancey's argument, and it was true, and John Henry, *knowing* it was true, let Yancey go, even though he'd also known he would never see Torrance again. Only after the fact had McAllen told the others. Why had he waited? Because he'd realized that the men would not have let Yancey "float his own stick," as the backwoodsmen say.

These men loved their families. They were devoted to making their farms and businesses prosper. But they were also prideful men who put great store by honorable conduct. And in their code of honor you simply did not abandon a comrade, no matter what the circumstances. McAllen was acquainted with them well enough that he understood this. So, concluded Tice, he also had to understand that Parton and Cole and the others were not able to leave him to his own devices this time. *And neither am I, for that matter. Of course, I have no family. If John Henry tries to get me to leave him I'll use that argument. I'll also argue that he might need a doctor along. Gideon might have been wounded . . .*

"Well," said Parton, disgusted. "Well." It was all he could say. He glanced at the others, and they looked at him.

Then, as one, they turned to their horses, mounted up—and started riding in a northwesterly direction, the way McAllen had pointed when he'd mentioned Caldero's home, leaving McAllen and Tice standing there.

Cedric Cole was the last in line as they rode single file past McAllen.

"Captain, we're going to Caldero's hacienda. Are you coming with us?"

Mayhew was singing. His was a fine baritone, in Tice's opinion.

> "It rained all night the day I left,
> The weather it was dry,
> The sun so hot I froze to death—
> Susannah, don't you cry.
> Oh Susannah, don't you cry for me
> 'Cause I'm going to Alabama
> With a banjo on my knee."

"What are you waiting for, John Henry?" asked Tice, turning toward his horse. "An engraved invitation?"

McAllen got aboard the gray hunter. Many things about the situation troubled him, but at the moment one question was foremost in his mind.

If Caldero's men had taken Gideon prisoner, why had they done so? In this kind of war, those kind of men usually showed no mercy. A captive was of no value; in fact, he often proved to be a hindrance. So why?

There was one other possibility. That Gideon had escaped the ambush. But if he had, and he was mounted, then he would have been back in Brownsville by the time McAllen arrived there. Unless he was lost. McAllen doubted Gideon could have lost his way. If a man could remember that the sun rose in the east and set in the west, and that the Big Dipper pointed the way to the North Star, he would be fine. In that scenario, the most likely explanation was one McAllen preferred not to contemplate. That Gideon had been wounded, and perished before reaching the Rio Grande, or that he had run afoul of Caldero's men at some other location, and that the turkey vultures were feeding on his corpse elsewhere in this godforsaken desert. *But I found no tracks, no sign of one person leaving the ambush site alone.*

No, Caldero's men must have taken him. As bleak as that eventuality might prove to be, it was preferable to the alternative.

The others had every right to be skeptical about their chances. Truth be known, so was he. Caldero had helped him once before and McAllen still wasn't sure exactly why he had done so; there had been no profit—but a great deal of risk—for Caldero in taking McAllen to the Palo Duro camp of the Quohadi Comanches who held Emily captive. Perhaps it had been because Sam Houston had made it a personal request. Houston was one of the few Americans that Caldero had any respect for. Maybe the only one.

This time McAllen didn't have Sam Houston to intercede on his behalf. What made him think Caldero would help him a second time? I have to give him a reason to help, decided McAllen.

Right off, though, he couldn't imagine how to do that.

Writing the letter to his mother was no easy task for Gideon. The letter's object was very simple—to tell her he was alive and well and would be coming home soon, not to worry. Also—and this was the hardest part—to apologize for causing her worry. At first, though, he tried to explain why he had left home in the manner that he had, to justify his actions, as young people are wont to do. That didn't work. He couldn't make any combination of words accurately reflect his feelings and motivations. Several times he tried; inevitably he would discard the unfinished letter. He even felt guilty about using up so much of Maura's paper and ink. These were luxuries that her grandfather occasionally obtained for her from the *tienda de raya,* so that she might write to her father. This she did religiously, even though O'Quinn had never written back. A regular and reliable mail service did not operate in war-torn Mexico, and Maura assumed that her letters got lost somewhere along the way. Even though by now she had given up hope of ever getting one through to her father, she continued to write the letters. She needed to do so for her own peace of mind.

Maura didn't complain about Gideon's wasteful use of her writing supplies, but after three abortive letters he resolved, for her sake if for no other reason, to make the fourth attempt his last. He wrote:

Dear Mother—

Rest assured that your loving son is well and safe. I am in Mexico, but please do not concern yourself about that, for my circumstances are comfortable and secure from danger. The border is too dangerous for me to attempt a crossing at this time. I will be better off remaining where I am, out of sight, until the present crisis has reached its conclusion. Then I will return to Grand Cane and tell you every detail of what has happened. Until that happy occasion when we are reunited, I hope it is sufficient to say how sorry I am to have caused you grief. Believe me when I tell you that this was not my intention. I have done a very foolish

> and irresponsible thing and I hope you and Father will find it in your hearts to forgive me.

Gideon hesitated, agonized over a difficult decision for some time, then continued to write . . .

> Quincy Yates is dead. If you feel you must relay this sad news to his father, tell him that his son died gallantly. I pray you will not let this cause you any anxiety with regards to my own safety.

He folded the letter, wrote Mrs. John McAllen, Grand Cane, on the outside, and gave it to Maura. Within an hour she was gone, bound for the Rio Grande and the home of the peddler whose wife would take custody of the letter and deliver it to Gideon's mother. She put a hat of straw on her head and a shawl that she would use as a blanket—the trip would take two days and she would have to sleep in the desert—around her shoulders. She carried a gourd filled with water from the well, and a small sack full of hoecakes made from maize. Apart from a knife this was all she would take with her.

At the last minute Gideon begged her not to go. It was just too dangerous. "I could never forgive myself if anything happened to you," he told her. Maura smiled and assured him that nothing would happen. The old man watched her go without expression, but Gideon sensed that this accomplished stoicism masked strong emotion, mixed with a dose of fatalism. Living a life full of hardship and unexpected tragedy, such people as Ramon Perez learned to accept whatever lay in store for them. When Maura was gone, her grandfather glanced at Gideon with dark, inscrutable eyes and then silently walked away, accompanied by his dog, to take the flock out to graze.

Left to his own devices, Gideon remained inside the adobe *jacal* most of the day. Maura had warned him to keep out of sight just in case some of the Maguey riders happened by to partake of the water in the well. But in a matter of hours he was too restless to abide any longer by such wise counsel. He went outside and gazed at the desert that encompassed him. In a way the desert was just as confining and claustrophobic as the adobe. There was no place for him to go. Nothing to do except think, and he didn't want to do that, because his thoughts were mostly of Quincy, dying in his arms, or of his parents, or of Maura, who was risking her life for his sake. So he went back inside the adobe and tried to sleep, but he couldn't. Finally the day grew old, and the sun sank reluctantly below the horizon in all its flaming glory, and he went out again to sit with his back to the jacal's wall, waiting for the old sheepherder to return with his flock. He had the distinct impression that Ramon Perez didn't like him, didn't want him around—but even his company was better than being alone.

Night fell and still the old man did not come home. Gideon decided Ramon had chosen to stay out in the desert rather than return for the simple reason that he disliked his American houseguest. All things considered, Gideon couldn't really blame him.

He awoke with the hot morning sun on his face, lying on his side with his back to the adobe wall. Sleep had crept up on him, claimed him with the unexpected finality of sudden death. Going to the well, he brought up a bucket of water and washed his face. When he happened to look down and see the scorpion scrambling over the toe of his boot he crushed it against the base of the well, shuddered violently, and walked glumly back to the jacal.

About midday the old man finally returned. Gideon was forewarned by the arrival of the dog, who appeared unexpectedly in the adobe's doorway, growled at Gideon, and then, like a sulky child, turned away. A few minutes later Ramon arrived with his flock. The dog helped him funnel the sheep into their pen. Gideon stood in the doorway and watched. He had never been so happy to see anyone in his whole life. The same could not be said of Ramon. The sheepherder was as impassive as before, and that undercurrent of resentment was still there.

The old man had a sack of coffee with him, and another containing twists of tobacco. He set about boiling the coffee in a pan at the fireplace. While he waited for the grounds to settle he bit off a chew of tobacco with the few yellowed teeth remaining to him. When the coffee was ready he poured some in a cup and went outside. The rich aroma of the coffee tempted Gideon, but he was too proud to help himself. Ramon hadn't offered him any—an intentional oversight.

Ramon spent the next several hours out near the pen, sipping his thick-as-mud coffee and chewing his tobacco, but he wasn't paying much attention to his sheep. Instead, he expectantly scanned the horizon, occasionally spitting a stream of brown tobacco juice. Gideon assumed he was watching for his granddaughter. If all had gone according to plan, Maura would be back today. If she did not return, Gideon had made up his mind to strike out for the Rio Grande in the morning; he would try to find her and, failing that, would at least be back in Texas. Assuming, that is, he could elude Caldero's men. Regardless of the risks, he simply could not linger here any longer in this wretchedly lonely hut with that hateful old man who would scarcely acknowledge that he even existed. He realized he was being completely unreasonable. After all, he had come here uninvited, had imposed on Ramon Perez and his granddaughter; certainly he had no right to expect hospitality, or to feel resentful because he wasn't made welcome by the old sheepherder.

And then Maura appeared, and Gideon ceased to brood. The dog ran to her, tail wagging so hard that Gideon thought the hound's spine would snap. Maura paused to pet the dog, then came on to the adobe, running up to her grandfather and giving him a big hug and kiss, and for the first time Gideon saw a glimmer of emotion on the face of Ramon Perez as he embraced her. Spotting Gideon in the adobe's doorway, she walked over to him, beaming, and Gideon realized he was grinning like a fool.

"All is well," she said. "I gave your letter to my friend, and she promised to take it to your mother. You can depend on her."

"I don't know how to thank you," said Gideon, overjoyed.

"You don't need to."

"Thank heavens you're safe, Maura. Did you have any trouble?"

Maura shook her head. Much to Gideon's amazement, she looked none the worse for two days of hard traveling on foot in the desert.

"I saw a few of the Maguey men, but they did not see me."

"Maura, you're absolutely wonderful."

She went inside the adobe and stood there for a moment, looking around with a frown on her face. "I smell coffee," she said.

"Your grandfather made some when he got back."

"Got back? Where did he go?"

"He took the flock out yesterday and only returned a few hours ago. What's the matter?"

Her smile had disappeared. Brows knit, she rushed outside, called to her grandfather and ran to him. Gideon watched from a respectful distance as they conversed. All he could discern from the exchange was that Maura was very upset. Perplexed, all Gideon could do was wait—he had no idea what it was that bothered Maura so.

A moment later she had rejoined him, and by her expression he could tell she was clearly afraid of something.

"My grandfather has gone to Maguey," she said.

"Maguey?" For an instant Gideon failed to comprehend. "You mean . . . you mean Caldero's place?"

Maura nodded, looking at him strangely—the way one would look at a condemned man. Or so Gideon imagined.

"I knew he had gone there," she explained, "because the coffee and the tobacco had to have come from the *tienda de raya*. We had none when I left. It is the only place he could have gotten these things. When I asked him about it, he confessed."

"But . . . but how is that possible? You said Maguey was a day's ride from here."

"He left the flock and walked all day and through the night. Don't let his years fool you. He is very strong."

Gideon looked past Maura at the old man, who was

still sitting on his heels near the pen, still watching the horizon, and Gideon knew now he hadn't been looking for Maura before—no, he'd been on the lookout for the Maguey vaqueros all along, the ones who would come and with his permission enter the adobe and remove his unwanted visitor. Realizing he had been betrayed, Gideon felt anger, resentment, fear, and resignation in quick succession. But most of all he felt sick to his stomach.

"You told me he wouldn't go to Caldero," he said. "You told me he'd given his word."

"He did."

Maura also felt betrayed, Gideon realized, and he felt sorry for her, because the bond of trust that existed between her and her grandfather was now broken, and such bonds were not easily repaired.

"Maybe he did it to protect you, Maura," he said. "Maybe he thought it was inevitable that I would be caught, and so he must have been afraid of what would happen to you if they found out you'd been helping me."

"It doesn't matter now. You must try to reach the border. I will go with you."

"Absolutely not! That would be too dangerous."

"I am going with you," she said, adamant. "There is no time to argue."

"No, Maura. Stay here. You've done more than enough for me already."

"Go inside and get your gun. I will tell my grandfather."

"You're not coming with me, and that's my final word."

Maura put her hand on his chest and turned her head, listening to something that he could not hear.

Then she threw herself down at his feet and pressed her ear to the ground. Startled and confused by this exceedingly odd behavior, Gideon could only stare. Bouncing to her feet, Maura looked west and said in a dull voice, "It's too late now."

They came over a low rise, silhouetted against the late sun, and Gideon experienced an unnerving sense of déjà vu, remembering the ambush in which Quincy had lost his life—the vaqueros had appeared just like this, their guns blazing. Today, though, they weren't shooting. And there weren't as many of them. Only four. But four was more than enough. Gideon considered getting his gun and making a fight of it. Better that than to be shot down like a dog. But then he would be putting Maura and her grandfather in the line of fire, and he could not do that, even to save himself. He wanted to run, but of course there was no place for him to go, and at the very least he could stand his ground and accept death with dignity; he didn't want to take the coward's way out, especially in front of Maura. She was so brave—could he be anything less?

As the Maguey men rode up to the adobe on their wiry desert mustangs, Gideon wondered if one of these vaqueros had killed Quincy. And he wondered, too, which one would be his own executioner.

But only one of the riders drew his pistol. This one swung a leg over the saddle horn and slid lithely to the ground and walked up to Gideon, raising the gun almost casually, and Gideon was astonished at the complete and sudden calm that came over him as he looked down the barrel of the gun, knowing he was about to die. Then two things happened at once. Maura jumped between him and the vaquero, and one of the other Maguey riders barked at Gideon's would-be killer, and even as Gideon pushed Maura aside, the vaquero lowered his weapon and just stared at Gideon without expression. The one who had spoken addressed Maura. When he was done she nodded and turned to Gideon.

"He says you are very brave. If you had tried to run they would have shot you down. They have no respect for cowards. But they admire courage. They will not kill you. They are going to take you to Maguey and let the hidalgo decide your fate."

So at least I have a little longer to live, thought Gideon. *However long it takes to reach Maguey.*

He had no doubt that Antonio Caldero would order his execution.

The vaquero who had almost shot him holstered his pistol, took strips of rawhide from his *mochila,* and tied Gideon's hands behind his back. While this was going on, Maura spoke to the leader. Gideon scarcely heard her. He was thinking about his mother and father, and was grateful that at least he'd been able to write that letter and apologize for the pain he had caused them. He supposed Maura was pleading his case—a waste of time. But he was wrong about that.

"He says I can come with you to Maguey," she told Gideon.

"Don't do it, Maura. I don't want you to. Stay here. Forget all about me."

"No," she said gravely. "I could never do that."

Chapter 10

Knowing that Judith was ensconsced in a hotel room almost within shouting distance of his own office was driving Samuel Burkin to distraction.

Occasionally she would emerge from the hotel for a stroll, accompanied sometimes by her husband, and always by a cadre of four to six men, all armed to the teeth, ruffians by the looks of them. Burkin found out they were Knights of the Golden Circle, hand-picked by Stoneman from the members of that secret quasi-military organization who had flocked to Brownsville when the call went out. Belonging to the Order of the Columbian Star—the elite group of KGC political leaders—Charles Stoneman had the authority to enlist as many Knights as he wanted to serve as his wife's bodyguards.

Burkin couldn't be sure how many of the men who had come to Brownsville armed and ready for war with Mexico actually belonged to the KGC. He could estimate that at least two hundred rifle-toting strangers had filtered into town in the past two weeks. Brownsville was a powder keg just waiting for a spark of fire. Some of the Mexican inhabitants had abandoned their homes and slipped across the river. The rest huddled in their adobes, afraid to step outside.

Several had already been gunned down by street patrols. Finally Burkin had given express orders to the Brownsville Tigers, who made up the majority of the men in the patrols, to cease and desist using innocent Mexicans for target practice. That had prompted a visit by Stoneman, who angrily accused Burkin of taking the wrong side.

"I'm just protecting the voters," Burkin had replied, sarcastically. "Remember, Charles, elections are just around the corner."

Stoneman didn't like his tone of voice, and what was even more infuriating from his perspective was the knowledge that Burkin obviously didn't give a damn whether he liked it or not.

"I see you've let fame go to your head, Samuel," said Stoneman icily. "What a shame. You could have had a great future. But you shouldn't try to buck me."

"I'll get by. I'm not worried about my future. What worries me now is that if something isn't done, if somebody doesn't start acting rationally around here, we'll have a bloodbath on our hands. Nerves are frayed and tempers are short, Charles. I don't want to see any more innocent people being slaughtered for nothing."

"For nothing? How noble of you. And how foolish. You seem to forget, we're waging a war here. We're creating the justification for the invasion of Mexico. We're trying to save the Union."

"It's not the Union you're worried about. But let's not debate politics. All I know is that things aren't exactly working out the way you'd planned, are they?"

Stoneman couldn't deny the truth of that. He was stalemated. Governor Runnels had sent only a handful of Texas Rangers who, after one foray into Mexico, were sitting it out in Brownsville drinking up Josiah Grindle's stock of liquor. Instead of the thousands of KCG members Stoneman had expected from the "castles" in Texas—not to mention those in other southern states—perhaps a hundred had showed up. Worst of all, the United States Army had dispatched only the one company of cavalry now garrisoned in Fort Brown, and its commander had orders to take any step he deemed appropriate to keep peace on the border. Captain Donaldson's vigilant details were not only trying to keep Caldero's men on their side of the river but also diligently prevented any of the trouble-seekers now infesting Brownsville from engaging in forays into Mexico.

Worst of all, from Stoneman's point of view, Antonio Caldero had been uncooperative. True, Caldero had shelled Brownsville with the two cannon captured earlier by his vaqueros, causing a modest amount of damage—his men were not trained artillerists. But the experience had caused a great deal of consternation bordering on panic. The only person who'd been happy about the bombardment, Burkin mused, was Charles Stoneman. Charles didn't care who suffered as long as his scheme was advanced.

Yet, since the artillery attack, Caldero had been quiet—distressingly so where Stoneman was concerned. Rumor had it that he had ridden into Matamoros to be hailed the conquering hero by crowds of adoring Mexicans. According to Stoneman's spies, however, he hadn't lingered long, disappearing into the trackless desert. Since then—nothing but an occasional sighting of bands of Maguey riders, sometimes on this side of the river in spite of the best efforts of Captain Donaldson and his patrols. No one knew what to expect from Caldero. Where would he strike next? Would he strike again? Or was he content to play cat and mouse with the Americans?

In spite of everything, Stoneman still had a few cards left to play. He had options and he could stir up plenty of trouble. The fact that some innocent Mexicans, legitimate and peace-loving inhabitants of Brownsville, were being killed worked to his advantage. If he could use this to goad Caldero into action, his purposes would be admirably served. If he could create a situation in which Brownsville's Mexican population rose up in self-defense, Stoneman could claim that Caldero's agents had instigated the insurrection. And if American lives were lost and American property destroyed, the Texas governor—and the United States Army—would have no choice but to take steps against Mexico.

That was why Stoneman was angry with Burkin for ordering the Brownsville Tigers to think twice before shooting a Mexican—and why Stephen Powers came to visit Burkin later that same day.

Burkin was downstairs in his office, thumbing idly through *Kent's Commentaries*. It wasn't that he had any cases to work on; such mundane things as legal suits and land claim disputes had gone by the board ever since Antonio Caldero had killed Sheriff Carnacky. The doctor had given him an official reprieve from the bed-rest order, but he had recommended that his patient stay close to home. No buggy rides, no excursions on horseback, no strenuous activity of any kind. That suited Burkin—now that Judith was here in Brownsville he had no desire to venture beyond the limits of town. He took two short walks a day, one in the morning and the other in the evening, and these forays inevitably took him in the vicinity of the hotel where the woman who possessed his soul and clouded his mind currently resided. Otherwise he seldom left his place except to get his meals and indulge in an occasional bath. Hence, though he came calling unannounced, Powers had a reasonable expectation of finding Burkin at home.

"I'm pleased that you have finally come to your senses, Samuel," said the rumpled, emaciated leader of the Blues. "You've managed to slip Stoneman's harness at last. Bravo! I'd always suspected you were too sensible to remain long in that scoundrel's orbit."

"I don't know what you are talking about, sir."

"Don't be coy, Samuel. It doesn't suit you. You know very well what I mean. I'm talking about the scales falling from your eyes. You can see what Stoneman is trying to accomplish and you realize he is in the wrong."

"I don't want innocent people getting hurt, that's all."

"Stoneman and his fellow Knights wish to destroy the Union, and you mean to tell me that this is no concern of yours?"

"So you know about the Golden Circle."

"Of course I do. The Good Book enjoins me to know mine enemy."

"Is it the Union's salvation you seek, Mr. Powers? Or the political high hand?"

"Both. With the political high hand I can do my part to keep the country together. At the same time peace is maintained, Mexico's sovereignty is secured, and innocent civilians stay alive. You must admit that everyone would be much better off if I have my way, and Charles Stoneman is prevented from having his."

"I'm not a Unionist. Nor am I a secessionist. None of that is of the least interest to me."

Powers shrugged. He'd folded his wasted frame into one of Burkin's secondhand chairs, making himself right at home, and Burkin wanted to order him out, but didn't. He had already alienated one of the two most powerful men in town, and he couldn't bring himself to cold-shoulder the second. But he wanted to be left alone in his misery.

"That's a shame," said Powers. "For too many of my countrymen seem to have adopted that very attitude. They don't want to believe that bloody civil war is imminent. They think that if they simply close their eyes the menace will go away. But it will not go away, sir. It most assuredly will not. And men such as yourself will know how precious the Union is only when it may be too late to save her."

Burkin fumed. He was really in no mood for preaching, and he nearly blurted out that the only reason he was breaking with Stoneman was because he coveted the man's wife. He wanted Stoneman to fail out of pure spite more than anything else, because Charles possessed what he wanted but could never have. He came to his senses in time; that was the kind of news Powers would dearly love to print on broadsides and distribute all over Brownsville if for no other reason than to humiliate his political arch rival. And Burkin had no desire to be the pawn in a high stakes game of dirty politics.

"I will let you worry about the Union, sir," he said briskly. "I have more pressing concerns."

Powers stood up to go. "I shall not give up hope," he replied cheerfully. "Good-bye for now, Samuel."

Late that afternoon, when the heat of the day was

beginning to subside, Burkin donned hat and coat and took up his walking stick and left the office for his evening stroll. Naturally he bent his steps toward the hotel, since there was always that slim chance that he might catch a glimpse of Judith. Luck was with him today, for as he approached the hostelry from across the square he spotted her, with her usual squad of bodyguards, one in front and three following closely behind. Stoneman wasn't with her this time. *He is probably at Grindle's*, thought Burkin, with a measure of self-pity, *telling McColley and Kennedy and the other Red leaders about my treason, and plotting how to ruin my life.*

Changing course and lengthening his stride, Burkin hoped to reach the boardwalk in front of the hotel before Judith and her gun-toting entourage neared the entrance. If he could only get a look from her, or even better one of those secret smiles. Some sign that she at least remembered that he was on this planet. The bodyguards saw him coming; the urgency of his stride alerted them. The one in front turned to speak briefly to the others, and Judith glanced in Burkin's direction—and looked quickly away as one of the men broke from the rest and planted himself firmly in Burkin's path. Burkin tried to go around, but the man blocked him.

"Where do you think you're going, friend?" asked the man.

"I mean to pay my compliments to Mrs. Stoneman. My name is Samuel Burkin. I'm a . . . friend."

"I'll pass your compliments along."

Peering over the man's shoulder, Burkin could see that Judith was nearly to the hotel entrance.

"Judith!" he called out. "Judith, it's Samuel! Please, wait!"

The desperation in his voice put the men charged with protecting Stoneman's wife on edge. One took her arm and hurried her toward the hotel entrance. She pulled free, but didn't acknowledge Burkin's presence, and continued on. Burkin again tried to outflank the man blocking his path. This time the man reacted more violently, slamming his fist into Burkin's midsection. Wheezing, Burkin dropped to his knees.

"It'll hurt worse next time," warned the man. "So don't let me see you hangin' around the little lady anymore, you hear?"

He walked away, rejoining his friends, who stood on the boardwalk with their hands resting meaningfully on the butts of their belted pistols. They gave him one last, grim look and then entered the hotel, following in Judith's wake.

Mustering what remained of his dignity, Burkin got up out of the dirt and glanced around, wondering how many people had witnessed their new hero's humiliation. That was when he spotted a familiar man loitering at the corner of a building diagonally across the square from the hotel. By his plain clothes and serape he was obviously a Mexican. The fact that he was out in the open meant he was a reckless fool or a man on an important mission—important enough to risk putting himself in the gunsights of the street patrols. Burkin knew the latter must be the case, for this was the same man he had seen a fortnight ago from the window of his room. This was the same man who had followed Charles Stoneman that night, like a wolf stalking big prey as Stoneman left Burkin's office.

Burkin thought the man was watching him, but he

stood in twilight's deepening shadows, so Burkin couldn't be certain. More curious than ever, Burkin considered confronting the man, asking after his motives. But he decided against it. He didn't want to scare the man off, or deter him in any way from his mission.

Especially if that mission was to harm Charles Stoneman, as Burkin imagined that it was.

So Samuel Burkin decided to mind his own business. He dusted himself off and walked away, thinking he still had a chance to have it all his own way. Sometimes it was better to just step back and let Fate play a hand.

Antonio Caldero had told the Maguey vaqueros that he would ride to Brownsville and capture the town. The idea of seizing United States territory—or rather what the United States *claimed* as its territory, since in Caldero's mind the Nueces Strip still rightfully belonged to the Republic of Mexico—had appealed to him. The capture of Brownsville would make a statement the whole world would hear. He knew he would not be able to hold onto the town for very long. But that wasn't the point. At least he would show the Americans that the Mexican people would not simply surrender their rights and property without a struggle.

It soon became apparent, however, that an attempt to make such a statement would be entirely too costly in terms of lives. The alacrity with which American volunteers had swarmed to Brownsville caught Caldero by surprise. These were followed in short order by a detachment of United States cavalry, now based in Fort Brown. Caldero thought he could still take Brownsville—a feint to draw off the American dragoons and then a quick strike at the town itself—but how many of his men would die in the attempt? Brownsville was of no strategic importance, really. So, for once, Caldero failed to do what he had said he would do.

Still, he had to act. He had to do *something*. Many men had come to join his cause. Some were poor farmers, others were bandits, and sixty convicts, inspired by a patriotic fervor, had broken out of a Tamaulipas prison to offer their services. He'd sent the convicts back to jail under armed guard, and sent the bandits packing, too, even though most of them swore they weren't after plunder, but merely wanting to strike a blow for their country. As for the campesinos, he kept only those he could arm and who were young enough to endure the rigors of a campaign, and who could convince him that they had no families that relied upon them. Thus the majority were eliminated. Even so, he had more than a hundred and fifty volunteers to fight alongside his vaqueros. From the mail that he continued to intercept, Caldero knew that the Americans were grossly overestimating his force. Their most conservative estimates placed his numbers at five hundred, and the most outlandish speculations gave him an army of five thousand!

Even a paltry one hundred and fifty volunteers presented Caldero with a host of dilemmas. He had stolen many horses from the gringo ranches in the valley of the Rio Grande, and so he was able to provide most of the new men with reliable mounts. As a rule, however, these farmers were not very capable horsemen. Feeding them also presented him with something of a problem. And he did not have enough guns to arm them all. The biggest problem, however, was finding something for them to do. They had come to fight, and if he wasn't going to capture Brownsville then he would have to think of something else.

He warned his lieutenants that they would have to take care. These were men like Manchaca, who next to Refugio was the one Caldero trusted most of all. Refugio was his right hand, and as such had been given the most important missions that required an independent command. It was to Refugio, then, that Caldero had assigned the task of defending the captured cannon used to bombard Brownsville. And it was to Refugio whom credit was to be given for defeating the Texas Rangers who had tried to take the cannon. But now Refugio lay wounded at Maguey, under the care of Caldero's oldest daughter, Teresa. Caldero had known for quite some time that Teresa had feelings for the dashing *segundo*, feelings she could but poorly conceal. She was afraid to let her father know, because she wasn't sure what his reaction would be. She didn't realize that Caldero would not object at all. A man could not ask for a better son-in-law than Refugio. Refugio could be relied upon to make sure Maguey prospered for Teresa and her little sister long after Caldero was gone. Assuming Maguey still existed . . .

"We must take care," Caldero would tell Manchaca and the others, "not to go too far, and attract too much attention from the United States government. They have sent one company of cavalry to patrol the border and defend Brownsville. If they send an army, an invasion of Coahuila will surely follow. We must do just enough to discourage such an invasion, to persuade the Americans that it would be too expensive in lives for them to try it. But if we go too far, they will decide that the only way to protect the border is to seize the whole province of Coahuila, and if that happens all is lost. Maguey is lost."

Stalemate. It was Caldero's only hope, and he had the foresight to know this was the case. He could not win this war. But by making the right moves he might be able to avoid losing it.

That was why, as he stood at the rim of a high bluff overlooking the Rio Grande and watched the riverboat through a spyglass, Caldero tried to predict the American reaction if he succeeded in his plan to seize and sink the vessel.

The steamboat was called the *Ranchero,* and was jointly owned by Mifflin Kennedy and Richard King, two ranchers whose empires lay upriver from Brownsville. Since the border had been relatively quiet for more than week now, the two men had decided to gamble on sending the *Ranchero* down the river with a cargo that, according to Caldero's spies, included sixty thousand dollars in specie. The *Ranchero* carried about two dozen heavily armed men and a small six-pounder cannon mounted on an iron swivel in the bow. The men were protected by ramparts of barrels and hay bales and sacks filled with river sand, all strapped together using stout rope and ringing both the upper and lower decks.

Caldero had decided to turn river pirate and attack the boat for two reasons. The first was that the men who followed him were aching for action, and here was a fight Caldero knew he could win with relative ease, and in which the inexperience of his volunteers where shooting and riding were concerned would not be a factor. Second, the thought of taking sixty thousand in gold and silver from a pair of American land barons and distributing it among the poor of Coahuila appealed to his sense of justice.

The place he had chosen for battle was La Bolsa Bend, about thirty-five miles upriver from Brownsville, where the Rio Grande described a large, horseshoe-shaped bend with the open part of the horseshoe to the south, on the Mexican side. A small village was located here; Caldero had evacuated the civilians and concealed many of his volunteers in the adobe jacals. His one regret was that he did not have his cannon with him; if he could put a few holes in the *Ranchero*'s hull just below the waterline he would sink the riverboat in the shallows. Here the river narrowed, and he could board her with ease once she was immobilized. As it stood now, he was forced to improvise in terms of finding a way to stop and disable the vessel.

From his vantage point Caldero watched the *Ranchero* swing lazily into the first curve. Here the narrowing channel brought the riverboat within thirty yards of the bank, and as near the village of La Bolsa as it would ever come. He turned to Manchaca and nodded. Manchaca swung aboard his mustang without fitting foot to stirrup, drew his pistol, and fired three times skyward in quick succession from the back of a pivoting horse. Then he straightened the mustang out and galloped it down the backside of the bluff at breakneck speed, leaving Caldero with two vaqueros at the crest.

Raising the spyglass to his eye, Caldero scanned the edge of town, and spotted the volunteers responding to Manchaca's signal. Popping into view from behind adobe walls, or emerging from the doorways of the jacals, the campesinos hurled their fire bombs at the passing riverboat. These bombs were made from tallow or turpentine poured into clay ollas which were then plugged with rags. The rags, doused with more of the flammable liquids, were lighted and then thrown bare-handed, or with the aid of rawhide slings, depending on the preference of the thrower.

Alerted by Manchaca's signal, the men on board the *Ranchero* began shooting at the campesinos. At the same time, the Maguey vaqueros, stationed on both flanks of the campesinos, began firing at the riverboat. They caused few casualties, but many of the Americans were forced to duck down behind their makeshift ramparts. Some of the fire bombs fell short, splashing harmlessly into the river, while others shattered onboard; a dozen small fires broke out almost at once. Even from as far away as the top of the bluff, Caldero could hear the shouts of alarm from the men on the *Ranchero*. The riverboat was tinderbox and they knew it. He could see them scrambling with blankets and shirts and buckets of water trying to extinguish the fires. But as soon as one was put out another would start. Some of the campesinos were running along the bank now, still throwing the bombs. Caldero grimaced as he watched several of them fall—a number of the *Ranchero*'s men were still managing to get off a few well-aimed shots. Some of the Americans were also falling. In the process of fighting the fires they were forced to expose themselves to Caldero's vaqueros, every one of whom was something of a marksman.

Try as they might, the Americans could not put out all the fires, and in a matter of a few minutes major conflagrations were blazing at bow and stern. The *Ranchero*'s pilot whipped his wheel around and steered his vessel toward the Texas shore. Caldero smiled tautly as he saw the riverboat swing sharply around. The pilot was going to run the boat aground in the shallows; that way the gold and silver would not end up at the bottom of the channel, and the men could get ashore, find cover, and perhaps keep their foes at bay until help arrived.

Watching closely through the spyglass, Caldero saw the *Ranchero* shiver and then tilt bow up. She was hard aground. The current swung her stern around but she held fast. The Americans began to scramble ashore. Now was the time to strike, before those men settled into defensive positions on the far bank. Would Manchaca's instincts for the ebb and flow of battle lead him to the same conclusion? With Refugio, Caldero would have had not a moment's doubt.

But Manchaca proved himself a worthy substitute for Refugio. The vaqueros leaped to their horses, which had been hidden behind the jacals of La Bolsa, and in a few short minutes were swarming across the river. The channel here was only four or five feet deep and, being narrow, could be quickly crossed by man and horse. Caldero's hope was that the Americans would be routed, leaving the riverboat undefended. Within an hour the *Ranchero* would burn to the waterline. Then, gather up the specie and vanish into the *malpais* before a rescue party from Brownsville could arrive on the scene—this was Caldero's plan.

Gunfire was a constant crackling cacophony of noise. Powder smoke drifted so thickly across the scene that Caldero could no longer view clearly what was transpiring below from the top of the bluff. By the sound of it the Americans were putting up stiff resistance. None of them wanted to have to explain to Kennedy and King how they had lost sixty thousand dollars but managed to save their own lives. Impatient, Caldero decided it was time to get a closer look. He snapped the spyglass shut and turned toward his horse. It was then that one of the vaqueros who stood nearby stepped forward, pointing downriver.

"Hidalgo! Look!"

Caldero saw what the vaquero was looking at, but at first he refused to believe his own eyes. A cloud of dust, downriver, on the Texas side—it could mean only one thing. Riders, and a lot of them, coming from the direction of Brownsville. Who were they? Texas Rangers? The Brownsville militia? Or United States troops? And how was it that they had appeared at such a crucial moment? Caldero's hopes dwindled. His heart sank when the riders came into view a moment later, for their uniforms identified them as United States dragoons. Where had they come from? Were these the soldiers who had recently been garrisoned at Fort Brown? Or had more soldiers come to the valley of the Rio Grande? For once his spy network on the other side of the river had failed him.

Scanning the battle scene below, Caldero realized that Manchaca and the other Maguey riders were all across the river now, locked in mortal combat with the men who had disembarked from the blazing *Ranchero*. There was no way to signal them to retreat.

Wheeling, Caldero vaulted into his saddle, raked the horse's flanks with his spurs, and galloped down the back of the bluff, followed by the two vaqueros.

Before he could reach La Bolsa and the river, the dragoons had closed with the unsuspecting Maguey vaqueros. The intensity of gunfire soared. As he guided his horse full tilt into the Rio Grande, Caldero heard one of the vaqueros who followed in his wake shout at him to stop. He paid the man no heed. The vaquero could tell that the battle was already lost, and that his hidalgo was almost certainly riding to his death. Caldero knew it, too, but he didn't care. If his men were going to die he would die with them, fighting at their side to the last cartridge, the last breath.

The sudden and unexpected appearance of the blue-coated dragoons threw the Maguey riders into momentary confusion, but Caldero's arrival heartened them, and they rallied. Firing at the nearest dragoons, Caldero roared at his men to withdraw across the river. Conditioned to obey his word without hesitation, they began to retreat. Caldero lingered behind, emptying one pistol and then another at the enemy, and clearing a few McClellan saddles in the process. Several dragoons concentrated their fire on him. He contemptuously wheeled his horse back into the channel while the vaqueros, now gathered on the Mexican side of the river, laid down a withering covering fire. Those who witnessed the remarkable scene and lived to tell of it would, in the days to come, attribute the fact that Antonio Caldero came through without a scratch to divine intervention.

With their beloved hidalgo safely across the river, the Maguey riders traded fire with the dragoons and the men from the *Ranchero,* keeping them at bay long enough for the campesinos to evacuate La Bolsa. This the vaqueros did even though they were outnumbered and outgunned and it cost the lives of a dozen more of their number. Finally, when La Bolsa was cleared, they retired.

The dragoons crossed over into the village, but they did not pursue Caldero into the chaparral. Instead, they searched the adobes for enemy wounded or stragglers. Finding none, they crossed back over to the American side of the river before night fell. By that time there was nothing left of the *Ranchero* but charred, smoking rubble. The dragoons camped there that night, and on the next day set about retrieving the gold and silver from the riverboat's wreckage. Lookouts kept an eagle eye out for Caldero in case he returned, but there was no sign of him.

When he was certain that there would be no pursuit, Caldero called a halt and the vaqueros made camp. They lighted a fire for the purpose of guiding the campesinos in, for the volunteers had scattered. Very few of them showed up that night. The vaqueros cast aspersions on their valor, but Caldero sternly silenced them. He didn't blame the campesinos for deserting the cause. They knew as well as he that a great disaster had befallen them all.

Caldero had lost twenty-five of his vaqueros, including Manchaca—nearly a third of his riders. Almost all who remained had been wounded, and some of them seriously. He fought mightily to keep despair at bay, but that was another losing battle. The vaqueros did not blame him, but he blamed himself; he had led these men into a trap, and too many had lost their lives. And for what? He wasn't sure anymore.

Thinking back on the past few weeks, Caldero concluded that in fact he had lost sight of the reason he had gone to war with the Americans. His original purpose had been only to protect Maguey by keeping the Americans occupied elsewhere—by making them realize that the cost would be too great if they dared venture deep into Coahuila. But the old hatred had flared, and he had tried to do more, too much more.

He had tried to make the Americans pay for all the wrongs they had done his people in the past. Tried to exact recompense in blood for all the suffering his people had endured in the past twenty years at the hands of the gringos. Now he knew he had gone too far. He had killed American soldiers. What's worse, American blood had been spilled on American soil—at least they said it was their soil. In 1845 the American president, Polk, had declared war on the Republic of Mexico using as justification the fact that United States troops had been slain by Mexican irregulars north of the Rio Grande border.

I have given them the same excuse today, thought Caldero. *I should have known better. Should have fought a strictly defensive campaign, striking only when the Americans crossed the river to violate Mexican sovereignty.*

Turning the captured cannon on Brownsville had been going too far; so was trying to steal sixty thousand dollars in specie. The temptation had been simply too much to resist. He had wanted to hit the Americans where it hurt them most—in their pockets. But he'd been outsmarted. Obviously Kennedy and King had sent for help in advance; they'd thought it likely that he would be tempted by specie, and they'd summoned the dragoons to meet the *Ranchero* in its passage downriver. The Americans had their excuse for an invasion of Mexico, now. He had given it to them on a silver platter. And if an invasion took place, Maguey would surely be lost. He would not be able to defend his home from an entire army.

Yes, he should have learned his lessons—there was more than one lesson here. Caldero wasn't sure who he hated more at this moment: the Americans or his own government. In all the time he had fought to keep the Nueces Strip, the government in Mexico City had not lifted a finger to help him. Neither would they help him this time. The Conservatives and the Constitutionalists were too busy killing each other to take notice of the threat at their northern border. The blind fools—did they care nothing for Mexico? He should have known . . .

Still, Caldero could not help but ponder cause and effect. If he hadn't gone into Brownsville that fateful day. If he hadn't been there to see Sheriff Carnacky abuse the old drunkard. If he hadn't put himself in a position where he'd been forced to kill the lawman. Then none of this would have happened. Why had he ridden into Brownsville in the first place? He'd known there could be trouble. But that hadn't deterred him. Put it down to pride. To a refusal to face facts and accept that the soil upon which Brownsville was built belonged to the United States now, whether he liked it or not. By his own actions he had put Maguey—and all of Mexico—in jeopardy.

He slept poorly that night, and in the dawn's light he stood before his men and informed them that they were going home to Maguey. The vaqueros were dismayed. Though many of their friends had died, and though most of those who'd survived were wounded, not a single man among them was ready to give up the fight. And that was exactly what their hidalgo was proposing. The campaign was over, and it had been a failure. Yes, they had beaten the Brownsville militia twice, and ambushed a small band of Texas Rangers. But they had not captured Brownsville, and had suffered defeat at La Bolsa. Caldero was accepting failure, but his vaqueros were reluctant to do likewise.

Still, he was the hidalgo, and they would obey without question.

Their progress was slow, since several of the men were seriously wounded. But they did not want to be left behind, and Caldero didn't want to leave them. About a dozen campesinos came along, riding double with the Maguey vaqueros. These men had sworn to fight to the death for Caldero and Mexico, and had refused to return to their homes. Caldero felt he had an obligation to them, and he let them stay.

Late in the afternoon a rider was spotting coming toward them from the direction of Maguey, and apprehension gripped Caldero. He had a hunch this messenger was the bearer of bad tidings.

It was one of the vaqueros who rode with Refugio, and he told Caldero that the Maguey *segundo* was in a very bad way. The *curandero* could do nothing more for him. A poison had entered his body, and no one thought he had long to live. The priest was preparing to administer last rites, and Teresa—Caldero's eldest daughter—was beside herself with grief.

Caldero was stunned by the news. Refugio, dying? It was incomprehensible. Refugio—who had spent his whole life at Maguey, whose father had been a vaquero riding for Caldero's father. Caldero had known Refugio all his life, had watched the boy grow into a man, and in past years had come to trust him as he would have trusted his own son. Refugio dying—it was almost too much for Antonio Caldero to bear.

The rider had more news. A young gringo had appeared at the jacal of the old sheepherder, Perez, and Perez had slipped away to Maguey to report him. Several vaqueros had gone out to capture the gringo, and they'd brought him back to the *casco* alive. The sheepherder's granddaughter had also come to Maguey, to plead with the hidalgo to spare the American's life.

"Who is he?" asked Caldero.

"He rode with the Texas Rangers, hidalgo."

"And you didn't kill him?"

"We wanted to, but Refugio said no."

Caldero told the others he was going to hasten back to Maguey with the messenger. They must follow as quickly as they were able.

Bent low in the saddle as his desert mustang raced across the *malpais,* Caldero gave the gringo prisoner no more than a passing thought. He could think only of Refugio, of making it back in time to be there when Refugio breathed his last. He owed the man that much, at least. It was his obligation.

Chapter 11

The day after finding Quincy Yates's body, McAllen and the Black Jacks reached Maguey. Their visit came as no surprise to the hacienda's inhabitants; long before they caught their first glimpse of the *casco* their presence was known. It was hard to imagine that anyone could remain out of sight for very long in this arid wasteland where a man could see a mountain range a hundred miles across the flatlands, but Caldero's vaqueros knew this country like the backs of their hands, and they could move across it without being seen. McAllen could sense their presence even though he couldn't see them. His instincts had been fine-tuned by two years of fighting Seminoles in the black-water swamps of Florida. He was certain the vaqueros were there, watching and waiting. But what were they waiting for? And when they did finally show themselves, would they shoot first and ask questions later?

When they were about five miles shy of Maguey, two riders suddenly appeared beyond rifle range to the west. They just sat their horses, black specks on the dun-colored desert.

"What do you reckon they're up to, Captain?" asked Lon Mayhew.

"They're letting us make the first move," was McAllen's prompt reply.

"I would've sworn we'd be attacked by now," said Mayhew.

"Why should they worry about us?" asked Morris Riddle, in his customary devil-may-care style. "There's only seven of us, Lon, in case you forgot to do the arithmetic. If there were *seventy* of us they might get a little worried. But the way it stands, they know they can take care of us any old time they want."

"They're a long way off, aren't they?" mused Cole. "But I think I could plug 'em, if you give the word, Captain."

Mayhew snorted. "You couldn't even hit Mexico from here, Cedric." Because he and Cole were the best shots in Texas, they had an ongoing if good-natured rivalry.

"No shooting," said McAllen. "My son's life may depend on it."

"What if they start shooting at us?" queried Buford Doss.

"No shooting, period!" said McAllen tersely. "You didn't have to come along, and you can turn back anytime you like."

Tice shot a glance at McAllen. It was rare for John Henry to be so abrupt with the men. But he was under a lot of pressure, and Tice knew for a fact that he'd gotten precious little sleep last night. McAllen had been up very late, writing a letter by the light of their campfire, and Tice assumed it was a letter addressed to Emily. One of those "if I don't come back alive" letters, most likely.

Onward they rode, following the trail of the men who had bushwhacked Tobias and the Texas Rangers. The sign made it plain that a few of the vaqueros had been gravely wounded, so they had made a beeline for home and they hadn't been too concerned about covering their tracks in the process.

A mile or so farther on, several more riders appeared, again at a safe distance, and this time to the east of the Black Jacks. The two on their left were shadowing them, and the trio on the right proceeded to do the same. A short while later Will Parton, who was bringing up the rear, calmly announced that more men had shown up behind them.

And then, a few tension-laden minutes later, twenty vaqueros seemed to simply rise up out of the ground directly in their path, so sudden and so close that McAllen's gray hunter snorted and shied away, startled. The Maguey riders had concealed themselves in an arroyo, and had waited until the Black Jacks were almost upon them before showing themselves. Instinctively McAllen's men reached for their weapons. The vaqueros raised their pistols and rifles. Their companeros closed in fast from left, right, and rear.

So why don't they shoot? wondered McAllen.

He held up both hands. "No *disparado*," he said. "No *disparado*. For God's sake, boys, don't shoot."

The Black Jacks held their fire. So did the Maguey vaqueros.

One of the Mexicans guided his horse forward. He held his pistol against his chap-clad thigh. Like most of the others, this one was young, lean, dark, with fierce eyes that seemed to bore right through McAllen.

"My name Lizamo," he said in broken English. "*Quien es usted?*"

"McAllen. John Henry McAllen. I didn't come here for a fight."

Lizamo smiled wryly. "This a good thing—for you."

"I want to see Antonio Caldero."

"The hidalgo expect you."

"Now how in the blazes can that be?" Riddle wondered aloud. "You reckon Caldero's got a crystal ball, boys?"

"It's simple," said Tice. "They reported seven men wearing black jackets. Caldero knows what these jackets mean. He knows who we are."

"So if he's expecting us he must have Gideon," breathed McAllen. "So he knows why we are here."

"Drop your guns," said Lizamo, and it wasn't a suggestion.

McAllen didn't hesitate. He slowly took his brace of Colt Patersons from their holsters and tossed them down. His rifle in its saddle scabbard was the next weapon to hit the ground. Tice and the others promptly followed suit—except for a dubious Morris Riddle.

"I don't cotton to this," admitted Riddle. "Not one bit, I don't."

"Do it!" snapped McAllen.

Riddle grimaced and shed his artillery.

"*Venga*," said Lizamo curtly, wheeling his horse around.

McAllen and the Black Jacks followed. Some of the Maguey riders tarried to retrieve their discarded weapons, while the others rode on either side of the Americans, keeping their eyes open and guns ready. McAllen knew that if he or one of his men made a wrong move it would all be over in a heartbeat. Nonetheless, he was elated. Gideon was alive. He was at Maguey. It had to be so.

Long before they reached the *casco* of Maguey they saw evidence of the extent of Caldero's empire. Vast fields of maize were nourished by an ingenious system of irrigation that wasted not a drop of water—a commodity as precious as gold in the Coahuilan desert. Conspicuously absent were the laborers who cultivated and harvested the Maguey crops.

The question of the whereabouts of Maguey's workforce was answered when they arrived at the *casco*. All of the people had been ensconced behind the well-guarded walls of the hacienda. McAllen and the others were astonished at their numbers—hundreds of Mexicans crowded the plaza to watch the procession of riders. They were grim, silent, alert to danger. These people, thought McAllen, were besieged both physically and emotionally. War was bad business in every respect, but worst of all was its impact on the innocent, the civilians who merely wanted to get on with their lives.

McAllen and his men were amazed, too, by the sheer scope of Maguey. It was a completely self-contained little city-fortress in the middle of a burning wasteland. Seeing it firsthand gave McAllen fresh insights into what Antonio Caldero was all about. The man fought with such fierce determination because he had so much to lose.

At a corner of the plaza Lizamo halted and ordered them to dismount. They were then herded into a small, barren adobe hut. The heavily-timbered door was slammed shut and a stout bar secured it from the outside. The solitary window's shutters were closed and also barred from without. A little light leaked in under the door.

"Well, boys," said Riddle, "we are in it up to our eyebrows."

"You should have gone home," said McAllen.

"What? And let you hog all the fun, Captain? Not a chance."

"I've stayed in worse places," remarked Cole, settling down with his back to a wall.

"That doesn't surprise me," said Mayhew.

"If they were gonna kill us they'd have done it already," said Doss, with less conviction than he had wanted to convey.

It was stifling hot in the room, and before long they were all sitting or lying on the cool hardpack. Will Parton had his Bible with him, and he lay near the door to capture the light and read passages out loud. Cedric Cole was soon fast asleep—there wasn't much that could faze him. McAllen paced the floor. He couldn't sit still, couldn't rest until he knew the truth about his son. Observing John Henry's anguish, Artemus Tice got angrier by the minute, and his anger was focused on Antonio Caldero. To keep a man in suspense about the fate of his own flesh and blood was cruel and unusual punishment.

An eternity later the door opened and Lizamo stepped in, backed by several vaqueros with pistols drawn.

"McAllen, you come." He spared the others a glance. "One of you is doctor?"

Tice got to his feet. "That would be me."

"You come, too."

The other Black Jacks were on their feet, and McAllen could tell they were all thinking the same thing—that maybe they'd be sorry if they didn't do something besides just stand by and let Tice and their captain be taken away. Though the odds were overwhelmingly against them they were ready, willing, and able to start a fracas. McAllen turned to them.

"I know what you're thinking, but you're wrong. Artemus and I will be okay. Just settle down and wait and maybe we'll get out of this. One thing's certain. We fight, we die. And so does Gideon."

"You come now," snapped Lizamo.

McAllen and Tice stepped out of the hut, waited while the door was once again secured, and then followed Lizamo across the plaza. The throngs of people were gone now. McAllen guessed that when he and the Black Jacks had been sighted an alarm had gone out, sending the population of Maguey to the protection of the *casco* walls. Now that he and his men were in custody, the people were being allowed to go about their business.

As they crossed the plaza, a passel of children playing stickball stopped to watch them go by. Women at the well, gathering water for cooking or washing, stopped what they were doing to observe their passing. McAllen wondered what would happen to these people if the men Stephen Powers had warned him about got their way. The Knights of the Golden Circle coveted Mexico because they thought they could carve new slave states out of the conquered territory, thereby securing the future of the Southern way of life. But then what would happen to these people? The Mexicans of Brownsville weren't slaves, but they might as well have been—they had no freedom and precious few rights. If citizens at all, they were most assuredly of the second class variety. They lived and died at the whim of their American overlords.

And what about Sam Houston? The Old Chief wanted to war against these people in order to unite Americans, north and south, in a common cause. In this way he hoped to avert secession and civil war and save the Union. That might have qualified as a noble sentiment, except that as the savior of the Union, Houston expected to garner enough political capital to pave his way to the White House. The end certainly did not justify the means. All along, McAllen had sought to excuse himself from this high stakes game of war and politics. But his prodigal son had drawn him into the vortex, and now that he was well and truly caught up in it, he found his sympathies were lying with the enemy. He had to smile—albeit somewhat bitterly—when he thought about what Sam Houston's reaction would be if the general could but know the sentiments of one of his most loyal and trusted lieutenants. For the first time in his life, John Henry McAllen stood four-square opposed against Houston.

Lizamo led them to the *casa principal.* They were kept waiting in a large downstairs hallway, under the guns of their vaquero guards, while Lizamo went upstairs—McAllen assumed to inform Caldero of their presence. As he waited, McAllen could look the length of the hall and out through open doors to a patio where a frail woman clad all in black sat motionless in a chair. She wasn't doing anything, and though McAllen could not see her face beneath a veil of exquisite black lace that matched the lace on the mantilla wrapped around her shoulders, he thought she was looking right at him. He could almost feel her eyes burning through to his soul. It was an unnerving experience, and he wondered who the woman could be.

The vaqueros were sweeping their sombreros from their heads, and this drew McAllen's attention away from the woman in black to the two men who stood at the top of the staircase—Lizamo and a man McAllen immediately recognized, even though nearly twenty years had passed since last they had met.

Antonio Caldero had not been much changed by the passage of time. His shoulder-length hair was gray like iron filings, and life's many burdens had etched more deeply the lines of his face. But he still possessed the eye of the hawk, and the sinewy grace of the panther. And he still had the singular aura of that rare individual—a man of destiny. A man, mused McAllen, not unlike General Houston. Someone who had the will and the drive and the vision to move the world.

"I always knew we would meet again, Captain," said Caldero as he started down the stairs.

McAllen waited until the Maguey hidalgo had reached the bottom of the stairs before responding.

"You know why I'm here."

Caldero nodded. At closer range McAllen thought the man looked very tired and forlorn and . . . defeated? No, not defeated. Not Antonio Caldero.

"Your son," said Caldero. "He is alive."

The stoicism that McAllen relied on failed him for a moment. "Thank God!" he gasped. "Where is he?"

"Nearby. You will see him soon. But first I must know if he is the only reason you have come here."

McAllen didn't hesitate in answering. "No, it is not."

Tice glanced at him, surprised. All along Tice—and the other Black Jacks—had been under the distinct impression that their captain's one and only reason for coming all the way down here to Mexico had been to find Gideon and take his errant son home. More than that, it had to appear to Tice as though the fact that their presence here was not connected in any form or fashion with the current border war must be a point in their favor, and perhaps the *only* thing that might serve to redeem them in Antonio Caldero's eyes—and, ultimately, save their lives.

"What else, then?" asked Caldero. "I'm listening."

"I have a letter from Sam Houston, and a message from Stephen Powers."

Now Tice was even more startled. McAllen had told him, in a very cursory fashion, about his visit with Powers in Brownsville. But John Henry had never made any mention of a letter from Sam Houston.

Caldero's smile was taut. "You keep good company."

"Powers would like to think he is your friend. And General Houston, as you must know, holds you in high regard."

"Both gentlemen generally keep their word. A rare trait in Americans. As far as I know, you are a man of honor, as well. That is why you and those who ride with you are still alive." Caldero nodded, as though he had just made up his mind about something important. "I will hear what you have to say. But not now." He turned to Tice. "You are the doctor?"

"That's right."

"You will come with me."

Caldero proceeded to climb the stairs. Tice glanced at McAllen, eyebrow raised in silent query, and McAllen nodded, so the old doctor followed Caldero, and McAllen trailed along behind him. He wasn't sure if he was invited upstairs, but he wasn't going to let Caldero separate him from his friend if he could help it. Nobody tried to stop him, and Lizamo tagged along. The other vaqueros remained in the hallway. Caldero led the way to a room on the second floor.

As soon as McAllen stepped inside he could smell the sickly sweet stench of death that permeated the room. A man lay beneath the covers on a four-poster bed, and a pretty, dark-haired young woman sat in a wing chair beside the bed, holding the man's hand. He wasn't conscious, and his breathing was ragged and shallow, and McAllen had seen enough of dying men to know that this fellow was on the threshold of the next life. If nothing else, the young woman's expression gave that much away. She obviously cared deeply for the dying man, and just as obviously she had little hope that he would recover. McAllen glanced at Caldero, whose own expression was as stricken as the girl's.

"Is this your son?" he asked.

"Not by blood. But he has been like a son to me. His name is Refugio. He was shot in the leg five days ago by a Texas Ranger."

"Five days," muttered Tice, moving quickly to the bedside. "Excuse me, miss," he said gently, smiling at the young woman, and she forced a smile in return even though her heart wasn't in it, and rose from her chair to step aside and give him the room he needed.

"*Esta un medico?*" she asked.

"She wants to know if you are the doctor," said Caldero.

"I am," said Tice, nodding to her, "and I will do everything in my power to save him."

Caldero translated for her, and a glimmer of faint hope appeared in her dark eyes.

Tice felt of Refugio's wrist, taking his pulse, measuring it against the keywinder he fished out of a pocket. Frowning, he threw the covers aside and examined the bandaged leg. Partially removing the dressing, he muttered something to himself, shook his head, and turned to glower at Caldero.

"I presume the bullet is still in him?"

"It is lodged too close to the artery. It could not be removed."

"And what is this beneath the dressing? Some kind of poultice?"

"The *curandero* made it to take away some of the poison."

"Well, it didn't work. You have no one here with medical training?"

"The nearest doctor is in Brownsville." Caldero smiled bitterly. "I don't think he would have come out. Otherwise, you must go two hundred miles to find another."

Tice glanced again at the leg, took a deep breath, and let it out slowly. "Gangrene is too far advanced to do anything besides take the leg. Then he might have a chance. I don't know. A slim chance, perhaps. Amputation is the only recourse, I'm afraid, and frankly it should have been performed days ago. He is in a weakened condition and the operation might be too much for him." Tice turned to Lizamo. "I'll need plenty of clean bandages. Hot water. Strong spirits. And the medical bag tied to my saddle. Be quick about it. There is no time to lose."

Lizamo didn't move. He was looking at Caldero.

"No," said Caldero.

"It is the only way, sir," said Tice curtly. "This man will surely die if his leg is not removed."

Caldero was very pale. He gazed sadly at Refugio's face. "You will not have his leg, Doctor. Even if he survived the operation he would not *want* to live if you took his leg."

"Nonsense. He would—"

"Listen to me," rasped Caldero. "He is a vaquero,

do you understand? No, I see that you don't. But I know him as well as I know myself. I know what he would want."

Tice was incensed. "And I'm telling you I've known many a man who led a long and fruitful life after losing an arm or a leg. It isn't the end of the world."

"It would be, for a man like Refugio."

"This is sheer madness. In a matter of hours the poison will reach his heart. He has at best twenty-four hours to live in his present state. And he will die an extremely painful death."

The young woman began to weep, leaning against the wall for support and covering her face with her hands. Caldero spoke to Lizamo, who went to her and escorted her from the room. She didn't want to go, crying out to Caldero, and he replied sternly, and she finally relented with a heartbroken sob and went with Lizamo. Caldero turned back to Tice.

"You want to take his leg, in the same way that your countrymen want to take part of Mexico, on the pretense of saving us from anarchy and destruction. You have Texas, now you want Coahuila. Perhaps Tamaulipas next. And then Sonora? Soon, if you have your way, there will be nothing left of Mexico. Not even the corpse. No. You will not operate on Refugio. He could not be the man he once was if you take his leg, Doctor, and he would not want to be any other kind of man."

"He will surely suffer and die. Why can't I get through to you?"

"Let it go, Artemus," said McAllen.

Caldero moved closer to the bed. "He will not suffer," he whispered. "I will see to that."

He drew his pistol and put the barrel to Refugio's temple.

"No!" shouted Tice, lunging forward in hopes of stopping Caldero.

Caldero backhanded him, and the old physician staggered. McAllen caught him. Tice wasn't through, and McAllen had to hold him back.

"God forgive me," said Caldero, and squeezed the trigger.

From beyond the door came a wail of anguish that made McAllen's skin crawl; he knew it came from the young woman.

Caldero's eyes were filled with tears as he holstered his pistol. But he let none of those tears fall.

"God damn you," rasped Tice.

Caldero ignored him. He was looking right at McAllen, and his eyes seemed to speak, to say *you understand why I have done this*, and McAllen *did* understand, and was deeply moved, just as he was deeply shaken.

"You are stronger than I could be," he said. "I couldn't have done that."

"I pray you never have to." Turning to the door, Caldero added, "I will have my men take you to where your son is being held. We will talk later."

While one of the vaqueros escorted Artemus Tice back to the jacal where the other Black Jacks were being held, another took McAllen to Gideon. His son was housed in a hut very similar to the one in which McAllen and his men had been incarcerated—a door barred on the outside, a shuttered window, a hardpack floor. At least this room could boast of a narrow bed in the corner with a thin straw mattress, and a rough-hewn table with a tallow lamp on it.

As he was let inside, McAllen was momentarily blinded by the bright afternoon sun that had been directly in his eyes while he crossed the *casco* from Caldero's house. The door was slammed shut behind him.

"Gideon?"

"Father?" Gideon had been lying on the ground beside the bed, and he jumped to his feet, gaping at McAllen as though he thought his father was an apparition. "Is that really you, Father?"

McAllen grinned, feeling both triumphant and relieved. He had done what he'd set out to do—what he'd promised Emily he would do—he'd found his son and Gideon was alive and well. He thanked God with his whole heart and soul.

"Have you been away so long that you've forgotten your own father?"

Gideon came toward him, faltered, and then proceeded as McAllen opened his arms and embraced him.

"I'm . . . I'm sorry," said Gideon, nearly in tears. "I know what I did was wrong. It was stupid. I didn't mean to hurt you and Mother."

"That doesn't matter now. All that matters is that you're safe."

"I am—thanks to Maura."

McAllen looked at the girl who had been sleeping on the bed. She was sitting up now, rubbing the sleep from her eyes.

"You're a prisoner, too?" asked McAllen.

"She insisted on staying with me," explained Gideon.

"Maybe you'd better tell me what's happened to you, son."

Gideon did just that, leaving nothing out—save for the part about Quincy Yates's display of cowardice in Brownsville when Caldero's men were shelling the town with the captured cannon. Quincy had been his friend, and even if he hadn't been it wasn't right to speak ill of the dead. When McAllen heard how Maura had risked her life to deliver Gideon's letter across the river he looked at the shy girl with new-found respect and expressed his most heartfelt gratitude.

"Don't worry, son," he told Gideon. "We'll all get out of here somehow."

Gideon glanced at Maura. For the first time, now that his father was here, he could seriously entertain the hope of going home. But what about Maura? The joy that he derived from the prospect of returning to Grand Cane was tempered by a profound sadness. The thought of parting company with Maura left a hollow emptiness within him. The expression on her face vouched for the fact that she suffered from similar apprehensions.

"How will we get out, sir?" asked Gideon. "You're a prisoner, the same as we are."

McAllen nodded. "We'll find a way."

Several hours later, Lizamo came to fetch McAllen back to the *casa principal*. The sun had set, and night was gathering its cloak around Maguey. The shadowy shapes of sentries moved slowly along the walls of the *casco*. A dog barked, a baby cried. The hacienda had a solemn aura about it, as though even the adobe walls and the Coahuilan desert mourned the death of the vaquero called Refugio. Entering the *casa principal* was like walking into a tomb. The gloomy stillness was oppressive. Lizamo escorted him into a modest downstairs room filled with a desk and a bookcase used primarily to store leather-bound ledgers. A map of Coahuila hung on the wall behind the desk, while the portrait of a white-haired man in vaquero garb hung above the cold fireplace.

Antonio Caldero stood looking up at the portrait, hands clasped behind his back. He did not turn around as McAllen and Lizamo entered the room.

"Leave us," he said.

"Si, hidalgo." Lizamo closed the door softly behind him. McAllen listened for his footsteps and heard nothing. He assumed the *vaquero* was lingering just outside the door. *I am the enemy,* McAllen reminded himself—he had to remind himself because he didn't consider himself to be the enemy of these people—*and they don't trust me, would just as soon kill me, and they don't understand why Caldero doesn't want to do the same.*

But McAllen had a pretty good idea. He thought he knew exactly what Antonio Caldero was all about. The master of Maguey was an old warhorse weary of fighting, just like himself. All he wanted was to be left alone. But events beyond his control had overtaken him and forever altered his life. And, too, Caldero was a man endowed with a strong sense of duty. The hundreds who lived and worked at Maguey depended on him. *Yes, I think I know Caldero pretty well—and I'm about to risk everything in finding out whether I am right.*

"It was Refugio who spared your son's life," Caldero told him, keeping his back turned, gazing into the eyes of the portrait's subject, to whom McAllen thought he bore an uncanny resemblance. "I wasn't here. The vaqueros would have killed your son because he was known to have ridden with the Texas Rangers. But from his deathbed Refugio stayed their hand. Do you know why?"

"No."

"I think I do. Because Refugio knew he was dying, and more than ever before he valued life."

"I'm sorry."

"It is I who should be sorry." Caldero turned, then, and spared McAllen a glance, and went to his desk. With a sigh he sank into the chair behind it and looked around as though he had never seen this room before.

"This was my father's office. This was his desk. He built Maguey. There was nothing here but the *malpais* before he came. Now I am about to destroy everything he gave his sweat and blood and life to create."

"You can save it. There is a way. I had a talk with Stephen Powers in Brownsville. He asked me to find you, deliver a message."

"And so you have found me." Caldero sounded supremely disinterested.

"He wants you to turn yourself in."

McAllen paused, watching Caldero closely, wanting to measure the man's response to the bare bones of the proposal made by Powers, free of any of Powers's assurances about providing Caldero with a capable lawyer and making sure he got a fair trial, because McAllen really didn't think Powers, as influential as the man was, could actually make good on those assurances. And McAllen refrained from starting off with all the reasons Powers had given for Caldero to surrender. They were good reasons but they wouldn't amount to a hill of beans if Caldero wasn't open to even considering what Powers had advised.

"Powers is a smart man," said Caldero calmly. "He is one of the few Americans I have known who has treated my people with the respect they deserve. Not just when he needs their vote, but all the time."

"He wanted me to tell you that it is the only way to prevent a full-scale war. And you know what happens if there is a war—another army, another invasion. And your government won't act until it's too late for the northern provinces."

Caldero nodded. He was looking at the portrait again. "Your soldiers came thirteen years ago. The only reason Maguey still stands is because my father made his own truce with General Zachary Taylor. My father swore his vaqueros would not take up arms against the United States, and that Taylor could have what he needed in the way of stock and grain for his army. Fortunately, Taylor was an honorable man. Even so, when Taylor was gone, other soldiers came and stole what they wanted. My father's vaqueros were proud men. They wanted to fight. Some of them could not remain at Maguey, even though they were devoted to my father, even though for many of them Maguey was the only home they had ever known. Those men left to fight the Americans. But my father kept his word to Taylor. It cost him dearly. But it saved Maguey."

"I've sometimes wondered why you didn't fight in that war," said McAllen. "You, and the men who rode with you in the Nueces Strip, could have wrought havoc on Taylor's supply lines. But you didn't—for your father's sake."

"For Maguey's sake, not my father's."

McAllen nodded. He understood perfectly. Maguey represented for Caldero what Grand Cane was for him. Grand Cane wasn't just *his* home—it was the home of all the freed slaves who lived on it, and worked on it, and made it prosper. He had a responsibility to them, and to Emily and his son—not to himself. So it was with Caldero, as it had been with his father before him. The livelihood—the very life—of every person on the hacienda depended on the hidalgo. He could not always do what he personally wanted to. Sometimes sacrifice was called for. Now Caldero was in a situation where the ultimate sacrifice was required of him.

"You said you have a letter from Houston," said Caldero.

McAllen took the folded piece of paper from beneath his shell jacket and laid it on the desk in front of Caldero, who gazed at it for a moment as though it were a viper that would strike if he reached out, would fill his veins with poison. Finally he picked it up, unfolded it, and read. His expression was inscrutable. When he was finished he folded the paper as it had been before and placed it back on the desk.

"I will let you know my decision," he said flatly.

"Regardless of what you decide, will you let my son—and my men—go free?"

"And what about you, Captain?"

"What you do with me is of no consequence, so long as the others are safe."

"I can see that you are sincere. Some men only play the hero."

"I'm no hero. Just a father, and a friend."

Caldero rose from the chair. "You are all free to go."

"Well, then, if I'm free, I'll ride with you to Brownsville if you decide to do as Powers suggests."

Taken aback, Caldero stared at him in disbelief. "Why would you want to do that?"

"To make sure you get the fair trial Powers has promised."

"That doesn't matter. All that matters to me is Maguey."

"It matters to me."

Caldero made a dismissive gesture. "You have your son. Now go home."

"I've got to go to Brownsville anyway. I have a score to settle with a man there."

"I don't need your help."

"I owe you—for Emily."

Caldero was chuckling. "So you are going to protect me from an assassin's bullet, or a lynch mob's rope? Is that what you think?"

"All a man can do is try."

When he had been returned to the hut where the other Black Jacks were being held, John Henry McAllen was besieged with questions. Was Gideon alive and well? Would Caldero let them all go free? Could Caldero be trusted even if he gave his word that they could go in peace? To all three questions McAllen was pleased to answer in the affirmative. When could they go? To that he could only say that he wasn't sure. He hoped it would be soon.

As the others congratulated themselves for having survived this den of lions, Artemus Tice pulled McAllen aside.

"How could you just stand by and let Caldero kill that poor boy, John Henry?"

"He was dying anyway."

"I might have been able to save him. Of course we'll never know, will we?"

"Listen, Artemus. Caldero did what he thought was best. It wasn't easy for him."

"Murder should never be easy. If that had been your son would you have blown his brains out to keep me from amputating his leg?"

"Of course not. But I'm not Caldero. And Gideon is not a vaquero."

"Pshaw! It was a cold-blooded execution, any way you look at it."

"You're wrong, Artemus. If anything it was a mercy killing."

"No, *you're* wrong. And another thing. What's this about a letter from Sam Houston? You didn't tell me the Old Chief had given you a letter to deliver to Caldero."

"Because he didn't. I wrote that letter last night. In fact, I think I did a pretty fair job of imitating the general's handwriting. I know I got his signature down pat."

Tice gaped at him. "What were you trying to do, John Henry?"

"I'm trying to stop a war."

"I thought you weren't going to become involved."

"I changed my mind."

Artemus shook his head. "That was a pretty underhanded trick. I didn't know you had it in you."

"Well, Artemus, if you liked that, you'll really appreciate this. I'm going back to Brownsville. I can't go home, not right away."

Tice squinted suspiciously. "What are you up to now?"

"If Caldero turns himself in I want to do everything I possibly can to see that he gets the fair trial Stephen Powers promised."

"Oh, well, that's simple," said Tice sarcastically. "But there's more, isn't there? Could it have something to do with Tobias and those Texas Rangers of his, by any chance?"

McAllen nodded.

Tice threw up his arms in despair. "I knew it. I just knew that look on your face. I've known you too long, John Henry. You can't fool me."

"Tobias left my son to die alone in the desert."

Tice turned to the others. "Listen up, men. I've got some great news. We're going to have our little scrape after all. You didn't come all the way down here for nothing, after all."

"Artemus," said McAllen.

But Tice wasn't listening. "John Henry says he's got a score to settle with that Captain Tobias. You just thought you'd be shooting at Mexicans. Instead, your targets are going to be Texas Rangers."

"Suits me," said Morris Riddle promptly.

"I've always wanted to try one of those high-and-mighty Rangers on for size," added Mayhew.

"Don't worry, Lon," said Cole. "I'll be right there to save your bacon when it needs saving."

"That *is* a comfort," retorted Mayhew. "I'll have to be sure to write my last will and testament before the shooting starts."

"What's gotten into you, Artemus?" asked McAllen.

"You really want to know? I'll tell you," said Tice, testily. "You've got what you came for, namely your son. Now you need to take my advice and leave well enough alone and take Gideon home to Emily like you promised."

"No, you're going to do that for me. And on the way you're going to locate Sam Houston and deliver a message for me."

Tice grimaced. "Your problem is you just don't know when to quit."

"I won't be wronged—or stand by while my son is wronged."

"Gideon won't like it that you see the need to fight his fights for him."

"He's just a boy. He's no match for the likes of Tobias. And besides, he won't know. I'm not going to tell him—and you won't either. Will you, Artemus?"

Tice grimly shook his head. "You've got me there, John Henry. You know I won't tell him. I can't. Not for your sake, but for his—and his mother's."

McAllen had to smile. "I've noticed you've been getting awfully ornery in your own age, my friend."

Early the next morning, following a sleepless night spent pacing the floor of his office or standing with eyes glued to the portrait of his father, Antonio Caldero went in search of Dona Petra, and as usual found his mother on the patio. Storm clouds had rolled in under cover of darkness, and the scent of rain was strong—rain that Maguey sorely needed, thought Caldero. The fields and the orchards and the livestock would all benefit greatly. It had been a long and hellish summer.

One of the house servants had brought Dona Petra her breakfast, which without fail consisted of a piece of fruit from the orchard and a cup of strong black coffee. She had finished this Spartan repast and the servant was taking the tray away as Caldero entered the patio. Sometimes Caldero forgot how much his mother had sacrificed to make Maguey a success. She had shed blood and tears and sweat the same as his father. She had sacrificed as much as Trinidad Caldero, in some ways perhaps even more.

The meager breakfast reminded Caldero of this, because for years, while she and her husband fought and toiled and suffered to make Maguey a reality, Dona Petra had survived on such simple fare—and sometimes less. Perhaps it reminded her of those days, mused Caldero; maybe she *wanted* to be reminded of sitting around a campfire or in the small adobe jacal that for a decade had served as the *casa principal* of Maguey, in the days when she had wondered if tomorrow would bring destruction, or one more small step closer to the realization of the dream she had shared with her husband.

She had shared the dream and the sacrifice, he thought. *She suffered much, and now it is my turn.*

He went to her, kneeled before her chair, and took one of her gnarled, age-spotted hands in both his own, and she touched his cheek with her other hand.

"My poor Antonio. What you did for Refugio—it was very difficult for you, I know."

"So you understand why I had to do it."

"Of course I understand. I am sorry you had to do this thing. You are very brave."

"No. Not nearly as brave as you, Mother. And now I must ask you to be brave again. I must go away, and I will not be coming back."

Her hand trembled against his cheek. "You will do what is right, Antonio," she sighed.

"I'm not sure if what I'm doing is right or wrong. I'm not sure of anything these days."

"I have faith in you, my son."

"I've decided to go to Brownsville and turn myself in for the killing of the sheriff."

Dona Petra gasped.

"It is the only way to save Maguey," he told her. "I realize this now. I was too proud to see the truth before. I thought I could fight the Americans. But they are too strong. I am only a man—I cannot make the sun stand still. I cannot turn back the tide."

She lifted the veil so that he could see the love and admiration in her eyes—could see, too, that she was indeed brave enough to endure, for she shed no tears.

"You are wrong about one thing, Antonio. You can turn the tide. With your blood you will save our people. Know this—no son has ever made his mother as proud as I am of you."

He captured her hand again and kissed it.

"Now go," she said sternly. "Do not waste your precious time on an old woman like me. Go and say good-bye to your daughters. They will weep, but do not let their tears turn you from what you must do. They are young and have yet to learn."

He nodded, not trusting himself to speak, and rose to go with a heavy heart.

"Antonio?"

"Yes, Mother?"

She lowered the veil. "No matter what happens, never forget who you are."

Chapter 12

Since he was approaching Fort Brown from the Mexican side of the Rio Grande, McAllen took the precaution of tying a strip of white cloth to the barrel of his rifle as a makeshift flag of truce. He didn't want to be filled full of lead by nervous sentries.

It was early in the morning—he and his party had traveled hard all day yesterday and had made very good time. They had camped a mile south of the river. Antonio Caldero had not spoken a single word since leaving Maguey, and McAllen wondered if the man was having second thoughts. In his shoes McAllen certainly would have. Because, in spite of all the promises, all the good intentions of men like Stephen Powers and McAllen himself, Caldero had to know he was a doomed man, condemned to die. So McAllen deemed it quite likely that Caldero might have a change of heart and slip away during the night.

Nonetheless, McAllen hadn't kept watch over him. Caldero wasn't his prisoner. The man had come of his own free will and as far as McAllen was concerned he could turn back anytime he wanted. And though McAllen had posted a night sentry—Mayhew, Doss, and Cole in three two-hour shifts—it hadn't been for the purpose of keeping an eye peeled for the Maguey vaqueros. Caldero had assured him that his men would not try to rescue him. He had given the order. They would obey without question. No, it hadn't been the Maguey riders who concerned McAllen, but rather the armed bands of Americans based in Brownsville. If any of them had eluded Captain Donaldson's patrols for a foray into Mexico, seeking trouble, they would hit a night camp on Mexican soil without pausing to identify its inhabitants.

But the night had passed uneventfully—and Caldero had not slipped away. So this morning, so early that gray shreds of night yet clung to the earth, McAllen rode across the Rio Grande with Tice and Gideon and Maura. His son and the Irish-Mexican girl rode Maguey mustangs.

The sentries spotted them as they reached the far bank of the river. They shouted the alarm and by the time McAllen's party had arrived on the other side a detail commanded by a lieutenant had ridden out to confront them. McAllen identified himself and informed the lieutenant of his earnest desire to see Captain Donaldson—it was an urgent matter.

"The captain is going to want to know what you were doing on the Mexican side of the Rio Grande, sir," said the suspicious dragoon officer.

"You wouldn't believe me if I told you, Lieutenant."

A short while later McAllen was being ushered into Donaldson's office. Fort Brown's commanding officer still had sleep in his eyes. He offered McAllen some coffee, which McAllen gratefully accepted—he hadn't lingered in his own camp long enough for a pot of coffee to brew.

When an orderly had brought them their coffee and departed, Donaldson motioned McAllen to a camp stool and sat on the corner of a desk fashioned of planks laid across a pair of hogsheads. He apologized wryly for the furnishings and explained that the army had taken everything—lock, stock, and chair—when Fort Brown had been abandoned some years ago. McAllen figured he was just being polite, engaging in a little small talk before getting to the point. His accent identified him as Virginia-born and bred, and McAllen could tell by the way he carried himself that he was a West Pointer.

"I have a hunch your lieutenant thinks I was up to no good down in Mexico," said McAllen. "But I was just looking for my wayward son."

"And did you locate him?"

McAllen announced that he had.

"Thank God for that."

"I found him at the Hacienda del Maguey."

Donaldson's eyes narrowed. "Isn't that Caldero's place?"

McAllen said it was.

Donaldson put his cup of coffee down. "You mean to tell me that you got your son out of Maguey and lived to tell the tale?"

"He's right outside. I've also got Caldero with me."

Two quick strides carried Donaldson to the window.

"He's about a mile south of here, Captain," said McAllen. "My men are with him."

Donaldson turned to gape at McAllen. "You *captured* Antonio Caldero?"

"Not exactly."

"Bring him to me at once, Captain."

McAllen shook his head. "Not so fast, Captain. I didn't capture him—he is giving himself up."

"Why would he do a thing like that? I wasn't aware that Caldero was a fool."

"He doesn't want war."

"He could have fooled me. He and his men killed a dozen of my dragoons at La Bolsa five days ago. They were attacking the riverboat owned by the ranchers, King and Kennedy. Mr. Kennedy had sent word to me of the riverboat's movements, and asked if I would come to escort it downriver. They should have waited until my men arrived before setting off down the river. My detachment arrived in the nick of time. The vessel was on fire and Caldero's men were attacking the crew—on the American side of the Rio Grande, by the way. The Mexicans were driven from the field with heavy losses. But the blood of American soldiers was shed on American soil, sir."

"I doubt that Caldero would have attacked had he known your troops would be engaged."

"But that's beside the point now, isn't it?"

McAllen nodded. "You've sent in your report, I suppose."

"Naturally. And I don't think it will amuse the War Department."

"Captain, at the risk of offending you I must ask a question. You are a Southern man. Your orders aside, do you *want* a war with Mexico?"

"I am a Southron, and a slaveholder. But no, sir, I do not want war," replied Donaldson curtly. "And I do find the question offensive."

McAllen smiled. "Good. Then I believe you."

"Just what kind of game are you playing, McAllen?"

"Caldero has been promised a fair trial. I'm going to make certain he gets one."

"Fair trial or no, he's going to die. From everything

I've heard it seems clear he shot the Brownsville sheriff in cold blood. A jury is bound to find him guilty of murder. They'll construct a gallows on the town square and hang him for certain."

"Maybe. But he *will* get that trial."

Donaldson sighed. "So why did you bring him here?"

"I think you know why."

"Okay. We'll keep him until the trial starts."

"You will guarantee his safety?"

"I won't let a lynch mob have him, if that's what you mean."

"And you will not under any circumstances hand him over to a state authority?"

"Not unless I am ordered to do so by my superiors."

"That won't happen." McAllen got up to leave.

"You sound right sure of yourself, Captain."

McAllen didn't respond. He thanked the dragoon captain and went outside where Tice and Gideon and Maura were waiting. They were sitting in the striped shade of a pole roof overhanging a narrow porch that fronted the post headquarters building. The sun had risen and though the day was still young the heat was the devil's hammer. A storm was coming up from the south—it had followed them from Maguey—and McAllen just hoped it would cool things off a bit.

Tice was smoking his pipe and regaling the youngsters with tales about fighting Seminoles in the Florida swamps, and McAllen noticed how closely Gideon and Maura were sitting together without even realizing it. She was pretty, he thought, and obviously had courage, and he couldn't help but wonder what the two of them had done to pass the time during their incarceration at Maguey. Then he shook his head ruefully and forced such thoughts out of his mind. Now was hardly the time to worry about such matters.

"What did Donaldson say?" Tice asked him, cutting his old war story short.

"They'll keep Caldero here until the trial," replied McAllen. "I'll ride back and get the others. It's time you got started."

Gideon stood up. "I want to stay with you, sir."

"No, son. You need to go home and apologize to your mother. Let her see that you are well. Then I'm relying on you to help Artemus."

"Help him do what?"

"Find Sam Houston," said Tice.

"Everything depends on it," added McAllen.

"I don't see why it should," said Gideon, reluctantly. "Truth is, you know there's going to be trouble down here and you're just trying to keep me out of it."

"Don't blame him for that," said Tice. "That's what fathers are supposed to do, boy." He glanced at Maura. "You'll have a son of your own someday, Gideon, and then you'll understand."

Gideon couldn't fail to notice the way Tice was looking at Maura, and he blushed. "Maura wants to stay with me, sir," he told McAllen.

"What about your grandfather?" McAllen asked her.

"He betrayed Gideon. I cannot trust him anymore. I do not want to go back to him. Please do not make me go. Let me stay with your son."

"Well what do you know," said Tice, beaming. "I have a hunch these two young people are in love, John Henry."

Gideon glanced shyly at Maura, and she glanced

shyly back at him, and then both looked quickly away and McAllen had to chuckle—he couldn't help it.

"You can't win if you stand in the way of romance, John Henry," warned Tice.

"Believe me, I'm not even going to try. Maura is welcome at Grand Cane, of course. But Gideon, I'll leave it to you to explain all this to your mother—and heaven help you."

"Okay," said Gideon. "I'll go home and I'll help Artemus find Sam Houston. But then, if you're still down here, Father, I'm coming back to help you."

The room above Grindle's saloon was the place where the leading lights of the Reds political machine met when they didn't congregate in the study of Charles Stoneman's mansion. They weren't meeting at Stoneman's place because Stoneman was still residing at the hotel in town. That suited everybody because Grindle's was more convenient, and Stoneman had spared no expense in turning the upstairs room into a posh sanctuary. The chairs and sofas were mahogany upholstered in velvet or black horsehair. The walls had been covered with rich damask and hung with costly landscapes imported from England in gilt frames. A Belgian carpet lay underfoot. The finest whiskies and brandies were stored in glass decanters and of course Stoneman had thought to lay in a stock of his Dosamygos cigars. So the others lacked nothing by meeting at Grindle's—except the long journey on the road to Port Isabel that passed in front of Stoneman's mansion.

Even though Stoneman had called the meeting at a moment's notice, and even though a rainstorm raged outside, turning the streets of Brownsville into a smelly morass of mud mixed with horse dung and human sewerage, everyone was present save for Kennedy, who was twenty miles away at his cattle ranch. Turnbull and McColley had braved the weather, and while they had been grumbling about the inconvenience as Grindle let them in, as soon as they saw Stoneman's expression they stopped complaining and started worrying.

Obviously something was terribly wrong.

Stoneman sat in a chair with a drink in one hand and smoldering cigar in the other, but the long nine and the double dose of liquid nerve medicine were forgotten; he was staring—no, glowering—at the tips of his mud-caked boots. It wasn't the mud, however, that upset him.

"What the bloody hell has happened now?" asked McColley. The gruff, burly Scotsman always liked to cut to the chase. "Oot with the bad news, Charles. Don't keep us in suspense."

"Caldero's in Fort Brown," rasped Stoneman.

"Good God in heaven!" exclaimed Turnbull. "He's taken the fort! How can that be? We're cut off from the coast! Why . . . why next he's bound to attack Brownsville! He'll . . . he'll surely kill us all! What are we going to do?"

Stoneman gazed at the merchant/mayor with unfettered disgust.

"No, you fool. He didn't *take* Fort Brown. He surrendered himself, and the army is holding him."

Turnbull—ashen the moment before—now blushed beet-red. "Oh, well . . . ," he muttered, casting about for something to say that would salvage his self-respect. Finding nothing that would do the trick, he could only stand there, shamefaced.

"This changes everything," said Grindle, morosely, breaking the uncomfortable silence with a statement of the obvious.

"But why did he do it?" asked McColley.

"John Henry McAllen brought him in," said Stoneman. "Not by force. From what little I've been able to learn, Caldero gave himself up. Stephen Powers promised him a fair trial and McAllen has made it known that he's going to be sure Caldero gets just that. Him and his damned Black Jacks."

"McAllen!" said McColley, with rancor. "He's a bloody Union man. He freed his slaves many years ago."

"And he's a Houston man besides," said Grindle.

"You think Sam Houston is behind this?" McColley asked Stoneman.

"I don't know. You can *never* know with any certainty what Houston is going to do."

"Houston says he's for the Union over everything," offered Turnbull. "Even his native South."

"Sam Houston will say whatever he needs to say," growled McColley. "It just depends on who the beggar is talking to at the moment, and what he's trying to get out of the poor sod."

"What Houston believes or doesn't believe isn't the problem, damn it," rasped Stoneman. "*He*'s not who I'm worried about. It's Caldero."

McColley helped himself to the whiskey decanter, which was laid out with glasses and other decanters atop a handsome cherry-wood sideboard beneath a painting of an English meadow with a few deer breaking cautiously out of dark woods. He thought that he and Stoneman and Turnbull and Grindle were all deer being forced out into the open, and he didn't like the feeling of being so exposed. With the connivance of Stephen Powers and John Henry McAllen, Caldero had played his trump card, and McColley wondered how long it would take Charles Stoneman to admit he'd been beaten. The Scots trader didn't like it, not one bit. He regretted having been drawn into this misbegotten scheme. Greed—that was what had lured him into such bloody foolishness. He'd gotten greedy because he had seen big profits stemming from a war that would transform the northern provinces of Mexico—at the very *least* the northern provinces—into American territories or even new states. If that had happened, and he could have secured the lion's share of the coastal traffic—and no one was in a better position than he to do just that—he could have retired in a few years and bought that castle overlooking some European river and lived out his life like a bloody king. Of course he was already rich enough to buy a *small* castle—he'd just wanted a big one. Greed. One of the seven deadly sins, and perhaps the most subtle in the way it destroyed a man.

Turnbull was babbling again. "So Caldero has given himself up. So what difference does it really make if he gets a fair trial. I mean, a jury will find him guilty of murder. There can be no doubt about that. They'll find him guilty and then we can hang him."

McColley glanced with pity at Turnbull. Stoneman looked at the merchant with absolute disdain.

"It isn't Caldero we want," said Stoneman, spacing his words out as though he were speaking to a slow-witted child. "Caldero dead doesn't help us attain our goals. Caldero alive and stirring up trouble works to our advantage."

"If he goes to trial and hangs, the border troubles

are over and done with as far as everyone else is concerned," McColley told Turnbull, just in case it still wasn't clear to the befuddled merchant just how serious their dilemma was.

"I see," muttered Turnbull, the dawn of understanding lighting up his face at last.

"That is exactly why Powers offered him the trial and McAllen delivered the message," said Stoneman sourly. "They knew it would ruin our plans. They don't want the Knights of the Golden Circle to succeed. They don't care if the South survives. They would just as soon see the institution of slavery destroyed."

McColley eyed Stoneman, wondering why it was that a New Yorker wanted so badly for the South and slavery to prosper. Only one explanation made any sense to the wily Scotsman. Again, it all boiled down to greed. It wasn't ideology that motivated Stoneman, who had invested heavily in the cotton trade and the "peculiar" institution of slavery. The slave South was prospering as it had never done before, and that prosperity was built on a foundation of money crops like cotton and the practical application of human bondage in labor-intensive agriculture. If the South suffered, so would Charles Stoneman. All the man's bold talk about states' rights and the threat posed by a federal government with the power to dictate to the slaveholding citizen—that was all just a smoke screen. *He is in it for the profit, same as I am*, mused McColley. *The difference is that I make no bones about where I stand.*

"So everything we've done is for naught," groaned Turnbull.

"Maybe Caldero's men will try to save him," said Grindle.

"He doesn't want to be saved," countered Stoneman, as an inch of ash fell on the expensive carpet from his neglected Cuban long nine. "Don't you understand? He's the damn Jesus Christ of flaming Mexico, Josiah. And he's the God Almighty of Maguey, too—which means his men won't save him if he told them not to. Which I am sure he has done."

"This just doesn't make any sense," Grindle complained. "He must realize that he's going to die."

"It's suicide, that's what it is," concurred Turnbull.

"You've got something up your sleeve, Charles," said McColley. He knew Stoneman, and had been watching him closely, and he'd seen Stoneman's expression change as an idea came to him.

Stoneman finally remembered his bonded whiskey and took a drink. "Yes, as a matter of fact I do. What if Caldero were to simply disappear?"

"How could he?" asked Grindle. "He's being kept under close guard by a company of United States cavalry."

"Josiah, your problem is you lack vision. He's got army protection now, but that's just until the trial. When the trial starts he'll be here in Brownsville, won't he?"

"I guess. But he'll still be guarded—if not by the dragoons then by McAllen and his Black Jacks."

Stoneman was on his feet now, pacing, his mind churning rapidly. "That's the beauty of it. We'll be able to kill two birds with one stone."

"You're being as clear as river-bottom mud, Charles," groused McColley. "Oot with it, now."

"We all know what Captain Tobias did to McAllen's boy. Lord knows Tobias has bragged all over town about how he avenged Eli Wingate's death at McAllen's hands. Tobias must know McAllen is planning to even the score. There's bound to be some shooting before those two are through with each other. We just make sure it doesn't happen until the trial starts. And while the Black Jacks and the Texas Rangers are busy killing one another, and everybody else is running for cover, we take Caldero."

"Take him?" asked Turnbull. "Take him where?"

The poor sod doesn't have a clue, thought McColley. "Oot in the middle of nowhere, of course, you bloody fool. Where he gets a bullet in the brain pan."

"And how does that help us?" asked Grindle, who didn't much care to be involved in cold-blooded murder.

"Dying a martyr is one thing," said Stoneman, his eyes gleaming, "but if Caldero simply disappears, everybody will assume he escaped back to Mexico."

"But he won't have," insisted Grindle, desperate now to dissuade Stoneman. This latest scheme to murder Caldero was going entirely too far, in the saloonkeeper's book. "He won't be in Mexico to stir up trouble."

"I've got men who will gladly go to Mexico and stir up trouble."

"The Knights," said McColley, nodding. He didn't like Stoneman, but give the man his due—he never gave up.

"Right. A hundred men with a license to rape, pillage, and burn. What do you think the Maguey vaqueros will do—stand by and watch all of Coahuila go up in flames? No. They'll strike back. They'll seek revenge. Why they might even come to Brownsville to find it."

"Good God, Charles!" exclaimed Turnbull, aghast. "This is madness. It's bad enough that Caldero shelled this town for the better part of two days with those cannon he took from Jarvis. But this—this is outrageous! You're talking about deliberately goading the Mexicans into a raid on Brownsville."

"Exactly. To be honest, I was a little disappointed that Caldero himself didn't pay us a visit."

"How many of our friends and neighbors would perish in such an attack? Why, all of us in this room might be killed, for heaven's sake."

"You can't have bacon unless you slaughter a pig," replied Stoneman.

"No. No, I won't let you go through with this, Charles. I can't."

Stoneman sighed. He doused his cigar in the whiskey and put the glass down and walked over to put an arm around Turnbull's shoulders.

"Old friend," he said, "you're either with us or you're against us. Do you *really* want to be my enemy? You know what happens to my enemies."

McColley saw the over-and-under derringer in Stoneman's hand. He had it planted in Turnbull's rounded belly.

"My God, Charles!" shouted McColley. "Don't do it. Have you lost your mind?"

Turnbull stared at the little pocket gun and tottered on the brink of passing out.

"You—you wouldn't," he stammered, and didn't sound at all convinced.

"Wouldn't I? I can't abide traitors and cowards, and I am beginning to think you're both. The cause for which we fight is bigger than all of us, and most assuredly more important than the life of a single man. I would sacrifice myself for the cause, and as that is the case you know I would certainly sacrifice you."

"You don't mean that!" gasped Grindle.

"He means it," snapped McColley. "Put the damned gun away, Charles. I'm sure the mayor didn't mean what he said. Did you, Mayor?"

"No, no, I didn't mean it. I—I won't stand in your way, Charles. You have my—my word on it."

Stoneman pocketed the derringer and slapped Turnbull on the back—a little harder than was necessary, in McColley's opinion. "Good, good," said Stoneman cheerily. "Can I pour you another drink? You seem to have spilled yours."

Turnbull noticed that the glass clutched in his hand was almost empty—he'd been shaking so severely that most of its contents had sloshed over the rim to splatter on his boots and stain the lush carpet.

"Uh, no thanks," he mumbled. "I think I'd better be going." He didn't want anyone to notice that he had soiled himself.

"Fine. But bear in mind, Mayor, that those forays into Mexico will need to be provisioned. I will expect you to take care of those details."

Turnbull nodded and beat a hasty retreat for the door.

"Hold on," McColley told him. "I'm leaving too."

When they had reached the street Turnbull paused on the boardwalk in front of the saloon and wiped the sweat from his face with a handkerchief. The rain was coming down in driving sheets and Brownsville's muddy streets were empty. Grindle's place, though, was doing a brisk business—filled with the men who had flocked to town hoping for a chance to kill a Mexican or two.

"He is insane," Turnbull told McColley resentfully. "Stark raving mad. He would have pulled the trigger, you know. He wasn't bluffing. What have we gotten ourselves into, Mac?"

McColley shook his head and stuck out a hand. "So long to you, Mayor. If I said we'd be seeing each other again it would be a lie."

"What do you mean?"

"I'm going to Port Isabel and taking one of my packets to New Orleans, and when I get there I'm removing every cent I own out of the bloody bank and set sail for Europe."

"You're—you're running away?"

"Aye, I'm getting as far away as I possibly can from Charles Stoneman and the bloody Knights of the Golden Circle. I'm going as fast as my legs can carry me. And I strongly suggest that you do likewise."

"But, I—I am the mayor. I have responsibilities. I can't just—just run away like that . . ."

McColley shook his head. "You're an idiot. You're mayor in name only. You're a flamin' figurehead, don't you realize? Stoneman owns you. He owns this town. He runs it, and he runs you. Are you too blind to see the truth? Get out while you still can, man, because there is going to be a lot of killing here in the days to come, and you might just get caught in the crossfire."

With these final words of warning, McColley turned up the collar of his longcoat and walked out into the rain.

* * *

When Stephen Powers came calling on Sam Burkin he brought John Henry McAllen with him.

"Oh yes," said Burkin, as Powers introduced him to McAllen. "I know about you. You're the one who went to Maguey and came back with none other than Antonio Caldero. Quite a feat."

"I had very little to do with it, actually."

"He is being overly modest, Samuel," said Powers. "He persuaded Caldero to turn himself in."

"It didn't call for much persuasion. I think his mind was already pretty well made up to stop fighting. He realized he couldn't win."

"Well, come in, gentlemen," said Burkin, only mildly interested in Caldero. He couldn't see how this could possibly have anything to do with him. "I have a bottle of whiskey somewhere, if you'd care for a drink . . ."

He proceeded to rearrange the careless piles of books and papers on his desk and, failing to find what he was looking for, began to search the drawers. Finally it occurred to him that maybe he'd spoken a little too soon in making that offer; he'd been drinking a lot more than usual lately. Could be that he'd consumed all the whiskey in the place.

"That's quite all right," said Powers. A peal of thunder rattled the windows of Burkin's office. "A real fence lifter, isn't it?" he asked as he cleared a chair of an untidy pile of newspapers and sat down. "Samuel, I have a case for you, if you're not too busy."

Burkin had to laugh at that. "Funny, but I haven't been getting a whole lot of business since I broke ranks with Charles and his crew."

"How would you like to represent Antonio Caldero at his trial?"

Burkin gaped. "You've got to be joking."

"Not at all. I am in earnest, sir. Mr. Caldero needs the best lawyer he can get."

"What he needs is a miracle worker."

"Caldero doesn't expect to walk out of court a free man," remarked McAllen, leaning against a wall with arms folded.

"That would be a highly unrealistic expectation on his part," replied Burkin, nodding.

"I just thought you might want an opportunity to fight for what's right," said Powers.

Burkin sank into his wobbly desk chair and didn't say anything.

"Of course you're bound to benefit greatly," added Powers.

"Sure," said Burkin wryly. "I'll forever be known as the man who represented the most notorious bandit and murderer in the Southwest. That ought to *really* help my business here in Texas."

"Actually, I think it would. Our Mexican citizens desperately need a champion to defend their rights. You could be that man."

"I see." Burkin turned the concept over in his mind. "God knows they *do* have cause to seek legal remedies for the wrongs done them."

"You wouldn't get rich with such clients, but you might sleep a whole lot better at night."

"I'd have to learn to sleep with one eye open, you mean. As for rich—well, I once thought I might marry into wealth. But I've given up on that notion."

"So you'll do it?"

Burkin smiled. A warm exhilaration was spreading through his body. "Yes, I will. Why not? If nothing else, I'll cherish forever what I imagine will be the look on Stoneman's face when he hears the news."

"Sounds to me like you've got a grudge against this fellow Stoneman," said McAllen.

Burkin shrugged. That was something he didn't want to get into.

Powers was leaning forward in his chair. "Understand this, Samuel—your job is to persuade a judge and jury that Caldero is not guilty of the murder of Bob Carnacky. We're not just going to go through the motions."

"I don't suppose you could get me a *Mexican* jury—"

"No chance of that, I'm afraid."

"Well," said Burkin, "if there is one thing I've learned, it's that you can't have everything."

Chapter 13

When he saw them turn off the river road and onto the lane, Jeb sent his son Joshua to the big house to tell the mistress of Grand Cane that her son had come home. Then the old ex-slave left the cornfield where he had been working and went out to meet the riders—Dr. Tice, Gideon, and a girl. But where was John Henry McAllen? Heart in throat, Jeb braced himself for the worst and hoped for the best.

So did Emily when she came out onto the porch to hear Joshua announce the arrival of the three riders, and she peered down the lane and the first thing she noticed was that her husband's gray hunter was not one of the three horses. And then, as the riders got closer, she confirmed the absence of her husband. Dread tempered her joy and relief at seeing Gideon again. Jeb was trotting alongside Tice's horse, and Tice was talking to him, and then Tice saw her on the porch and turned to speak to Gideon and Gideon urged his horse into a gallop. Emily hurried down to the gate set into the hedge of Cherokee rose that encircled the house. She didn't breathe again until Gideon had assured her that his father was alive and well, and she nearly wept with joy as Gideon leaped from his saddle into her arms.

Gideon introduced Maura O'Quinn Perez as the girl who had saved his life, the one who had given him shelter when he was alone in the Coahuilan desert, the one who had made certain the letter he had written reached Grand Cane, and the one who had risked her life to accompany him to Maguey after Caldero's men had captured him. Emily gave him a curious look as he spoke; there was something in Gideon's voice that betrayed the powerful feelings he had for this Irish-Mexican waif. When Emily took Maura's hands and thanked her from the bottom of her heart, Maura answered with a sweet smile and a modest disclaimer that she had done nothing, really.

Emily turned her attention next to Artemus Tice, and the old physician knew her too well not to accurately read the query in her eyes, and he nodded with what he hoped was a reassuring smile.

"John Henry will be home soon, my dear. He had some business to take care of first."

"You can't fool me, Artemus. He's in danger, isn't he?"

Tice shrugged. "Probably. But is that so unusual? And it isn't anything he can't handle. I've seen him in worse trouble, believe you me."

"You must tell me all about it—over dinner. You will stay for dinner, at least, won't you, Artemus?"

"Have I ever been able to turn down an offer to sit at your table, Emily?"

"I would like for Maura to stay here with us, Mother, if you have no objections," blurted Gideon.

"Why of course, she is welcome to stay for as long as she likes."

"I'll show her up to the spare room," Gideon said, and held out a hand, and Emily saw the look on

Maura's face as she took the hand, and after the two of them had gone inside Emily said, "Oh dear."

Tice smiled. "She might be staying a lot longer than you think, Emily."

"Yes. Yes, I can see that. Oh, Artemus! Gideon went away a boy, but he's come home a man."

"It was bound to happen. And he could do worse. That gal is something special."

"You must tell me everything."

"After dinner, Emily. I'm starving. Haven't eaten a decent meal since we left."

When they sat down at the dinner table an hour later, Emily made sure Maura was seated beside Gideon, and Tice took that as a sign that she had accepted the situation. Maura was barefoot, and wore the same threadbare calico dress because that was all she had to her name, but she had washed her face and brushed out her hair and she'd found a pale yellow flower somewhere and wore it in her hair over one ear. Tice thought she was as pretty as a picture. Obviously Gideon thought so too—the poor boy could hardly keep his eyes off her.

After they had eaten, Emily insisted that Gideon tell his story, which he did, leaving nothing out, including the grim details of the tragic death of Quincy Yates.

"I have a letter Quince wrote to his father," he said. "Father found it and gave it to me. Tomorrow I should go into town and give it to Mr. Yates."

"You won't find him, dear," said Emily sadly. "After receiving your letter I paid Memucan a call and gave him the news. He was devastated. The next day he was gone. Left everything behind. No one knows where he went."

"Poor man," said Tice.

Gideon went on with his tale, describing how he had stumbled upon the jacal of the old sheepherder, Ramon Perez, how Maura had delivered the letter, how Perez had betrayed him, and how Maura had come with him to Maguey, where they had been found by his father.

"And so I guess it should come as no surprise," he said, blushing just a little, "that I am in love with Maura. I hope . . . I hope she will marry me—when I come of age, of course."

Maura was stunned. Emily took pity on her, because Gideon had put her on the spot. "Tact and good timing are not McAllen traits, my dear," she told the Irish-Mexican girl. "But since the subject has been broached, I want you to know that I approve most heartily of the match. You must consider Grand Cane your home."

Tice looked at Emily with pure admiration.

"I'm sorry if I embarrassed you," Gideon told Maura, mortified. "It's just that . . . well, I—I don't want you to go away."

She smiled shyly. "I won't. I will stay."

Gideon couldn't restrain himself; he jumped to his feet with a whoop of joy, overturning his chair.

"Gideon!" said Emily sternly. "Mind your table manners, if you please."

Tice laughed.

Emily gave him a stern look—she wasn't amused—and then suggested to Gideon that he show Maura around the plantation before it got too dark. It wasn't *really* a suggestion, but Gideon didn't mind at all. He thought it was a good idea. When he and Maura had gone, Emily turned to Tice.

"Tell me about John Henry, and leave nothing out."

Tice obliged her, and gave a thorough, unadulterated account of everything that had transpired since their departure on the trail of Gideon and Quincy Yates. When he got to the part about Captain Tobias leaving Gideon to die in the desert, the color drained from Emily's face.

"How could a man do such a thing? *Why* would he do it?"

"Remember Eli Wingate?"

"He was the Texas Ranger my husband killed in Palo Duro Canyon."

Tice nodded. "Seems Wingate meant a lot to Tobias. So Tobias has been looking for a way to avenge his death."

"Vengeance? Against a sixteen year old boy who never did him any harm?" Emily was furious. "I suppose that must be why John Henry hasn't come home. He wants to settle the score with Tobias."

"That's part of it."

"Well"—Emily looked at her hands, clasped tightly together in her lap—"I hope John Henry kills the bastard."

Tice was startled. "Emily! You never cease to amaze me."

"If Tobias is capable of doing what he did to Gideon, none of us are safe until he is dealt with. Unfortunately, there is only one way to deal with such men. You said that was part of the reason John Henry stayed behind. What else?"

Tice continued with his narrative, describing their experiences at Maguey. At this point he *did* leave something out—the part about Refugio. That incident still bothered him greatly, and he saw no reason to shock Emily with the tragic details of the young vaquero's death. He went on to explain Caldero's decision to give himself up, and John Henry's commitment to making certain that the Maguey hidalgo got a fair trial.

"I see," said Emily. "The men who want war with Mexico can't be too pleased that Caldero surrendered."

"No. But Caldero is just trying to protect his home and his people. And your husband wants to prevent a full-scale war. That's why he's asked me to find Sam Houston."

"The general? I believe he is in Austin."

"I will leave in the morning."

"When the general was here he did not speak of his real purpose in my presence, but I could tell that he had said something to upset John Henry. Did it concern Caldero, by any chance?"

"He offered your husband a brigadier's commission. You see, Houston wants to raise an army of Texas volunteers as soon as he becomes governor. He thinks he can save the Union by invading the northern provinces of Mexico."

"Then for the first time in his life John Henry stands four-square against Sam Houston," said Emily gravely.

"That's what bothered him when Houston was here. And it still bothers him."

"Is that why he wants you to see the general? To explain his actions?"

"Now, you know John Henry better than that, gal. When has he ever bothered trying to explain his actions? He knows he's in the right. He wants a guarantee from Houston."

"What kind of guarantee?"

Tice told her.

Emily was astonished. "If he wants war, the general will never do it."

"I've got to give him a reason to."

Emily was silent for a moment.

"I think I know a way you can persuade him," she said.

As Gideon walked with Maura along the lane that sloped down from the big house on its bluff overlooking the Brazos to the fields and the river road below, the Grand Cane freedmen who had spent the day working in the corn and the sugarcane were trudging home to their cabins. All welcomed him home, and their sincerity touched him. But for Joshua, old Jeb's son, he had intentionally removed himself from any more contact with the blacks than had been necessary, deeming it unbecoming of a young southern cavalier to fraternize with such people. Loathe though he was to admit it to himself, he'd even been rather aloof where Joshua was concerned in the past year or so, a shameful way to treat a childhood friend and companion. Now the sincerity with which the ex-slaves expressed their happiness in his safe return moved Gideon deeply.

And when Maura asked him what the slaves were doing in the fields, Gideon hastened to explain that his father had freed all his slaves twenty years ago; he omitted any mention of the fact that he had previously resented this act. At the moment he was quite relieved that it had been done, because he could see that the news pleased Maura immensely.

"To keep other people in bondage is such cruelty," she said. "Don't you agree?"

"Why, uh . . . yes, of course I do," he replied, and

to his amazement he realized that indeed he *did* agree. He understood now what had completely escaped him before—that this business of seizing Mexico and turning it into new slave states was altogether wrong and misguided, particularly since it was predicated on the notion that people whose skin happened to be of a darker hue than that of the Anglo-Saxon race were in every way inferior. He now knew this notion to be as false as it was pernicious. The girl he loved was dark-skinned, and she was in no form or fashion inferior. The people of Mexico were in every respect the equal of his own race, and so it followed that *his* people had no right to take what rightfully belonged to the Mexicans. It followed, too, that neither did his people have the right to keep blacks in bondage. Memucan Yates and Quincy and all those who thought that way were wrong. Gideon was ashamed that he had ever been in accord with such a wicked concept. He was ashamed, too, of the way he had acted toward his father because of the manumission of Grand Cane's slaves. His father had been right all along. He usually was. The only excuse Gideon could come up with was that he had been a naive child who hadn't known any better. Maura—and his experiences in Mexico—had opened his eyes.

He showed her the mill, where the sugarcane now being harvested was processed, and then they strolled down to the river where the water glimmered in the late summer moonlight and bullfrogs sang in chorus with crickets. The ferry was lashed to its moorings on this side of the Brazos. Maura sat on the edge of it and let her legs dangle in the cool water. At her prompting, Gideon stripped off his shoes and socks and rolled up the legs of his pants and joined her.

They sat there for quite some time, enjoying the moonlight and the night sounds and the murmur of the river, and most of all each other's company. It was Maura who at last suggested that they ought to be getting back. Gideon reluctantly agreed. Hand in hand, they traipsed along the footpath that zigzagged up to the rim of the bluff. From the quarters came the sound of voices raised in song; he explained that the ex-slaves often got together around a fire to sing and dance and play music, whiling away the cares of life. With a smile on her face Maura paused to listen.

"Do you think you will like it here?" asked Gideon.

"Yes, I'm sure of it." She squeezed his hand. "But you are worried about something. What is it? You can tell me."

"I have to go away for a while, Maura. My father needs my help."

"I know."

"I sure hate to leave you, though," he confessed. The very thought of leaving made him feel almost physically sick.

She pulled him closer and wrapped her arms around his neck and with her lips very close to his she whispered, "I will be here when you return."

He kissed her, and one kiss led inevitably to another, and the world around Gideon seemed to fade away entirely. By an exercise of supreme will, just as he thought he was about to lose control, Gideon broke away, and they stood there for a moment, staring at one another in breathless wonder. Then they both began to laugh. Gideon couldn't stop laughing. He laughed because he was filled with the sheer wonder and joy of it all. When they were all laughed out, they walked back to the house, not saying anything—

nothing needed to be said—and they held hands all the way.

"Rise and shine," said McAllen as he nudged Cedric Cole with the tip of his boot, and as Cole groaned and stirred, he moved on to Buford Doss, repeating the process. He made the rounds, waking them all, and then went to the center of the hay-strewn carriageway in the livery stable and put down the lantern he'd been carrying to light his way. He took a watch from his pocket and consulted it. Buford Doss sat up and rubbed the sleep out of his eyes and looked around, and when he realized the sun wasn't even up he looked sourly at McAllen.

"What the hell's going on, Captain? It's still nighttime. I just went to sleep."

"It's half past five, gentlemen," said McAllen. "Time to make our appointed rounds. You boys have been sitting around for nearly a week, grumbling because you didn't have anything to do. Well, today we do something."

Accompanied by a symphony of groans, coughs, and muttered deprecations, the Black Jacks began to roll out of their blankets. Morris Riddle got up, hawked, spat, and stumbled over the empty whiskey bottle he'd helped the others polish off last night.

Since Brownsville was busting at the seams with volunteers, and all the hotels and boardinghouses were packed to the gills, they had been forced to settle for accommodations in one of the local liveries. The proprietor of the business hadn't minded the arrangement at all. Like most residents, he'd been more than a little concerned by the sudden influx of strangers. And though he'd never met McAllen or the Black

Jacks before, he'd heard plenty about them. Along with their fighting prowess one thing stood out about them—they were honest men. So the livery owner had offered to let them stay in the stable. He even let them keep their horses there. That way he could rest assured that his property, and the livestock housed therein, would be safe from less honorable men—of which Brownsville seemed to have more than its fair share these days.

"I sure could use some coffee," said Cole.

"You could use a bath, too," said Mayhew.

"Don't start with me, Lon. I ain't in a good mood."

"So what's new?"

"No time for all that," said McAllen curtly. "And no time for coffee, either."

"You're just getting soft in your old age, Cedric," said Doss as he brushed the straw off his clothes and checked the loads in his revolver. "We once went six weeks without coffee in the Everglades, chasing those cussed Seminoles to hell and back. All we had to drink was swamp water. I remember. Still get the remittent fever now and again. Not to mention the runs."

Impatient, McAllen turned to the stall holding the gray hunter. He had already saddled the horse. The Black Jacks knew he was through exhorting them to get a move on—if they wanted to go with him they would have to move fast.

A few minutes later they left the livery and rode the dark and silent streets of Brownsville, heading for the Mexican side of town.

McAllen had in hand a list of names prepared for him by Sam Burkin. Advanced scouting had located the people on the list, so he wasted no time this morning. He had eight people in five households to collect, and they were expecting him. McAllen was a bit surprised that the seven who were cooperating voluntarily agreed to come with him; they were frightened, and had every right to be, but not one chose to back out.

At the last house a man and a woman emerged in answer to his summons. The man wore the plain and threadbare garb of a common laborer, with sandals on his feet and a straw hat on his head. The Black Jacks did not recognize him until he raised his head to take a cautious look around.

"Well I'll be," muttered Buford Doss. "It's Antonio Caldero!"

"Keep it quiet," said McAllen dismounting. "And I suggest you keep your head down, sir," he told Caldero.

Caldero nodded and joined the other Mexicans, who stood together, surrounded by the mounted Black Jacks.

McAllen stepped to the threshold of the adobe and glanced inside. Captain Donaldson was standing near the hearth, sipping a cup of coffee.

"Thanks, Captain," said McAllen.

"You're welcome," replied Donaldson. "I must say I'm relieved he's off my hands. Some of the men very nearly mutinied when they found out Caldero was in the brig. It was their opinion that he ought to be executed. You see, to a man they had friends who'd lost their lives at La Bolsa."

McAllen nodded, turned back to his horse, and climbed into the saddle. The sun was just now rising in all its searing glory.

"Okay, boys," he said, "let's go to court. Just remember, no shooting unless you're shot at."

They moved out, maintaining a protective ring around Caldero and the Mexicans.

The Brownsville meeting hall, opposite the hotel on the square, was used for trials. McAllen had hoped to arrive before the crowd gathered, but in this he was disappointed. The square was already teeming with people, residents as well as a good number of the armed and idle strangers who so worried the livery owner. Though some of the war-seekers had headed for home after hearing of Caldero's surrender, under the assumption that the border troubles were over, plenty yet remained.

McAllen focused his attention on a knot of men at the doors to the meeting hall. Burkin was there, standing alongside two men McAllen knew as Slattery, the judge presiding, and Benjamin Revell, the prosecuting attorney. Charles Stoneman was a few feet away, and near him was Captain Tobias and his small band of Texas Rangers.

"What's the meaning of this?" Slattery asked Burkin. "What are those Mexicans doing here?"

"Those are my witnesses, Your Honor."

"Witnesses!" Slattery was a beefy, white-haired, red-faced man, and his complexion was very nearly crimson in hue as he watched the Black Jacks approach with their wards. "Mexican witnesses? What game are you playing, Burkin?"

"No game, sir."

"I don't think it will do to have Mexicans in the courtroom, sir. No, sir, that won't do at all."

"But these are my witnesses, sir. And they are citizens of the great state of Texas, as well. They all reside right here in Brownsville. In fact, some of them have been here longer than you have, Judge. Surely you don't mean to deny them their rights as citizens. They have the vote, and therefore I think their testimony is as valid as anyone else's."

"Do you mean those people claim to have witnessed the murder of Bob Carnacky?" asked Revell, a short, slender, impeccably dressed man with angular features sharpened further by the neatly trimmed goatee on his chin.

"Surely you don't expect me to divulge my case," said Burkin, smiling.

Revell's answering smile was cold and calculated. "Let him have his witnesses, Judge. He'll learn what weight a jury of white men will give greaser testimony."

"Oh, very well," huffed Slattery. "In any case, I am more concerned with the whereabouts of the defendant. I do not intend to try Caldero *in absentia*, Mr. Burkin. Produce your client, sir, or mark my words, you will suffer the court's wrath. I intend to be done with this by supper time."

"Caldero will be here before you know it, Judge."

Slattery grunted and walked into the meeting hall. Revell lingered, eyeing Burkin with pity.

"You were a fool to take this case, Sam. You can't possibly win."

"You don't have anything to worry about, Ben. You've got your hand-picked jury, and I'm sure Judge Slattery has already received his instructions from Charles Stoneman."

"Better be careful what you say." Revell started to turn away, paused, and added, "And you'd be well advised to start packing your belongings. Brownsville will not be a good place for you after this, I fear."

As McAllen neared the meeting hall he noticed that Tobias was watching him like a hawk.

"Glad to see you're still here, Captain," said McAllen. "We have some unfinished business, you and I."

"I'm at your service anytime, McAllen," growled Tobias. Then he glanced at Stoneman, and McAllen noticed how Stoneman answered the Ranger captain's silent query with an almost imperceptible shake of the head. Stoneman had his own coterie of four grim, heavily-armed men—members of the Knights of the Golden Circle, no doubt. *So the lines of battle are clearly drawn,* mused McAllen. Tobias and the Rangers were siding with Stoneman and the KGC. McAllen glanced at the Ranger who had told him what Tobias had done to Gideon, providing him with that first clue and leading ultimately to the recovery of his missing son. The expression on Mase Williams's face was inscrutable.

Dismounting, McAllen led the way into the meeting hall, followed by the Mexicans and all of the Black Jacks except Cole and Mayhew; these two had already been made aware of their job, which was to watch the horses and keep an eye peeled for trouble outside.

The meeting hall-turned-courtroom was already filling up with people. Burkin had reserved one of the front pews, directly behind the defense table, for his witnesses, and McAllen made sure all the Mexicans were seated, then posted his men—Morris Riddle at one end of the pew and Buford Doss at the other, with Will Parton stationed at the back of the room. That left McAllen free to roam at will.

Slattery was already behind his desk, a gavel and Bible in front of him. The new sheriff of Brownsville, a surly looking man named Simmons who sported a sweeping mustache and whose black button eyes were darting here and there, missing nothing, stood off to one side of the judge, his back to the wall. Stoneman and Tobias came in and sat down in the front pew directly behind Ben Revell's table. One of Stoneman's KGC bodyguards came in, too, to stand in the back not far from Will Parton. McAllen circled around through the crowd to position himself against a side wall, near a window, and behind Tobias.

A few minutes later Slattery hammered the table with his gavel and the people packed into the pews—McAllen figured there had to be almost two hundred people in the room—fell silent. All but one man, that is, who was seated near the back, too busy talking in a high-pitched voice to the woman who sat beside him to notice how quiet it had suddenly become. Slattery glowered, but that didn't work because the man wasn't paying him any attention, and then the judge snarled, "Corbett, shut your trap!" The man obeyed, shamefaced, and someone laughed at his discomfort, but Slattery cut the laugh short with another glower.

"Fine," he said at last. "Now let's get on with this. Mr. Burkin, I told you I wanted the defendant here on time—"

"Mr. Caldero is here, Your Honor." Burkin turned and nodded at Caldero, who stood up and removed his hat.

McAllen watched Stoneman's head jerk around as he looked in astonishment at Caldero, and then jerk back the other way as he fired an angry glance at Tobias.

"Why the shenanigans, Mr. Burkin?" rasped Slattery.

"Just a precaution, Judge. There are some people in these parts who would like to see my client dead."

"I expect they will get their wish soon enough," said Slattery, a comment that evoked murmured assent from some of the onlookers.

Burkin motioned for Caldero to sit beside him at the defense table.

"Mr. Revell, you may proceed with your case."

The prosecutor rose and approached the twelve men seated on two benches, one behind the other, at right angles to the judge's table and along the wall on the prosecution's side of the room.

"Gentlemen," said Revell, "you all know why you're here. To do your civic duty, to Brownsville, to Texas, to God and country, and most of all to justice. This man"—he gestured sharply across the room at Caldero—"is a bandit, a thief, and a murderer. He has no respect for our laws or our customs. He refuses to recognize our right to this land. He has spent his entire life at war with our race. And two months ago he rode into our town and in cold blood, with malice aforethought, gunned down one Robert Carnacky, then acting as our sheriff. I am confident you will avenge Mr. Carnacky's murder. I have but one witness, Mr. Josiah Grindle, a man you all know, a respected member of our community, an honest and forthright and God-fearing gentleman. He saw the brutal act committed by the defendant in this case. He will tell you all you need to know to make a well-reasoned and responsible determination of Caldero's guilt, and I am certain you will be prompt in returning a verdict that will restore law and order to our land. Thank you."

As Revell returned to his table, the crowd broke into applause mingled with some shouts of approval. Slattery beat the table with the gavel, making the Bible jump, until silence again reigned. Then he looked at Burkin.

"Do you have any remarks to present to the jury?"

"I'll save my remarks for closing, Your Honor."

"Good. Call your first witness, Mr. Revell."

"I call Mr. Josiah Grindle to the stand, Your Honor."

Grindle approached the judge's table.

"Put your left hand on the Good Book, Josiah," said Slattery, "and raise your right hand. Do you swear to tell the whole truth and nothing but the truth, so help you God?"

"I do."

"Sit down."

Grindle sat in the witness chair beside Slattery's table, facing the crowd and nervously tugging at his ill-fitting broadcloth suit.

Revell stood up. "Josiah, tell the jury what you saw in the street in front of your place of business at approximately nine thirty in the morning of June twelfth, 1859."

Grindle cleared his throat. "I saw Sheriff Carnacky arresting an old drunk named Lopez. That's when Caldero rode up and told him to let Lopez go free. Bob said he wouldn't do that. When he told Caldero he was under arrest, too, Caldero drew his pistol and fired. He hit Bob square in the chest. Bob was dead inside of a minute."

"Then what happened?"

"Caldero took the old man and put him on his horse and just walked away."

"Did Caldero display any remorse for having shot Mr. Carnacky?'

"Nope. He just shot him down like you would a mad dog."

"That's an appropriate simile," said Burkin.

"What was that?" asked Slattery.

"Nothing, Your Honor."

"Thank you, Mr. Grindle." Revell sat down.

"Do you have any questions for the witness, Mr. Burkin?" asked Slattery, as though he would be very unhappy if Burkin said he did.

"Just a few."

"Well, be quick about it," said Slattery, disgusted.

Burkin strolled over to the witness chair. "Josiah, you mentioned that Sheriff Carnacky tried to arrest my client."

"He sure did."

"What for?"

The question caught Grindle off guard. "What for? Why, because he's a bandit. An outlaw. We don't want his kind in Brownsville."

"No, I'm afraid you're wrong. You see, Mr. Caldero received a full pardon for all his wrongdoings from the state of Texas. He had every right to be on the street that morning."

"I object, Your Honor," said Revell. "This isn't relevant. It isn't even correct. Carnacky was arresting Caldero because Caldero was interfering with the arrest of the old drunk, Lopez."

Burkin smiled at Revell. "Oh, so you were there, were you, Ben?"

"Of course I wasn't there. But everybody knows that's what happened."

"How does everybody know that, Ben? Josiah was the only witness, wasn't he? And he says different."

Revell breathed an annoyed sigh. "He is simply mistaken as to the reason the sheriff was attempting to arrest the defendant."

"If that's the case, you can't have much confidence in your only witness."

Someone in the pews chuckled. Slattery raised the gavel threateningly and the chuckling stopped.

"Josiah, did you actually hear what Carnacky said when he told Mr. Caldero he was under arrest?"

Grindle saw a way out of his predicament and jumped at it. "No, I didn't actually hear it."

"And yet you claim to have heard Mr. Caldero tell Carnacky to let Lopez go free."

Grindle scowled. He was tired of being put on the spot. "Yes, I did hear that."

"So you heard what Mr. Caldero said, but not what Carnacky said."

"That's right."

Burkin glanced at the jury with a raised eyebrow. "No further questions." He went back to his table and sat down.

"Stand down, Josiah." said Slattery. "Mr. Revell?"

"No other witnesses, Your Honor."

As Grindle went to his place in the pews he studiously avoided meeting Stoneman's disapproving gaze.

"Mr. Burkin?" said Slattery.

"As most of my witnesses do not speak English very well, Judge, I'll require the services of a translator."

Slattery stared at him, then said, begrudgingly, "Sheriff Simmons speaks the language."

"Then I call Antonia Delgado to the stand."

A young and attractive woman rose from the pew guarded by Doss and Riddle. Simmons swore her in and she took the chair Grindle had just vacated.

"Miss Delgado," said Burkin, "please tell us how you came to be, um, acquainted with Sheriff Carnacky."

Simmons translated the question, and her answer. "She says that the night before he died Carnacky told her that if she didn't come to his bed her brother, who was in jail at the time, might meet with an accident."

Revell shot to his feet. "I object! This is an outrage, Your Honor. Mr. Burkin ought to be ashamed of himself, attempting to besmirch the good name of the man his client brutally murdered."

"I wholeheartedly agree," said Slattery, "and your objection is sustained."

Burkin didn't argue the point. He called his next witness, a fourteen-year-old boy named Ricardo Islas.

"You were arrested by Sheriff Carnacky on several occasions, were you not, Ricardo? Can you tell the jury why?"

Simmons translated. "He says he didn't do anything wrong. Carnacky just threw him in jail every time he wanted the boy's mother to sleep with him—"

"Objection!" shouted Revell.

"Sustained!" roared Slattery. "I'm warning you, Mr. Burkin. I will not tolerate any further so-called evidence of this sort. It is irrelevant to the charge against your client."

Burkin apologized and called his next witness, an older woman named Margurite Soto.

"Mrs. Soto, please tell us what you saw on the morning of June twelfth in front of Grindle's saloon."

"She says she saw the sheriff kicking the old drunk, Lopez," translated Simmons. "He kicked—"

"For God's sake, Your Honor," said Revell, exasperated. "I object."

"Mrs. Soto was a witness to the alleged crime, Judge," remarked Burkin.

Slattery grimaced. "Go ahead, then."

Burkin nodded at Simmons, who continued. "She says Carnacky kicked the old man in the stomach, and then in the back, and then he hit Lopez with his rifle."

"What happened after that?"

Simmons posed the question to her, and translated the answer—he seemed highly amused by it all.

"Caldero rode up and asked the sheriff to stop before he killed the old man. Carnacky turned his rifle on Caldero, and that's when Caldero shot him."

"Shot him," said Burkin, with a glance at the jury, "in self-defense."

"Objection!" snapped Revell, again on his feet. "It is customary, I believe, for a peace officer to cover a man—especially a dangerous man like Antonio Caldero—as he is taking that man into custody. Caldero's actions were most certainly *not* self-defense."

"Having witnessed the way Carnacky was treating Lopez in the process of arresting him, I contend that my client most assuredly *was* acting in self-defense," countered Burkin. "Caldero would not have survived a single night in Carnacky's jail. He knew it."

"I strongly protest, Your Honor."

"Protest all you want," said Burkin. "It's the truth. I know it and so do you, Ben. So does everyone else in this room."

"It is *your* truth, Mr. Burkin," said Slattery.

"I'm sorry, Your Honor. I was under the impression that there is only *one* truth. And that is what I am trying to bring to light."

"I don't think I like your tone of voice, Mr. Burkin."

"My apologies, Judge. May I call my next witness?"

"Mr. Revell, do you have any questions for this witness before I excuse her?"

"No, Your Honor." Disgusted, Revell sat down.

"Call your next witness, Mr. Burkin."

"I call Charles Stoneman to the stand."

Chapter 14

"Good morning, Charles."

"Samuel."

"Charles, do you recall our visit to Bob Carnacky on the morning of June twelfth?"

"I remember," was Stoneman's diffident reply.

"Do you also recall the purpose of that visit?"

"It was a social call," said Stoneman, smirking. He had been wondering, of course, why Burkin would call him as a witness for the defense; now he thought he knew where Burkin was trying to go with this line of questioning.

"A social call," said Burkin wryly. "You and Bob Carnacky moved in the same social circles, then."

"I object, Your Honor," said Revell wearily. This time he didn't bother getting to his feet. "This is completely irrelevant to the matter at hand."

"Sustained," said Slattery.

"No," said Stoneman coldly. "I'll answer his questions."

"There is no need for you to," said Slattery. "I have sustained Mr. Revell's objection."

Stoneman shot him an angry look.

Slattery shrugged. "As you wish."

"It wasn't a question, anyway," said Burkin. "Just a comment."

"Then ask me a question or sit down," said Stoneman.

"So you deny going to Sheriff Carnacky with me on the morning of the day he died for the purpose of instructing him to refrain from his rough treatment of Brownsville's Mexican citizens?"

"I don't recall talking to him about anything like that. Why would I presume to dictate to the sheriff how to do his job?"

"Perhaps because the elections were coming up and you wanted the Mexican vote."

"Your Honor," said Revell plaintively.

"Shut up, Ben," snapped Stoneman. "This is between me and Burkin."

"So I take it you don't recall the conversation you and I had after leaving Carnacky's house," said Burkin.

"Why don't you refresh my memory?"

"Glad to. I told you that Carnacky was a liability as sheriff because he abused the rights of our Mexican citizens, that he was a wicked and brutal man who would someday do something incredibly stupid, and you agreed, and said that when the time came you would get rid of him, and you expected the Mexicans to be eternally grateful to you for doing it. You said that for the time being, though, Carnacky stayed because the white residents of Brownsville were afraid of the Mexicans and they liked having a man such as Carnacky around. To keep the Mexicans in their place, is the way you put it."

"You either have a good memory or a good imagination," said Stoneman.

"So you deny to my face that the conversation ever took place."

"I emphatically deny it, sir."

Burkin stood there for a moment, arms folded, staring straight into Stoneman's eyes. Then, putting a hand on the back of the witness chair, he leaned over Stoneman.

"I remind you, Charles, that you are under oath."

"I am telling the truth, the whole truth, and nothing but the truth, so help me God."

"And I suppose you deny being the leader of a conspiracy to start a war with Mexico in order to justify an invasion of our southern neighbor for the purpose of establishing new slave states there."

"I don't have any idea what you are talking about."

Burkin raised his voice. "And I suppose you deny having even heard of a secret organization of traitors known as the Knights of the Golden Circle."

Stoneman bristled at the word *traitor,* but he kept his composure and answered with a surly smile. "I've never heard of such an organization. But of course, if it was secret, and I were a member of it, I wouldn't be able to tell you, now would I?"

Burkin sighed and stepped back. "Thank you, Mr. Stoneman. I think we have managed to demonstrate beyond a shadow of a doubt that you are a liar, sir, since every person in this courtroom knows full well that you are in fact the leader of a conspiracy such as I have just described, and that you are in fact a member of the Knights of the Golden Circle, and that you would go to any lengths to have your damned bloody war—even to the point of sacrificing the town of Brownsville and everyone in it."

"You're the traitor," shouted Stoneman, gripping

the arms of the witness chair and leaning forward, as though he were about to lunge at his tormentor.

The audience was in an uproar. Men were shouting and gesticulating angrily at one another, at Judge Slattery, and at Sam Burkin. Slattery was furiously hammering his table with the gavel—so furiously that the head of the gavel broke away from the handle and flew through the air so close to Simmons that the sheriff had to dodge it. His jowly face purple with rage, Slattery yelled something at Simmons, who promptly drew his revolver and fired, putting a bullet hole in the roof of the meeting house. The crowd quickly settled down.

"I will have order in my court!" shouted Slattery, spacing the words out and instilling a terrible menace into each one.

"I have no further questions for this witness," said Burkin, who had remained an island of icy calm in the recent tumult.

Stoneman came out of the chair and walked straight at Burkin, but Burkin held his ground and at the last instant Stoneman veered and brushed past him. He did not return to his place in the pew behind the prosecutor's table but stalked out of the meeting hall without looking to left or right. Tobias got up and went after him. McAllen watched the Ranger captain all the way and was just about to turn his attention away from the door when Gideon walked in.

Covered with trail dust, looking haggard and bone-tired, Gideon scanned the crowd. Spotting his father, he smiled with a weary relief and circled around behind the pews to join McAllen.

"Did you see the general?" asked McAllen, pitching

his voice low—calm had been restored and now Slattery was asking Burkin if he had any other witnesses.

"Yes, sir. Dr. Tice and I found him in Austin. He wrote you a letter." Gideon produced a piece of heavy blue vellum, folded twice and sealed with red wax.

"I have other witnesses," said Burkin, "but I don't feel as though I need to call them."

"I take that to mean you are finished," said Slattery hopefully.

Burkin turned, found McAllen, and gave him a questioning look.

McAllen held up the letter he had only briefly scanned.

"I have a letter I would like to read to the court," said Burkin.

"A letter? From whom?"

Again Burkin glanced at McAllen, and McAllen nodded.

"From Sam Houston, Your Honor."

Perplexed, Slattery glanced at Revell. "I presume you are going to object," he said dryly.

"No, Judge. Let him read his letter. He can do handstands for all the good it will do him or his client. The facts are clear, the defendant's guilt readily apparent to any reasoning man, and Mr. Burkin's transparent attempts to obfuscate those facts and that guilt with attacks upon the character of a murder victim will avail him nothing."

"Well said," agreed Slattery, nodding. "Go ahead and read your letter, Mr. Burkin."

McAllen came forward and handed the letter to Burkin. Seeing that it was McAllen who had possession of the letter, Revell said, "I would, however, like the court to verify that this instrument does in fact bear the genuine signature of General Houston."

"Are you suggesting that Captain McAllen would be a party to some sort of skulduggery, Ben?" asked Burkin. "That he would forge General Houston's signature?"

McAllen thought, *It wouldn't have been the first time,* remembering the letter he had written for Caldero's benefit.

Revell glanced warily at McAllen. "Well, I—"

"Does anyone here feel he is capable of vouching for the signature of Sam Houston?" asked Slattery.

"I am," said McAllen.

Beaten, Revell made a throwaway gesture. "Never mind, Your Honor. I withdraw my request."

"Get on with it, Mr. Burkin."

Burkin unfolded the letter and began to read:

" 'To Whom It May Concern. It having come to my attention that Antonio Caldero has submitted himself to American justice, facing a charge of murder, I make the following earnest declarations on his behalf.

" 'While Caldero is responsible for the deaths of many of my fellow Texans, I hold no rancor towards him, for in my opinion he is a soldier rather than a bandit. He fought for his country, more particularly to maintain that portion of land lying between the Nueces River and the Rio Grande after that territory had been ceded to the Republic of Texas by the legitimate convention of a treaty signed by Santa Anna, President of Mexico. Caldero's refusal to acknowledge our rightful title to that territory known as the Nueces Strip does not in my mind make of him an outlaw. Baseless rumors to the contrary notwithstanding, Caldero never waged war on innocent women and children, and if harm came to any at the hands of the men who fought with him, I am confident that the crimes were committed without his knowledge or consent. Antonio Caldero was an honorable enemy, and I regarded him then, as I do still, with respect.

" 'Being acquainted with recent events along our border with Mexico, I am persuaded that whatever Caldero may have done, he was justified in doing. Such a man could not commit murder. If he killed, it was as a soldier who must take the life of his enemy. Caldero has always fought in defense of his country and it is common knowledge that in the present circumstances there is a movement afoot to seize by force of arms the northern provinces of the Republic of Mexico. Caldero would resist such aggression to his last breath, just as I or any patriot would resist a foreign aggression upon the sacred soil of our Union.

" 'Let me add that it has never been my intention to seize the northern provinces of Mexico for the establishment of new territories or states. When I spoke of a Mexican protectorate in the Congress, it was always my intention that if such a measure became necessary, as a result of conditions of anarchy in those provinces occasioned by the civil war currently raging there, the protectorate would be a temporary expedient designed solely to protect the lives and properties of peace loving Mexicans therein residing until such time as a stable government could be formed in Mexico City. It is the duty of a good neighbor to come to the aid of his fellow man, and that is no less true among nations sharing a common border. The protectorate would serve a humanitarian purpose, and no other.

" 'Therefore I, Sam Houston, do solemnly avow that

were I the governor of the state of Texas, it would be incumbent upon my sense of fairness and honor, knowing what I do of the character of Antonio Caldero and the extenuating circumstances which must surround his recent actions, to provide him with a full pardon. As I am not yet governor, however, I have prevailed upon Mr. Hardin Runnels, by appealing to his better nature and sense of decency, to take that step for the sake of peace, if not for the life of an old soldier whose only crime is that he loves his country more than life itself. I have it from the governor's own lips that a pardon will be issued Antonio Caldero forthwith.

" 'Your Obedient Servant, Sam Houston.' "

Burkin slowly folded the letter and handed it to Slattery. The judge stared at it as though he couldn't quite figure out what it was. Then he handed it back to Burkin, unopened.

"I rest my case, Your Honor," said Burkin.

Slattery glanced at Revell. "Any closing remarks?"

Revell shook his head. *He knows he can't top Houston's letter,* thought McAllen. *He's smart enough not to try, because anything he might say would fare poorly by comparison.*

Slattery glanced at the twelve men of the jury. "You may proceed to discuss among yourselves. The court will await your verdict."

Burkin gave the letter to McAllen and without a word sat down at the defense table next to Caldero. A murmur of subdued conversation rippled through the onlookers. McAllen rejoined Gideon, who was watching the jury, now gathered in a huddled knot.

"What do you think their verdict will be, sir?" he asked his father.

"I'm not sure," replied McAllen—even though he was. "But tell me. How in heaven's name did you and Artemus persuade the general to write such a letter?"

Gideon grinned. "Isn't it what you were hoping for?"

"It was everything I hoped for and more."

"Actually it was Mother's idea. She said to tell General Houston that Memucan Yates was bound to find out about the plot by the Knights of the Golden Circle, if he didn't know already, and he wouldn't hesitate to connect the general to it."

"That would be something you might expect from the Brazos *Intelligencer*," agreed McAllen. "Even though Yates must approve of the plan, he'd know how much damage it could do to Sam Houston to be associated with it. Your mother didn't mention exactly how Yates would find out, did she?"

"She didn't have to."

McAllen smiled. "I never knew your mother could be so devious."

"Even more than you know, sir. Because Memucan Yates left Grand Cane over a week ago. When he heard about Quince he just disappeared."

"I guess the general was pretty annoyed."

"If he was, he didn't show it."

McAllen nodded. Houston would accept the inevitable with good grace and keep his true feelings concealed. That was the Old Chief's way. He would realize that if his name was linked with the Knights of the Golden Circle in a conspiracy to expand the boundaries of the slave South at the expense of the Republic of Mexico, he would pay a high cost politically. Such a connection could not hurt him—indeed, it would probably help—in Texas, but he would lose credibility as a man committed to Union in the North, and if he lost his support in the northern states he would never occupy the White House—never reach that pinnacle of power from which he thought he might be able to mend the rendered seams holding the sections together. It had been a brilliant idea on Emily's part. Of course Houston was bound to be extremely disappointed in both Emily and her husband, and McAllen felt a twinge of guilt for opposing a man he respected above all others. But Houston had taken the wrong side on this issue, and McAllen could assuage his conscience by remembering the women and children he had seen in the streets of the Maguey *casco*.

"But I wonder how the general got Governor Runnels to agree to Caldero's pardon?" he asked.

"Dr. Tice said he thought it was because Runnels knows he is losing the election on account of his extreme secessionist views. He's trying to mend his political fences and appeal to the moderates who have deserted him for Houston."

"It's too late for Runnels," said McAllen, with satisfaction. "Sam Houston will be our next governor."

"I think we'd be better off for it."

McAllen was mildly surprised. "I would have thought your politics were more in line with Runnels's."

"I see things a whole lot differently now. I want to apologize to you, Father. You were right and I was wrong. I'm glad you freed the slaves at Grand Cane. And I'm glad you stand for the Union and not its destruction."

McAllen put a hand on his son's shoulder. "And I apologize to you for not respecting the fact that you've grown up. I guess I didn't really ever want you to. Because if you're grown up I've grown old."

Gideon laughed. "You're not old, sir."

The jury foreman rose.

"Your Honor, we've arrived at a verdict."

A hush fell over the crowd.

"Antonio Caldero, stand up," said Slattery.

Caldero stood, and Burkin got up too.

"On the charge of murder, how say you?" Slattery asked the foreman.

"We find the defendant guilty as charged."

McAllen had been expecting it, and thought he'd prepared himself, but the verdict hit him like a punch in the midsection. The crowd was oddly subdued; he had thought they would raise the roof in fierce jubilation. Caldero had frightened them badly in past weeks. Now their tormentor would pay the price. But there were no cheers, or shouts of approbation. The woman named Margurite Soto sobbed softly into her hands.

"No," breathed Gideon, shocked. "It's not right."

"This was bound to happen, son."

"But he let us live, Father. He could have had us killed. His men wanted to kill us but he wouldn't let them. We've got to help him somehow."

"He knew what he was getting into."

Slattery looked at Caldero with a certain amount of smug satisfaction written all over his face.

"Mr. Caldero, I am happy to say that your career as a marauder is finally drawing to a close. Never again will you prey on the good people of Texas. The sentence I am prepared to render will not only balance the sheets for the murder of Bob Carnacky. It will see justice done for the many widows and orphans you have produced during your long and bloodstained campaign of violence and terror. Do you have anything to say?"

Caldero was completely composed. He shook his head.

"Then I sentence you to hang by the neck until you are dead. The sentence will be carried out at dawn on the fifteenth of this month, one week from this day."

"I would remind Your Honor that a pardon for my client is on its way from the governor," said Burkin.

"Then it needs to get here before the fifteenth." Slattery looked with disfavor at his broken gavel and lifted his bulk wearily from the chair. "This court is adjourned. Sheriff Simmons, you will take the prisoner into custody and hold him until execution of sentence."

"Stay here, Gideon," said McAllen, and headed for the defense table, meeting Simmons there. The sheriff's hand was resting on his pistol.

"Don't try anything, Caldero," he warned, "or you'll cheat the hangman."

Caldero smiled with faint disdain. "You need not concern yourself on that score."

"You don't understand, do you?" McAllen asked Simmons. "This is what he wants."

Caldero turned to McAllen. "Now your debt has been paid. As you would say, we are even."

As Simmons led Caldero out of the meeting hall, Burkin turned to McAllen. He was trying to act as though the trial's outcome didn't bother him, but without much success.

"They were bought and paid for," he said, with a trace of bitterness in his voice. "The judge and the jury both."

"You did a good job."

"We can only hope that pardon gets here on time." Burkin shook his head and turned away.

A shot rang out, followed by a quick flurry of gunfire.

McAllen broke into a run, shouting at Doss and Riddle to come with him. He could see that Will Parton was already making for the door, Bible in one hand and pistol in the other. Everyone in the meeting house was on their feet, and McAllen lost Gideon in the crowd. Pushing and shoving his way through the melee, he paused for an instant in the doorway to survey the scene before him.

Sheriff Simmons was on the ground, writhing in pain. His arm had been shattered by a bullet and he was bleeding profusely. Out in the square, Cedric Cole and Lon Mayhew were engaged in a gun battle with several men, using their horses to shield themselves. McAllen recognized those men—they were Texas Rangers, part of Tobias's crew. Closer, Will Parton was joining in, sounding off with Scripture at the top of his voice to be heard above the din: " 'The truly righteous man attains life, but he who pursues evil goes to his death.' "

A man came around the corner of the meeting hall, his pistol blazing, and McAllen shouted a warning to Parton, but it was too late. The preacher was knocked sideways, and McAllen muttered a curse—only to feel vast relief when Parton scrambled up to one knee and fired back. McAllen's Colt Patersons spoke, too, and the man performed a jerky pirouette as the bullets struck, then sprawled lifelessly on the ground. Even as he killed the man McAllen realized he was a stranger, not one of Tobias's Rangers; that meant he had to be one of Stoneman's KGC men.

"Praise the Almighty," said Parton, amazed at his survival, and holding up the Bible for McAllen to see the bullet hole. The thick, leather-bound Good Book still held the slug meant for the preacher.

McAllen knelt beside Simmons. "Where's Caldero?" he asked.

"Two men," said the Brownsville sheriff through teeth clenched at the pain. "Took him around back."

McAllen turned to Doss and Riddle, who were coming out of the meeting hall. "Take care of this man," he said, and took off running. As he reached the corner of the meeting hall he saw two men dressed in the plain garb of the poor Mexican laborer, sombreros on their heads, just turning the back corner of the building, dragging Caldero along between them. Caldero was hurt, unsteady on his feet. McAllen shouted, and the two men stopped, turned, and, seeing him, dropped Caldero. When McAllen spotted their pistols he knew he was too far from the corner of the meeting hall to dodge back out of sight, so he hurled himself to the ground. A Colt Paterson in either hand, he blazed away at the pair. He didn't know who they were, but he could be sure of one thing—they meant to kill him. Their bullets made a crackling sound as they passed over his head. One struck the ground inches from his head and threw dirt in his eyes. McAllen rolled to the left and kept firing. One of the men jackknifed forward, clutching at his belly, and fell. The other turned to run, but one of McAllen's bullets caught him in the side and slammed him against the meeting house wall. He tried to make the back corner, but Caldero was on his feet now, and the Maguey hidalgo grabbed the man's gun and wrestled for it. The gun went off between them, and McAllen pounced to his feet and started running again—before he could reach Caldero the other man slumped to the ground, the front of his shirt covered with blood.

"Are you hit?" McAllen asked Caldero.

Caldero put his hand to the back of his head—his fingers came away smeared with blood. "They were waiting in front. One of them shot the sheriff. The other hit me over the head with his pistol."

Four horses were tethered behind the meeting hall—they had been the destination of the men who had seized Caldero. But why? McAllen turned his attention to the dead men, rolled the nearest corpse over on its back. In spite of his garb, the man was no Mexican. It all came clear to McAllen then.

"Who is he?" asked Caldero.

"If I had to guess, I'd say it was one of Stoneman's men."

"Cuidado!" shouted Caldero, and he shoved McAllen to one side, raising his pistol, and McAllen saw Tobias, then, but before he could shoot the Ranger captain had fired, and Caldero was thrown backward, reeling. McAllen turned his pistols on Tobias. The Ranger had shooting irons in both hands. As he walked forward he fired one and then the other. A bullet splintered the meeting house wall behind McAllen. Another struck him in the shoulder, driving him back against the wall. He fired his Colts, and Tobias staggered but kept coming on.

"Time to finish our business, McAllen!" he roared. "This is for Eli Wingate, you damn son of a bitch!"

McAllen kept shooting. He was sure he'd hit Tobias several times, but the Ranger captain refused to go down. Then the hammers of McAllen's Colts fell on empty chambers. His eyes burning from the powder smoke, all he could see was the triumphant grin on Tobias's face.

"You're a dead man, McAllen," he rasped, stopping at last six feet away, swaying slightly and raising his pistols slowly, as though they were heavy as anvils, and McAllen knew the bastard was dying. He just wasn't dying fast enough.

A gunshot rang out, very loud in McAllen's ears, and to his astonishment he realized it wasn't Tobias who had fired, and then the Ranger captain pitched forward at McAllen's feet. Only then did McAllen see Gideon standing some distance away, gripping a smoking pistol with both hands. Taking a deep breath, McAllen went to his son and pried the gun out of the boy's hand.

"Is he . . . ?" Gideon was too shaken to finish.

"He is," said McAllen. "Thank God."

He turned to Caldero, who lay on his side in the Brownsville dust at the corner of the meeting house, and he knew at a glance that the Maguey hidalgo was dead. The Ranger captain had shot him through the heart.

The sounds of the battle that had been raging in the square were subsiding. McAllen shoved Gideon's pistol in his belt, holstered one of the Colt Patersons, and reloaded the second as he walked to the front of the meeting house. He scarcely felt any pain from the wound in his shoulder; that would come later. At the moment he was more concerned about his men.

Parton and Doss were near the door to the meeting house, and Doss was sitting with his back to the wall, applying his neckerchief as a tourniquet around his leg just above where a bullet had struck. Out in the square, lying near a dead horse, Lon Mayhew stared with lifeless eyes at the burnished sky. Morris Riddle was checking the bodies of three men farther out in the square, while Cole covered him, scanning to left and right and back again. But the Rangers and their KGC accomplices were gone. Now that the shooting was over some of the more audacious of the people in the meeting house began filtering cautiously outside; a few lingered to gawk at the carnage, while others slipped away. Judge Slattery and Ben Revell came outside together.

"What happened here?" Slattery asked McAllen.

"Must have been Caldero's men," offered Revell.

"So you were in on it," rasped McAllen. "The men who tried to take Caldero are dead. They weren't Maguey vaqueros. They were Stoneman's KGC boys."

"That is a reckless accusation," warned Revell.

"It's the truth. It was just meant to look like Caldero's men rescued him. The bodies are over there. See for yourself, Judge."

"This is ludicrous," said Slattery. "Why would they do something like that?"

"You're a smart man, Judge. You can put it together. But the scheme won't work now. You see, Antonio Caldero is dead. He didn't just disappear, the way they'd planned. When I'm done, everyone in Texas will know who killed him and why. Caldero is dead, but he won. I don't think there is going to be an invasion of Mexico after all. Do you, Revell?"

The prosecutor grimaced and wisely said nothing.

A few days later, when Charles Stoneman stepped out of the hotel lobby with his wife, followed by two of the men he had selected for bodyguards, he was surprised to find Sam Burkin waiting for them. The pair of bodyguards quickly inserted themselves between Burkin and the Stonemans, reaching for their guns, but Burkin calmly stood his ground and smiled disdainfully.

"Really, Charles. I just came to say good-bye. You're not afraid of *me,* are you?"

As Stoneman told the bodyguards to stand aside, Burkin glanced at Judith. She was more radiant than ever, clad in a sky-blue muslin dress adorned with white lace, a bonnet bedecked with flowers, and a parasol to match. He couldn't read her expression, but her eyes were very wide as she stared at him the way a frightened deer might stare at a hunting dog.

"I hope you will find New York to your liking, Mrs. Stoneman," he said cordially.

"I'm certain I will," she said in a small voice, and the voice triggered painful memories for Burkin—memories of their stolen moments together, at the abandoned adobe down by the river, and Burkin still couldn't be sure whether he hated Judith or loved her. Maybe it was both.

"My suggestion is that you leave Brownsville, too, Samuel," said Stoneman. "A lot of people resent you for defending Caldero."

Burkin shrugged. "It seems pretty quiet around here now. Almost all the men who came here looking for war have gone home. McAllen and his men took Caldero's body back to Maguey. It's all over, isn't it? But I'm curious as to why *you're* leaving, Charles. Could it be you're afraid someone south of the border will seek revenge for Caldero's death?"

"I don't know what you mean," replied Stoneman stiffly. "Antonio Caldero was killed trying to escape. My wife needs a change of scenery, that's all. The events of the past few weeks have weighed heavily upon her."

"That's what I admire about you, Charles. You're a devoted husband."

Stoneman gave him an odd look, wondering if he was sincere. "I don't think we have anything further to say to each other. Come along, dear." He took his wife's arm and began to turn to the surrey that would take them to Port Isabel and the coastal steamer, and in spite of everything Burkin felt his heart breaking because he knew he would never see Judith again.

"There is one other thing," said Burkin. "Something I think you ought to know, Charles."

A gasp of terror escaped Judith's lips, and Stoneman glanced at her, bewildered.

"What is it?" he asked, frowning at Burkin.

Judith's eyes were begging him not to do it, and at that moment Burkin realized that he had the power to destroy, the same power Stoneman possessed—and he didn't like it.

"I just want you to know," he said slowly, "that I harbor no hard feelings, Charles."

"That's very generous of you," sneered Stoneman. "Now, if you'll excuse us, we're on a tight schedule—"

At that moment one of the bodyguards shouted a warning, and Burkin was struck from behind and stumbled sideways, catching a glimpse of a man rushing past him, right at Stoneman, and Burkin recognized him as the Mexican who had been shadowing Stoneman, and Stoneman cried out in terror as he saw the knife in his assailant's hand, and he thrust Judith into the Mexican's path. Burkin watched the knife plunged into Judith—the Mexican could not react in time to avoid it. *"Madre de Dios!"* gasped the Mexican, shocked, and he stepped back, watching in horror as Judith fell, clutching at the knife. Then he saw the bodyguards, drawing their pistols as they came toward him, and he turned to run. He didn't get far. The pistols spoke, and the Mexican staggered and fell. He twitched once and died.

Stunned, Burkin stared at Judith. She was writhing on the hotel boardwalk, reaching out to him and whispering his name. *She's calling out to me, not to her husband,* he thought. He took her hand. It was smeared with warm blood but he gripped it tightly—and then she smiled at him and closed her eyes and put her head down and died.

The bodyguards were standing over the body of the Mexican. Stoneman had turned to run back into the hotel; now that the danger had passed he stopped and stood there and looked at his wife, and then at Burkin, and all Burkin could read in his expression was vast relief. No remorse, no grief—the only thing Charles Stoneman cared about was his own survival. A burning rage overcame Burkin. He stood up, trembling violently, and reached under his coat, brandishing the little single-shot Briggs. Stoneman watched in disbelief as he raised the pistol. Burkin was dimly aware of the bodyguards to his left. He could see them out of the corner of his eye, whirling, turning their pistols on him, but he didn't care. He took two steps closer to Stoneman.

"Go to hell," he said, and fired.

The bullet struck Stoneman an inch above the bridge of his nose, and the impact hurled him violently backward. Burkin didn't live long enough to see him fall. Each of the bodyguards fired several times at point-blank range, and Sam Burkin was dead before his body hit the boardwalk. He fell beside Judith, his head resting on her outflung arm, and one of his arms thrown over her, and it occurred to one of the KGC men—before he turned to walk quickly away—that it looked as though the pair of them were locked in a lovers' embrace.

Epilogue

What really happened along the Texas–Mexico border in 1859 . . .

This story is based on actual events—an extraordinary but little-known piece of American history.

General Zachary Taylor established Fort Brown in 1845, at the outset of the war with Mexico, and the town of Brownsville grew up rapidly around the stronghold; by 1859 it could boast of a population of two thousand, most of them Mexicans. Of course the Americans controlled the town, and two political factions, the Blues and the Reds, sprang up. The leaders of these factions were men of power and influence. Stephen Powers, a friend of former president Martin Van Buren, and a former minister to Switzerland during the Van Buren administration, was the leader of the Blues, while Charles Stillman and Samuel E. Belden, the latter an attorney, were leaders of the Reds. Richard King and Mifflin Kennedy, local ranchers, were also members of the Reds political machine.

Since the majority of the population were Mexicans, the Blues and the Reds needed their votes to win elections, and made lavish promises at election time. These promises were almost always broken, and for the rest of time the Mexicans were not treated well at all. It was obvious that a double standard applied in the application of the law. The wealthier Mexicans were sometimes robbed of their property in American courts. Poorer citizens were victimized in other ways. They desperately needed a champion.

That man was Juan Nepomuceno Cortinas (or Cortina). Son of a ranchero, Cortinas did not avail himself of the quality education that his brothers and sisters enjoyed. He preferred the company of vaqueros to that of the upper class. By the age of twenty-one he was an accomplished border bandit, stealing horses and freight in Texas and spiriting whatever he purloined back across the Rio Grande to sell in Mexico. Contemporary accounts portray Cortinas as an intelligent, intuitive, and charming man, with brown hair, green eyes, and a reddish beard, which made his appearance quite distinctive. He could also be a contrary and dangerous man.

In 1859, Cortinas was living on his mother's ranch on the Texas side of the Rio Grande, about seven miles west of Brownsville. Nearly every morning he would ride into town for a cup or two of coffee. On July 13, during one of his visits, he saw the city marshal, a man named Robert Shears, arrest an inebriated Mexican with whom Cortinas was acquainted. Shears was a brutal man, especially where Mexicans were concerned, and Cortinas intervened. When Shears insulted him, Cortinas drew his pistol and shot the sheriff in the shoulder, lifted the drunk onto his horse behind him, and galloped out of town. For the next two months no one could—or would—say for sure where Cortinas was hiding.

He reappeared in September, on the occasion of a ball held in Matamoros; though this town was south of the river, many Texans from Brownsville were in attendance. Late that night, as the partygoers were returning to their homes, Cortinas and a hundred armed men thundered into Brownsville and seized the town. They killed several Americans, though the personal enemies whom Cortinas sought, Shears among them, managed to escape. A dozen prisoners were broken out of jail. Fort Brown, recently evacuated by United States troops called upon to fight Indians, was briefly occupied by the bandits. Cortinas sought to justify his actions with a proclamation stating that he was fighting for Mexican rights. *"Our personal enemies shall not possess our lands until they have fattened it with their own gore,"* he declared. It is unlikely that Cortinas was as dedicated to this crusade as he claimed to be, but the Mexicans were delighted. He became their hero, their knight in shining armor. "Viva Cheno Cortinas!" was a cry disgusted Americans often heard.

Cortinas did not linger long in Brownsville, vanishing into the desert, and the Americans dispatched frantic pleas for protection to Texas Governor Runnels and U.S. President Buchanan. A guard of about twenty men, calling themselves the Brownsville Tigers, joined forces with about forty Texas-Mexicans commanded by Colonel Loranco and set out with two small cannon to engage Cortinas in battle at his mother's Santa Rita ranch. Cortinas captured the cannon and sent the Tigers and their allies fleeing back to Brownsville.

In the weeks that followed, Brownsville was a town under siege. Cortinas threatened to shell the town if his enemies were not turned over to him, but he acted with restraint, and apart from firing a few rounds just to scare the townsfolk, he did not bombard Brownsville. He did steal some cattle, and intercepted the mail, but he left a due bill for the cattle and always returned the mail, resealed.

The first help to reach Brownsville was a band of Texas Rangers led by Captain W. G. Tobin, who, according to historian Walter Prescott Webb were "a sorry lot" whose "conduct . . . reflects no credit on the organization." At that time, one of Cortinas's lieutenants, a man named Cabrera, had been captured, and it is rumored that Tobin's men instigated a lynch mob which cut short poor Cabrera's life. Cortinas had his revenge. When Tobin sent a few Rangers to meet Captain Donaldson and his contingent of United States regulars, who were on their way to Brownsville, Cortinas ambushed the Ranger contingent at Palo Alto Prairie and killed three of them.

In November 1859, Tobin, his Rangers, and about two hundred volunteers set out to beard Cortinas in his Santa Rita den, but as before Cortinas was victorious. By now his prestige had soared and many Mexicans flocked to his banner. They believed he would drive the Americans north of the Nueces, reclaiming the disputed strip of land between that river and the Rio Grande for Mexico. It is uncertain what goals Cortinas set for himself. He issued another proclamation (which is referred to in this novel), referring to his American enemies as a flock of vampires:

> Some, brimful of laws, pledged to us their protection against the attacks of the rest; others assembled in shadowy councils, attempted and excited the robbery and burning of the houses of our relatives on the other side of the river Bravo [the Rio Grande]; while

> others . . . when we entrusted them with our titles, refused to return them under false pretexts; all, in short, with a smile on their faces, giving the lie to that which their black entrails were meditating. Many of you have been robbed of your property, incarcerated, chased, murdered, and hunted like wild beasts, because your labor was fruitful, and because your industry excited the vile avarice which led them. . . .
>
> Mexicans! Is there no remedy for you?
>
> Mexicans! My part is taken; the voice of revelation whispers to me that to me is intrusted the breaking of the chains of your slavery, and that the Lord will enable me, with powerful arm, to fight against our enemies, in compliance with the requirements of that Sovereign Majesty, who from this day forward will hold us under His protection. On my part, I am ready to offer myself as a sacrifice for your happiness.

More volunteers joined Cortinas, including sixty convicts who broke out of prison at Victoria, Tamaulipas. At this point Cortinas had enough men to perhaps drive the Americans out of the Rio Grande valley, if he acted before the United States Army sent reinforcements to the area. But he did not go on the offensive. Instead, he expressed confidence that Sam Houston, recently elected governor of Texas, would provide Mexicans with the necessary legal protection when he replaced Runnels in that office.

Before that could happen, however, Major S. P. Heintzelman arrived in the Brownsville area with a second and much larger American force. He marched upriver with three-hundred men, including about one hundred of Tobin's Rangers, and engaged in an indecisive skirmish at La Ebronal—the name given a barricade of ebony logs—with Cortinas's forces. But Cortinas remained as elusive as ever and escaped the army's clutches.

In the state capital of Austin, Governor Runnels heard with alarm rumors that Cortinas was on the march, burning one Texas town after another, and he ordered Major John S. "Rip" Ford of the Texas Rangers to hasten south and take command of all state troops. Ford and his fifty men arrived too late to partake of the fracas at La Ebronal, but they were on hand a few weeks later when another foray led the Americans to the Barstone ranch, where Cortinas was said to be headquartered. The ranch buildings had been sacked and burned, and there was no sign of Cortinas. Then the Americans got word that Cortinas had plundered the town of Edinburg, and there they rushed, but once again Cortinas was gone, hiding in the vast canebrakes along the river.

The day after Christmas, Heintzelman received intelligence indicating that his foe was at Rio Grande City, a small town eighteen miles farther up the river. Ford set out to circle around Rio Grande City and cut off Cortinas's retreat. But Cortinas anticipated this tactic and blocked Ford's encircling maneuver. Ford settled down and waited for Heintzelman and his regulars to come up.

In the battle that followed, the Texas Rangers commanded by Ford and Tobin did all of the fighting. They struck the Mexican lines so hard that Cortinas's men faltered, and when they saw the U.S. regulars marching forward they broke and ran. Cortinas and his bodyguard quit the fleeing remnants of his army and sought refuge in Mexico. Sixty Mexicans were slain; the Americans lost not a man.

He was next spotted at La Bolsa, on February 14,

1860, where he attempted to wreck the steamboat *Ranchero* and steal sixty thousand dollars' worth of specie which he knew to be onboard. This battle is fictionalized in this novel. The *Ranchero* was not burned, and the Mexicans did not use firebombs. In addition to the arrival of two companies of U.S. cavalry, Rip Ford and his Texas Rangers also made an appearance at a most opportune time. Ford and a handful of Rangers crossed the river and moved upstream to engage the Mexicans, who had formed their lines in the village of La Bolsa. Ford and his men distinguished themselves with incredible valor, rolling up the Mexican lines and causing the Mexicans to flee. Cortinas tried desperately to rally his men, but they would not heed him. In disgust, Cortinas emptied his revolver at the Rangers and was the last to leave the field. The Texans fired dozens of rounds at him; miraculously, he was unscathed. Against Ford's wishes, some of the Rangers set fire to the village of La Bolsa.

Cortinas found refuge in the Burgos Mountains, but he was reported to be in the Mexican village of La Mesa, with the result that Ford's Rangers and Heintzelman's cavalry participated in a raid south of the border. After a brief melee, it was learned that the men the Americans were fighting belonged to a unit of the Mexican national guard. "We have played hell now," Ford said. "We've whipped the Guardia Nacional, wounded a woman, and killed a mule."

The Americans engaged in several other raids—including one on the village of Reynosa, whose inhabitants reputedly challenged the Texas Rangers to try them on for size. Never one to walk away from a dare, Rip Ford took his men to Reynosa and raised a ruckus. But the excursions across the Rio Grande were curtailed by Colonel Robert E. Lee, recently appointed commander of the Department of Texas. Lee's arrival in the spring of 1860 marked the end of the so-called Cortinas War. A hundred people had lost their lives. Farms, ranches, and villages all up and down the Rio Grande had been destroyed, some by Cortinas, many others by Texas Rangers. Cortinas was still at large. He would become a brigadier general in the Mexican army and then governor of Tamaulipas. A very wealthy man in his later years, his hatred for the Americans never abated; it was said that until the day of his death he financed numerous depredations across the border.

The secret quasi-military organization known as the Knights of the Golden Circle existed in fact; its origins and mission are as I have described them. It is also true that Sam Houston entertained the notion of establishing a protectorate over the northern provinces of Mexico. I surmise that he hatched this scheme in order to start a war with Mexico that would divert his fellow Americans from their preoccupation with those sectional differences which would ultimately lead to civil war. As a U.S. senator he spoke of the protectorate on several occasions, making the scheme part of the public record, and when he became governor of Texas he gave the appearance of making plans in earnest to invade northern Mexico, which he claimed to be a land gripped by anarchy and violence. It was, he claimed, the duty of every civilized and compassionate American to bestow upon the poor people of the northern provinces the blessings of liberty and republican government. The Knights of the Golden Circle expressed keen interest in participating in the invasion, but Houston kept them at arm's length. Nothing came of his plan in the end because the Buchanan administration refused his request to sanction it.